KobiKobis Island

The Journey Begins

Aimee Linde

PublishAmerica
Baltimore

At the specific preference of the author, PublishAmerica allowed this work to remain exactly as the author intended, verbatim, without editorial input.

ISBN: 1-4241-9007-X
PUBLISHED BY PUBLISHAMERICA, LLLP
www.publishamerica.com
Baltimore

Printed in the United States of America

Dedicated to my children and all my nieces and nephews.

Many Thanks go to my children, Zachary, Madison, & Johnathan who inspired this book, my sister Michelle Rasmussen who urged me to finish it, my nephews' Adam & Gabriel Jolly, who read it with enthusiasm and gave me great suggestions and ideas, my sisters' Crystal and Nikkole my Dad (Rick Crowther) and my friend Becky Barrett who all assisted me with editing.

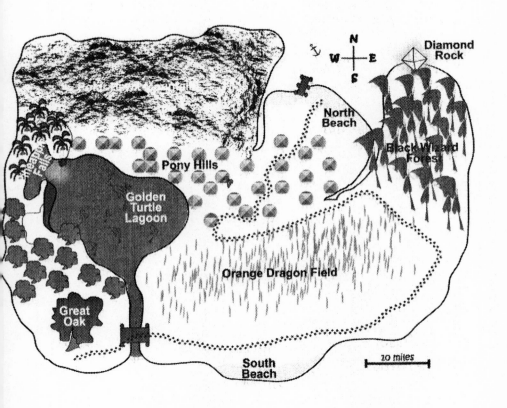

KobiKobis Island

Chapter 1

Teag stood with his nose in the window next to the door, trying to catch a glimpse of the storm just outside. His fascination with natural disasters made him more curious than ever now that he was right in the middle of one. He desired to step out into the high winds and rain to see for himself; to experience what he would call *a thrill* after watching a disaster film. The tropical cyclone was just starting and the ship kept sailing through. Teag could hear several of the passengers talking amongst themselves; they were concerned, the Captain wasn't turning around to escape the storms path. The strong wind was becoming ever so powerful as it tossed the ship about. The large ocean waves barreled over the bow and crashed onto the deck. Spindrifts sprayed the salty mist and rain, causing it to clatter on the windows like hail.

Outside, the crew raced about trying to secure the ship for the stronger winds and waves ahead. A bell rang, Teag noticed as one crewmen ran door-to-door telling everyone to gather in the dining hall. The chatter in the room was as loud as the waves crashing on the deck.

Teag could barely see through the windows while the rain and spray pelted it. Knowing that his mother would never let him get far, he had been inching his way to the door for the last ten minutes, hoping she wouldn't figure out what he wanted to do.

"Teag!" Milly yelled over all the noise, "Stay inside! It's too dangerous out there! Why don't you come and sit by me?" She motioned him over.

"I just want to watch," Teag shouted while pointing to the large window. He watched and waited for his mother to say something else. She suddenly turned her attention too his younger sister and brother who were fighting over a card game. While she tried to break it up, he knew it would be his only chance. He opened the door and walked out.

The deck outside was wet and slick. Two inches of water lingered whirling around his feet and soaking into his sneakers. A chill ran up his spine as the ice cold water saturated his socks. The spindrift's stung his face and hands. Teag fought the pain convinced it would stop when he got to the Bow of the ship. He held the railing while he made his way to the stairs that lead to the lower deck. Lightning flashed and made it easy to see the waves as they headed towards him. Leaving him only seconds to brace himself before the ocean flooded over him, he held on for dear life. Regardless, Teag was not detoured from wanting to be outside in the storm. He quickly made his way to the bow of the ship, hanging on he was feeling free. He held his breath each time the ocean came crushing down on him. The strength and sheer velocity of the waves amazed him; to him it was like they were willing him closer.

With each blast, Teag was being tossed about the deck. Trying not to slip overboard, he held the side railing with all his strength. Quickly growing tired, he looked back to where he had come from. He couldn't see the door to the dining hall, and knew it would be too hard to go back.

'How am I going to get back,' he thought, 'I'm in trouble.' A sudden loud boom of thunder hit like a hammer and then cackled through the sky causing Teag to jump with surprise. Another wave crashed over his head. The spindrift's hit his shivering body making his chattering teeth click so hard and fast he thought they might crack. Several large lightning bolts flashed all around the ship lighting up the sky. The light was so bright Teag wanted to look away, but before he did something caught his eye. Behind the bright light he watched, panic flushed through him as his adrenaline burst through his body.

Unable to move he yelled in terror, "OH, NO!" 'I'm not gonna make it this time,' he thought as he stared at the fifty-foot wave heading right for him. 'Maybe I can run back to the dining hall,' he thought, but the wave was moving too fast, it was now right on top of them. Riding the wave straight up into the air for what seemed to be minutes, Teag feared the worst. The higher and higher the bow of the ship climbed straight up into the air. Teag lost his footing and was only hanging from the wet railing. His cold hands started to slip and he knew he couldn't hold much longer, it seemed the wave couldn't either. It tipped and folded the ship into the sea like taffy.

Teag's throat was burning for air, kicking and swimming as hard as he could to make it to the top. But he didn't know which way was up. The pain in his chest was immense as he was kicking and fluttering around, hoping to reach the top for air. All he wanted to do was breath in. The ocean whirled around him as if trying to tear him apart. He struggled, but at last couldn't hold it any longer, and breathed in.

Teag sat straight up, gasping for air and grabbing his chest and throat with pain, only to realize he had just had the worst nightmare of his life. Jacob was walking past Teag's bedroom door when he heard the commotion from inside.

With fatherly concern, Jacob went over to him and asked, "are you okay?"

Milly heard his panic from her room, and ran in to see if everything was all right.

Teag's heart was pounding, he was trying to shake the awful dream, but remnants of it lingered while he tried to understand what had just happened, "I think so. I just had the worst nightmare."

"What happened?" Milly asked him, alarmed at the excitement as she entered the room.

"Teag just had a nightmare," Jacob informed her. He was anticipating her exaggerated worriment.

"Oh, well what happened in your dream?" Milly asked, trying not to make a big deal about it for Teag's sake.

Knowing his mothers belief in dreams and their meanings and thinking about their upcoming cruise, he didn't want to stress her. She had a habit of thinking that bad dreams were more than just a dream. She believed it was a message from your sub-conscious trying to warn you of future events. Teag thought the better of it. He didn't believe that the big scary monsters that came out of his closet in his dreams when he was little, were really anything to worry about.

"It was just a bad dream. I'll be okay," Teag forcefully smiled.

"Are you sure you don't want to talk about it? Sometimes it helps," Milly coaxed curious at what could have happened. It just so happened she had been reading her book about dreams moments before. She was still holding it in her hands. She looked at it and then asked, "I can look it up for you, it might make you feel better."

"No, mom, it was nothing, I'll be okay," he said politely, hoping she wouldn't force him to share or listen.

"All right, but if you want to talk, I'll be packing," Milly said as she walked out of the room.

Jacob was still standing there. He walked over and sat on the edge of Teag's bed, "so what was that really about?"

"It was just a dream. It wasn't real," Teag said as he rubbed his eyes. He glanced over to his alarm clock, hoping to find the time, but it was unplugged. 'I must have yanked the cord out when I woke up,' he thought.

Jacob wasn't going to press it any further. He stood up and started to walk out.

"Dad?" Teag called out.

"Yeah?" Jacob turned to look at him.

"Can I ask you something?" Teag asked still unsure if he should share his dream.

"Sure," Jacob was curious.

"Can dreams come true? I mean, can they really happen?"

"No."

Well what about deja vu?"

"Well, some people have said that daja vu is experiencing something that you feel like you've seen before or have already been through. Its also been said that most people have dreamed it before it happens. That is why they think they remember whatever it was when it really happens. At least that is how it was explained to me when I was a kid."

"So you're sayin' it's possible for dreams to come true then?"

"No, I'm just telling you what I know about daja vu, they say that sometimes, in some situations, its happened to some people, or so I've heard.""Has it ever happened to you?"

"Yeah, I've had daja vu before."

"What happened?"

"Oh nothing big, actually I can't remember now, but you'll know it when it happens. What brought on these questions? Are you worried about your dream?"

"Well," Teag started, and then decided he really didn't want to talk about it, "nothing. I was just wondering."

"Are you sure? Because I know a good therapist, and she's on call all day everyday. In fact, she's sitting in the other room, I'm sure her bible of dreams can help you," Jacob joked knowing that Teag didn't care for his mother's book.

Mostly Teag didn't like hearing someone else's boring nonsense about how, 'a drowning dream is really your sub-conscious telling you that you're feeling helpless and out of control,' Teag could hear his mother say in his mind. He shook his head at the thought.

Teag laughed, "I'm sure dad, I'm good now, it was just a stupid dream. What could happen? It was no big deal, really," Teag said out loud, but didn't really feel that way. He started to wonder if that was all it was, him feeling out of control, after all, he didn't have any friends. His final grades came way down from last year, and there really wasn't anything he liked to do except play his gameboy and read. His rambling thoughts were interrupted by Jacob's voice once again.

"You're sure that's all you wanted to talk about?" Jacob asked, inquisitively.

"Yes, I'm sure. It was really nothing."

Jacob took off his glasses and cleaned them carefully with a cloth he had pulled out of his pants pocket. When he was done, he carefully placed them back on his face and turned to walk out of the room, "okay, well…go to sleep quickly because morning comes early."

"What time is it?" Teag asked looking at his clock again. He had forgotten that it was unplugged.

"It's ten-seventeen."

Teag leaned over, plugged in his clock and set the correct time, "thanks, dad. Oh, would you mind shutting the door on your way out?"

"Sure," Jacob smiled. As he started to close the door, he opened it again with one more question, "Oh…are you done packing?"

"Yeah, except I have a few more things to finish in the morning."

"Okay, well, you'd better get up early to take care of it all, I don't want to be late tomorrow," Jacob smiled, shut off the light, and then closed the door as he walked out of the room.

Teag thought a little bit longer about his dream. It was hard to believe that a dream like that could really come true, but something in his gut told him something bad was going to happen. Not wanting to consider it any further, he tried to think about something else and soon fell back to sleep.

Somewhere far away, in a dark and chilly room, sat a man and a woman. The draperies were drawn keeping the sunlight out. The only light in the room was a small, slow burning candle that burned on the coffee table in between them. The illumination from the small candle was so dim it was hard to see anything. The smell of burning matches lingered in the air like the candles were lit moments before. The woman's voice broke the long silence; it was calm and collected, even sweet, "do you know why I chose you?" She asked quietly.

"No," came the deep voice of the man.

"Because I know that you will keep a secret, and I also know that I can trust you."

"Yes, I'll do as you ask, but are you absolutely certain it has to be done this way?" He asked with an Australian dialect.

"I'm sure, I told you I saw him. I know it's him this time, the one we've been searching for all these years, but the parents will be in the way. No one else will understand why things must be done this way, but you know, you know what's at stake. You understand what must be done, for the good of our kingdom, and your family," She looked at his silhouette knowing he would obey her, but slightly aggravated that he was asking questions.

"But, with all due respect, isn't there another way, a better way? I'm sure if we just talk to them and help them understand they'll…" he broke off feeling the tension in the room rise and suddenly realizing he had crossed the line.

She slightly changed her position sitting up a little straighter. Her eyes were wide and full of fury. In an aggravated voice, "have I not been good to you? Have I not given you everything you have asked for? Have I ever been wrong?"

"No…, no on all counts, I'm sorry, it won't happen again," he quaked with fear.

"Do you understand your instructions?" She barked back at him.

"Yes," he replied knowing he had better not push her any further.

"Remember, just take care of the boy's parents, and make sure they are not found, you'll know what to do with them. And don't forget to return the crew to their homes. I don't need them in the way either."

"Consider it done."

"And speak of this to no one. I do not wish anyone to know until it is time."

"Yes 'em," he stood up and slowly walked toward the door, opened it and looked back at the woman sitting alone in the dark. She was starting at the wall with no expression on her face. She slowly turned to look at him leaving. He bowed his head as if ashamed then walked out, carefully closing the door behind him.

She waved her hand over her face then stood up and walked to turn on the lights. There stood a beautiful woman with silky light olive skin and long dark brown hair. She was wearing an elegant red evening gown that accentuated her slender waist and made her feel beautiful and glamorous. Her light brown eyes danced in the light as she grinned wickedly at the thought of her brilliant plan.

It was June first. The morning was warm and beautiful like a warm fuzzy blanket, the sun had just come up, Teag opened the blinds on his window to take in the warm light. The night had been chilly. A gust of cool wind blew through his already open window. Teag went to close it but took a moment to look at the beautiful landscape around the back yard. There wasn't a cloud in the sky. The fresh air that whizzed past him smelled clean and crisp like the night rain had washed away the filthy air. He could hear birds chirping and the sounds of busy life moving all about. The tall evergreen trees chattered lightly in the soft breeze. The excitement of the long-awaited cruise filled the air. Knowing they had to leave soon Teag closed the window and began to rush around his room to pack his last minute items.

The Tragers' were minutes away from leaving their home in Bellevue, Washington. Teag stood by his bed and went over all the things he had packed a week ago, making sure everything was there. When he was finished checking off his list, he sat on his bed and began playing his gameboy.

Something flashed out of the corner of his eye. He quickly looked up for a moment to see what it was, but only caught a glimpse of himself in the mirror. He stood up and tossed the gameboy aside then started admiring himself. His dark brown hair was short in the back but long on top and dangled in his eyes. He brushed it back carefully admiring himself more, his brilliant blue eyes and deep smile were strangely attractive. His tall thin build made him feel puny compared to the other boys at school. He fell deep in thought about the problems he had in class; he was different from the other kids, a loner, though he tried so hard to make friends. He looked deep into his own eyes 'Maybe they don't like me because of the light blue star around my left pupil.' He wondered as he stood there staring. He was used to it, but 'maybe it freaks them out.' While the rest of his eye color would change from a brilliant blue to gray, the star would always stay light blue.

His mind drifted off as he sat on his bed. All he ever wanted was to be liked, to fit in and have someone other than his family to talk too. His mind drifted to a phone call he had gotten the day before:

"Hello?" he answered.

"Hi...Teag?" The girl on the opposite end of the phone asked hesitantly.

"Yeah?" There was a pause. Teag didn't know who she was, so he waited for her to say something else.

"Um, I hope I'm not calling too early. I didn't wake you, did I?

"Uh...no, it's okay."

"Oh, good. Umm...I was wondering...I mean...I don't do this very often, but...well...do you wanna catch a movie with me tonight or something, and then hit the Bortan House Party after?" She asked. Teag knew that the Bortans' always had the bomb of parties and anyone who was anyone, was always there, and you had to be one of the elite to even be invited.

"Well, who is this?" Teag asked, a little confused at the call.

"Oh, I didn't tell you? I'm sorry. This is Cara Taylor from school."

"Oh. Hi, Cara. I didn't recognize your voice," Teag was a little excited because she was the most popular girl in school, and he was, well, nothing. He didn't even know she knew he was alive, "Listen, about tonight..."

"Yeah?" she interrupted cheerfully.

He was afraid to say yes, the kids in school had terrorized him, made him believe they liked him and then played horrible pranks on him, even humiliated him in front of everyone, but she sounded so sincere, and he really did think she was cute so he agreed, "Sure, what time should I pick you up?"

"Well, uh-oh, my dad has to use the phone, can you like, call me back in like, five minutes?" she asked. Teag thought he heard giggling in the background.

"Sure, what's your num…" He started but heard a click. She had hung up the phone before he could get her number. He hung up his end of the phone and sat on his messed up bed. He looked around the room, but wasn't really looking; he was contemplating what had just happened. 'Was it a joke? She didn't say it was, she did say to call back in five minutes. Maybe she was forced to hang up, maybe she thought he knew her number. He looked at the clock on his night stand and stared at it, but it wasn't moving. Time felt as though it was standing still. Driving himself crazy thinking about what her real intentions might have been he started pacing his room. Then he remembered a week before the whole school got phone books with everyone's phone numbers in them. He quickly ran to his closet and looked at the heap of papers on the floor. He started rifling through them searching for the booklet. When he didn't find it there he looked in his backpack that was hanging off his doorknob just waiting to be cleaned out from the previous year of school. He rummaged through his notebooks and folders and at last found it. He pulled it out and brushed off a few crumbs that had become glued to the front page. He flipped through and found her name and then quickly dialed her number. He found himself, unintentionally, breathing heavy, like he had just run a marathon. The other side was ringing, "Pick up, Pick up, Pick up," he said as he tried to calm himself down.

"Hello?" came a girls voice from the other end of the phone after the fifth ring.

"Cara?"

"Yeah?"

"This is Teag," he paused for a moment, "I'm just calling you back," when there was still silence he added, "we were going to go to a movie and then the Bortan house party."

"Who is this?"

"Teag Trager, you just called me a few minutes ago," Teag was confused, why didn't she know who he was. Then dread hit, it had to be a joke. This knowledge was confirmed when she spoke again.

"Is this some kind of joke?" She paused for a moment (there was giggling in the background) and acted like she didn't know what he was talking about, "I haven't called anyone at all this morning and anyway I'm going with my boyfriend, Tom Erick, to the Bortan party, sorry," her voice was harsh and rude.

Angry that he was a joke to them he slammed down the phone. "Dang it," he felt so stupid for trusting her. His heart was pounding; he was horrified and humiliated once again. It seemed to be a ritual now; there wasn't a day that went by that they didn't tease him in some way. School was out and they were still laughing at him, and he fell for another one of their tricks.

So there he was now, lying on his back on his unmade bed, tears filled his eyes. He wanted revenge, justice, but no one would listen to him. His parents told him he wasn't trying hard enough, and that there is always someone who gets it worse. He refused to tell his teachers because that would just make it worse. After holding back the tears of emotional pain, he took a deep breath, but it was no use, he turned over and let out a few muffled cries into his pillow.

After a few minutes he settled himself down, He wiped off his eyes and then stood in front of the mirror once more. Thinking of all the things he wanted, he began to imagine he was popular "And here he comes, the man of the year, the most handsome tenth grader in the world: Teag Trager," he announced to himself, and then made cheering sounds, imagining a crowd cheering him on. He whistled the catcall, and screamed in a higher-pitched voice, "I love you, Teag. Will you go out with me?" He then nodded his head and pointed to himself in the mirror, flexing his muscles like he was the greatest thing to come to earth.

"Ha, ha, ha, ha," Teag jolted around to find his younger brother, John, mimicking him and laughing.

"What are you doing in my room Johnny?" Teag yelled, chasing him away, "That's it, you're getting a swirly."

John tried to apologize, "Teag, I won't tell anyone. Please don't flush my hair in the toilet, no stop it," they wrestled as Teag tried to drag John into the bathroom. After a long struggle and tumbling into walls they stumbled into the bathroom. Teag struggled to keep hold of his brother who was now half way dangling over the toilet and trying desperately to get away.

Teag was only teasing, but didn't want his brother to know it yet.

"What are you doing?" Suraionee asked with a gasp as she saw Teag struggling to push John's head in the toilet. She quickly turned around and ran to her mother's room that was just around the corner from them, to tell her what was happening.

"Teag," Milly started with a calm but serious tone. She wasn't really listening to what Suraionee was saying about what Teag was doing, so her orders weren't as sharp as they would have been. "Stop it right now, and get down stairs. The shuttle will be here any time," She yelled from her room.

"Mom, he was in my room again," Teag tried to defend himself after letting his brother go and walking into the hallway he stood in his mothers' doorway, but his mother wasn't listening to him either. She was too busy rushing around gathering last minute items and stuffing them in her suitcase.

"Johnny, leave your brother alone, and stay out of his room," she looked back at Teag, "Now he's younger than you, so please set a good example," Trying to neutralize the problem without knowing the details.

"It was just a joke, I wasn't really…," Teag was interrupted

"Teag, just do as your mother asks. Now please," Jacob insisted as he stepped up the last step of the staircase and entered the hallway.

"Humph, fine." Knowing there would be consequences if he didn't do as he was told, he went back to his room for his gameboy shaking his head. John followed him.

"Milly," Jacob started as he stood in the doorway of their room. "If you don't hurry, we're going to be late. Traffic at this hour is going to be bad," his nicely combed, dark brown hair and well built physique stood in the doorway looking at his wife. He turned around and looked at his sons whispering in secret just down the hallway. He took off his stylish, thin black glasses to clean them, and then placed them nicely on his face. He pulled out his checklist and skimmed over it again, making sure he had everything.

"I know honey, I just have to finish Suraionee's hair, we'll only be a second more," she replied. Milly had long auburn hair that was always in place, even after just waking up in the morning. She had an air of elegance to her that others tried to emulate but failed horribly. She loved her family, and had the rare luxury of staying at home to raise her children.

A horn honked in the background.

"The shuttle is here, I'll take down the luggage," Jacob said as he picked up the luggage from his bedroom and walked down the hall and started down the stairs.

Teag took the large duffel bag from his room and then followed his father out the door. Just outside the front door was a small porch and walkway that lead to the curb of the street where the shuttle sat idling. The grass on both sides of the walkway were dark green and freshly cut. Flowers sat in pots on both sides of the door. The flower garden was well taken care of and had brightly colored blooms. The neighboring houses were connected like town homes and each with their own colorful but tasteful designs to them. Teag dropped his bag at the trunk of the big white shuttle van, and then ran upstairs for more.

John was at the top of the stairs challenging Teag to be the first one down the stairs to the shuttle. They both picked up two bags each, then tried to race to the bottom and out the door. John followed close behind Teag. They were pushing and shoving each other down the stairs to be the first one out the door, when John lost his balance and started to fall dropping his bag; grabbing Teag and pulling him down along with him. They tumbled for a moment laughing, and then kept going. After they reached the doorway, they stumbled through, both thinking they had won; which gave them something new to argue about.

John was a striking, fourteen-year-old boy. His short, light brown hair, flawless face, stunning brown eyes and timeless smile could captivate even the most unresponsive person. It was hard to tell he was the younger of the two because he could easily keep up with his older brother.

Jacob was standing by the drivers' door talking to the shuttle driver through the window, when Teag and John appeared stumbling through the doorway. The shuttle driver opened the door and stepped out. He walked passed Teag and John and started loading the suitcases in the back of the van. Teag followed John and climbed into the back seat. Teag found his seatbelt and put it on. Then the two continued wrestling and teasing one another, growing louder by the second.

"Boys," Jacob spoke firmly. "Calm down," checking his watch, he started pacing back and forth on the sidewalk. "What could she possibly be doing? Does it really take that long to fix Suraionee's hair?" He mumbled under his breath.

Moments later Suraionee ran outside. Her long natural auburn highlights glistened in the sun against her dark brown hair and made her big green eyes stand out more than usual. Her lips were a naturally deep pink and her eyelashes so long that even her mother envied them. She held the dark brown, fuzzy-soft teddy bear her father gave her when she was five under her arm. The bear was worn and tattered, but Suraionee insisted that she couldn't leave home without it, "this is going to be our best vacation ever," she remarked in excitement, climbing into the back seat next to Teag.

"Where is your mother?" Jacob asked, worried they were never going to get out of there. He put his left hand on his hip and used his right hand to scratch his head through his hair. His tall mass was standing there anxiously awaiting Milly's appearance.

"Here I am," Milly said with a warm smile on her face. She turned to lock the door, then swiftly got into the shuttle. Jacob slid the door shut behind her, climbed in on the other side and sat next to her. As soon as he shut the door, the shuttle pulled out and raced to the pier.

On the Freeway the vehicles were at a quick pace and several passed them on the left speeding into the distance. Teag pulled out his gameboy and started to play it while John and Suraionee watched out the window as they passed all kinds of cars and trucks and the thick layer of large evergreen trees that bordered the freeway.

The game felt boring at the moment he knew it so well he didn't really need his full attention to play anymore. He suddenly found himself envisioning his dream, the crashing of the waves and how the mist stung his face. A bad scenario came to his mind, instead of himself he watched, while wide awake, as his mother drown. He shook it off, but then another vision of his father drowning. He shook his head as if it would clear his mind, it helped for a moment and then he thought about something else. 'I'm not crazy, I'm not crazy...it's just my imagination,' he thought, then he forced himself to think about the birds chirping while he stood in the window. The thought successfully took out the horrible images and thoughts.

It wasn't long before they reached the Evergreen Point floating bridge. The water was high and choppy. Several boats were already out and floating around on the lake. The bridge moved slightly from side to side from the shifting water giving a light sense of insecurity. The view was beautiful. All the millions of trees that landscaped the terrain were so vibrant with life. A few clouds lined the sky but the sunny day just kept getting better.

Milly riffled through her purse and pulled out the tickets looking at them again. Over the top of the large rectangle ticket it said Princess Ruby Cruises to Juneau, Alaska on June first. Leaving at seven am. The ticket also said they were in suite Three Hundred Fifty Nine and Three Hundred Sixty. Milly smiled as she remembered her friend insisting that she and her family take the tickets and go on this *"well deserved trip."* It was hard for Milly to accept such an expensive trip, but her wonderful friend would not take, *"No,"* for an answer and had said, "Besides, we can't get the vacation time to go and it expires, so someone better make use of them, and who better than you and your family?" Milly knew that they would never be able to afford going on a trip like this because it was way out of their budget, but she felt better about accepting when she was told that the tickets were free to her from her boss for making top sales woman of the year.

Twenty minutes after they had left their home, they were at pier sixty six and unloading. The air had the fragrant of salt and fish. Suraionee got out and started walking toward the large building. Milly, not paying attention to her, said, "oh good, we still have ten minutes and there's no line. I knew everything would be alright," she hoped it would please her tense husband. Then noticing Suraionee, Milly called out, "Sura, stay by me please. We don't need you wandering off and getting lost," Milly motioned her back. John grabbed a bag from the back and then walked with them.

"I'm ten, Mom. I'm not a child," Suraionee said, annoyed that her mother still treated her like a baby.

"Sura, you're Nine—you'll be Ten in five days, and you're still my child...and we don't have time to play this silly game," Milly said, taking Suraionee's arm and following Jacob to check in. "This is going to be so much fun. You're just going to love the cruise," she added with a big grin on her face.

Suraionee wasn't upset with her mother long; especially when she saw the huge Cruise Liner they were getting closer to, "Wow!" she and John exclaimed simultaneously.

John ran to catch up with Teag who was leading the group with Jacob, his duffel bag over his shoulder.

"Look Teag," John pointed at the Cruise liner. They both stopped walking.

"Just a minute. I almost have it..." Teag paused the game, then looked up from his gameboy. "Whoa," he said, taking a step back to get the full picture. A big grin filled his face. "Is that the ship we're going on?" he asked John.

"I guess so, Mom was just talking to Sura and..."

"I'm gonna beat ya there," Teag teased his brother, running closer to the Cruise Liner entrance.

"Wait boys," Milly yelled after them, "come back! We need to check in first."

Teag and John quickly turned around and ran back to stand with their mother. They were standing a few feet behind Jacob, waiting and chatting amongst themselves. Milly could tell there was something wrong and tried to listen in, but John was now teasing Suraionee, and Teags gameboy was beeping too loud.

"What do you mean it's the small ship? The tickets said the Princess Ruby, and the whole family was included," Jacob said in protest pointing to the tickets he held in his hand, faced at the woman behind the counter.

The woman took the tickets and turned them to face Jacob and pointed, "I'm sorry, sir, but your tickets say otherwise. It says here a family of three and the ship is *The Treasure* and you have two rooms number five and six," The large woman behind the counter said apologetically.

Jacob was perplexed, he looked back at Milly and then shook his head, "I'm sorry my wife said it was something totally different,"

Aftertaking a moment to think, he asked, "well how much is it to add my other two children?" Feeling stupid for not looking at the tickets himself earlier.

"It will be Twelve Hundred Dollars."

Jacob grunted, "Twelve Hundred each?" He shrieked, "No! no, we can't do that," his cheeks grew red with frustration.

"No, I'm sorry, sir. It's Twelve Hundred for both of them."

"Well, how much more is it to upgrade to the Princess Ruby?"

"Let me just see what I can do here," she stared at her screen and began typing fast, "it looks like I can get you on the Princess Ruby, I only have two suites left and I'm afraid you'll have to pay an extra two thousand per person. It leaves tomorrow morning, would you like to change your plans?"

Not even hesitating Jacob replied, "no, let me just pay for my other two children and we'll go on *The Treasure*," there was a short pause as Jacob pulled out his money to pay, "but out of curiosity, where is the Princess Ruby going?" Jacob asked, knowing they had just enough money to buy food and gifts while staying in Alaska, and paying the extra money would eat that all up.

"Juneau, Alaska," she nicely replied.

"Oh, I'm sorry I meant where is *The Treasure* going?"

"To Anchorage, Alaska," She smiled back at him.

Jacob nodded and then handed her his money. She handed him a receipt and his tickets and then pointed him in the right direction.

After they were all checked in, they started toward their ship. Milly asked Jacob what had happened. When the kids walked ahead of them, he told her.

"No, I looked at the tickets while I was sitting in the Shuttle, I know what they said, I'm not crazy," she exclaimed thinking back.

"Well the lady showed them to me and that isn't what was printed on them at all."

"Maybe she switched them."

"How? When? She didn't have time to do that, and anyway, why would she? Why do you always think so negatively? You just read it wrong. Next time, I'll make sure I read it carefully."

"I don't always think negatively," she defended, "and I wish you had looked at them, because you would have seen that I'm not crazy."

"I know dear, lets just get to the ship." Jacob nodded in agreement but was frustrated at the mistake. Milly felt bad that the trip wasn't what she had thought, but they agreed that they wouldn't tell the kids because they knew they would beg to go without food if it meant taking the larger ship. "I guess that's what we get for free tickets. Where did we get it from again?" He asked.

"From my friend Sally, she got them from work as a prize but they couldn't get the holiday time to go, so she gave it to us."

"Oh, well, that was nice," Jacob said as they walked.

Teag watched in amazement as they approached the cruise liner. The ship had to be the same size as the Titanic. He had learned about the shipwreck in school last year. His ninth grade teacher, Miss Washburn, made him redo his report. She said it had no feeling, lacked in facts and, he hadn't made the proper notations as she had previously asked him to do. He remembered that, before his dream, it alone had made him afraid to get on a ship. Now the memory of his dream reminded him of the panic of not being able to breath, and then the pain of breathing in the water. The excitement that was once thick on his mind, was now gone and left an intense fear. His stomach turned and twisted as he tried to relax and forget about it. He closed his eyes tightly and took a deep breath. When he opened his eyes he looked around to make sure no one noticed.

Teag looked back at the large ship. The cruise liner had what appeared to be eleven levels. It was huge and so beautiful. The white paint was so brilliant with the sun hitting the side that he had to look away. As they approached, he watched his father walk past the entrance. Teag, Suraionee, and John stopped.

"Dad, where are you going?" Teag asked, confused.

"To our ship. It's this way," Jacob replied, looking at his kids crushed faces.

"But dad, I thought this was our ship," Suraionee said with obvious discontent.

"Nope, that would have been fun, but way too expensive for us right now," Jacob said, "but you should like the one we get on."

Milly pointed to the tiny ship that dwarfed the massive Cruise liner. It was such a difference in size that they were all disenchanted. Teag took a good long look at the small ship. It was old and dilapidated, and it appeared as though it had seen many years and even more storms. The name on the side of the ship said, *The Treasure*. 'Some Treasure,' he thought. One of the windows on the bridge was cracked. When he walked on board, the deck creaked as though it was ready to break beneath him. He even noticed a small trace of slime on the railing and a bit of seaweed on the deck here and there. He slowly inched his way forward and then caught the smell of food cooking in the dining hall. Teag, John, and Suraionee peaked inside. It was decorated like a cabin. There were only four small tables in the middle of the floor that seated four people. Along the walls were several booths with large brown panels on the walls separating them. Suraionee read aloud a note on the wall. It read:

In case of a severe storm,
everyone must report
to the Dining Hall.

The thought of his dream crept back into Teag's mind, 'Even though this is a smaller ship, the same thing could still happen,' he thought, 'that is if we don't sink before we leave the dock first.'

Jacob took the bags to their room while Teag, John, Suraionee, and Milly stepped on the deck to watch the pier slowly drift away as they departed. The engine, though old, made light, *sh...sh...sh*, sounds in a rhythmic sort of way.

There weren't many people on the ship. Teag counted four other small families that had young children. They hadn't gone far when he caught the excitement on one small child's face after he spotted a family of Orca whales swimming close by.

"Kyle," his mother called him, "lets get closer," they quickly walked past the Tragers' and slipped out of sight.

John and Suraionee raced each other down to the bow of the ship. Teag watched them as they played tag and other silly games. He looked down below and one level lower was a small pool that looked like it was as old as the ship. It was full of clear water but the tiles

26

inside appeared to be lightly stained with mold. There were deck chairs all along the side of it but no one was using them.

The smell of salt water was in the breeze, then suddenly, the smell of rain. The once sunny day was now turning into another rainstorm. The ocean, though rainy, was quiet and calm. 'Something doesn't feel right,' Teag thought to himself, noticing he was standing alone under the overhang. He glanced around to find his mother. She was standing at the railing about twenty feet away, staring off into space, and getting wetter by the minute. Her long auburn hair, flowing gracefully in the wind just moments before was, now stuck to her face lashed by the rain. Her light brown eyes looked troubled. She was always nicely put-together and seemed to always have everything in order. Even in the worst situations, she always had a smile on her face. Yet as she stood there, it was as if she knew something the rest of them didn't. For the first time in his life, she was showing concern. Teag walked over to her, "Mother," he started, "why are you just standing in the rain?"

Milly looked at him, then pulled him close with one arm and replied, "oh, it's nothing dear. Everything will be fine, just fine," she said calmly trying to shield Teag from her fears. She had an overwhelming feeling that something bad was about to happen that enveloped her as soon as she set foot on the ship. Yet she didn't know what or even understand why she felt that way. She stood there looking off into the distance as if the ocean and clouds were talking to her, trying to tell her something important.

Teag could feel her apprehension, and could tell she wasn't being truthful. He knew she was just saying it to protect him, but she wasn't a very good liar. "You're worried, aren't you?...about the storm, I mean," Teag questioned, calling her on it in a nice way.

Milly and Teag looked over to John and Suraionee who were now standing near them on the same level. John was playing and wrapped his arm around her pretending he was going to toss her over the rail into the pool below.

Suraionee fought back, trying to loosen his grip and get away, "stop it. You're hurting me," she complained.

Looking back at Teag, Milly said, "No, no, it will pass. You'll see," she tried to convince herself. Noticing the noise John and Suraionee were making she, glanced back over to John and Suraionee, and yelled, "John! Leave her be!"

John released Suraionee and then grinned, while poking at her. He saw his father peek out of a nearby room, then he looked back at Suraionee, who started walking back down to the Bow of the ship because she wanted to stay outside in the rain. John started grabbing at her trying to make her go inside.

Struggling to get free, Suraionee kept yelling at him, saying, "Let me GO!"

Irritated that they weren't listening to her, Milly ignored them and was concentrating on her conversation with Teag and trying to tune out the background noise her children were making.

"How do you know? Mom, I just have this feeling...," Teag started, but was interrupted when his father called to them.

"Hey," he said to all of them, "I can't have you all getting sick. Come in here where it's nice, warm, and dry," then directing his attention to John and Suraionee, he warned, "John, let go of your sister and get in here. You're soaked."

When they got to their room, Suraionee said in surprise, "wow, is this room all mine?"

"No, Suraionee. The bed is for your mother and me, and the small couch you see over there," he pointed to the couch at the foot of the bed, "well, you pull the pillows off, and that becomes your bed," Jacob was half laughing.

Suraionee was so used to having her own room and a big bed that the thought of sleeping on a couch in a room the size of a large walk-in-closet appalled her, "you're kidding, right? Ha, ha, ha, daddy. Really, where is my room?" She demanded.

"Really, Sura, I'm not joking, this was all they had," Jacob noticed the tears in her eyes, then added with his hand on her shoulder, "listen, it isn't going to be that bad. It's only for three nights, and we don't have to stay in here all the time, just to sleep...and maybe when it's raining outside, but that's all. The rest of the time you can spend up on deck enjoying the sun, air, and your brothers."

"Daddy, how can you expect me to sleep on a couch the size of a peanut? All I have to do is roll over and I'm on the floor."

"Now, really Suraionee. You're exaggerating. You roll over on that couch, and you will be wedged between the queen bed and the couch, you won't ever touch the floor," Milly jumped in, suddenly feeling jovial.

Suraionee glared at her mother. Then, realizing that there was nothing she could do, she stomped over to the couch and sat down, "I can't wait till this is all over," she pouted under her breath.

Jacob and Milly laughed.

"Why are you laughing?" Suraionee asked, very annoyed.

"Well, you never asked where your brothers were going to sleep," Jacob said, getting a kick out of teasing her and the fact that she was taking the bait.

Suraionee's fury overwhelmed her, and her eyes grew dark, "they'd better be sleeping on the floor," she demanded.

Jacob tried to contain his laughter. Suraionee had never let him get to her like this before. She normally just brushed it off, and knew he was joking. Making one last attempt to tease her and make her realize that he was joking, he said, "well, actually, all three of you are going to sleep on the couch together," This time Teag and John joined in laughing, knowing that Jacob was teasing.

After a moment of steaming, she couldn't hold a straight face any longer and joined in laughing, "very nice Dad, but you wont be so lucky next time. You won't get that close."

"We'll see," Jacob said, wiping the fresh tears of laughter off his face, "we'll see."

"You two have a sick sense of humor," Milly said as she lightly hit Jacob on the shoulder.

"You joined in too," he defended.

"Yeah, well…if you can't beat 'em, join 'em," Milly explained, still laughing, "come with me, Suraionee. You and I will sleep in the room next door. This should be the door here," she unlocked an adjoining door from inside. Then she walked into a room the same size and design as the first.

"Dad and Teag will sleep on the bed, and John will sleep on the couch. You and I are in here," Milly clarified.

John, catching the conversation teased Suraionee, "Oh, so now I have to sleep on the couch?" Then he stomped around the room, trying not to laugh.

Teag looked at his father and said, "if it's all the same to you, I'd rather sleep on the floor."

Jacob didn't hesitate. He nodded in agreement and handed Teag his pillow.

Suraionee pretended not to hear John. She sat on the bed in her room and glanced around. The room had a sort of warmth to it; small and cozy, yet, if it were her own, it would have felt comfortable. There was an old musky smell to both of the room, as if they hadn't been used in many years. It reminded her of her grandmother's house. The walls were an old velvety red, brick color, as if someone was trying to create an elegant-type royalty room and was not succeeding. Above the queen bed was a copy of Monet's Rough Sea 1883. It was a painting of a ship on the stormy seas, "Funny," she said to herself.

"What?" Milly asked

"What?" Suraionee then asked her mother as she snapped out of her trance.

"You said *funny* so, what's so funny?"

"I said that out loud?"

"Yes."

"Oh," there was a short pause as Suraionee thought about it again, "I was just looking at the painting and thinking it was funny that they would put a picture of a storm on the ocean in a room on a ship," Suraionee replied.

Teag laid upside down on the bed with his head at the foot. He heard her talking from the other room and took a look at the painting over the bed in his room. It happened to be the same painting. The more he thought about it, the more he worried that the storm was going to get a lot worse. He closed his eyes and wished himself to Hawaii. But when he opened them again, he was still in the small, cramped room. His father was sitting on the edge of the bed close to the door to his sisters room. He was reading today's newspaper which he had brought from home. He must have been really involved, because Milly came back in and talked to him for over 15 minutes, and he never even looked up. She didn't seem to mind though.

John threw the pillows off the couch and then sat down. Suraionee closed her eyes and fell asleep.

John and Jacob were talking while sitting on the couch. Teag's thoughts were consumed with the ocean and the storm ahead. On his back and with his head at the foot of the bed, he stared at the painting on the wall. The rocking of the ship was somehow soothing. He looked to his left and could see the door to leave the room, there was a porthole on the left for the door. Directly behind him was the sofa that John was going to sleep on but on the Left of that was the full bathroom and tiny closet. On the right of the sofa was a little table with a phone that was bolted down. There was just a little walking room between the queen bed and the wall on Teags' right that lead to his sister's room. The door was open and Teag could hear her snoring.

Milly riffled through her luggage and pulled out a page of activities. She sat down on the bed next to Teag and started to read it to herself, "Are you interested in some activities?"

"Like what?" Teag closed his eyes feeling that there couldn't be anything on the ship that he would want to do.

"Well, it says here that there are crafts, looks like they're making necklaces and bracelets."

Teag turned and looked at her like she was crazy, "do you really think I want to make a necklace or a bracelet?"

"Well, you could make it for Sura, she would like it and you could give it to her for her birthday."

"Yeah, but if I show my face to something like that I wont have any chance of making any friends on this ship. And if anyone back home got wind of it, I'll never hear the end of it," Teag was annoyed that she would even think he would enjoy something like that.

"Okay, well, there is bowling and also swimming, but the weather would have to clear up for that one." Milly scratched the top of her nose then kept reading, "here's one, there's a wood shop somewhere around here and you could make anything you want with the teachers help. That would be nice, I know you like your shop class back home, you get good grades in it, wouldn't you like to do that?" Milly stared down at him in hopes to see some kind of reaction from him.

"Fine, if I must, I'll go bowling, and maybe later I'll head down to the shop and see what they have."

"I know you're just going to love it."

"Right, thanks mom."

"Right after lunch we should go bowling, that would be a great family activity," Milly commented to the room of people. Teag had already told her he would go so he didn't bother to move or say anything else, he just closed his eyes and allowed the smooth rocking of the ship lulled him to sleep.

Chapter 2

Suddenly gasping for air, Teag sat straight up on the bed and realized that his father and John were looking at him.

"You alright there?" Jacob asked with concern.

"Fine, just a bad dream, sorry to bother you," Teag said hoping his father wouldn't ask any further questions.

"Same dream as before?" Jacob asked, guessing he was right before Teag answered.

"Yeah, but it's no big deal," Teag nodded and then leaned back and laid his head on the pillow. His brother John was watching and Teag didn't like it. His brother was always so irritating, wanting to know his business and sticking his nose where it didn't belong. So he turned his body to lay on his side away from John and his father.

"Do you want to talk about it?" Jacob asked.

"No, not really," Teag answered, looking back at John who was anxiously awaiting an answer. He glanced over at the clock on the night stand by the bed and read the time 'lunchtime.' he thought. With his heart still pounding and still worried about his dream, he walked over to the small porthole by the door and saw the ocean calm and serene. Only little ripples poked to the surface as the light rain fluttered down to meet the sea. He took a deep breath and started to calm himself. His stomach began to growl and churn when he remembered he hadn't eaten breakfast.

"What's the dream about?" John asked curiously still waiting to hear more.

Jacob looked over at Teag to see his reaction to the question. When Teag just shook his head, Jacob knew Teag didn't want to talk about it, "nothing, it was just a silly dream." Jacob told John.

The lunch bell rang. Voices of cheerful children and their parents grew louder as they walked past the Trager's room towards the dining hall.

Teag announced to his father, "I'm going to eat," and then he bolted out the door.

John and Suraionee were waiting for Milly, "hurry, mom or we'll be the last ones to get there, and there won't be anything good left," Suraionee said impatiently.

"I'm coming," Milly replied, slipping on her shoes and walking towards the door. "Slow down, or you'll slip and fall out there," she commanded while Suraionee was pulling her by the arm. "Jacob, are you coming?" She called out, half way out the door.

"I'll only be another minute. I'll meet you there," he called back to her as he turned the page of his news paper.

The dining hall smelled of tacos and beef enchiladas, and the line was already backed up to the door. Suraionee was frustrated. The line was moving too slow for her, and she was growing impatient. After a minute of standing there with no movement, she caught a glimpse of Teag five people up in line. John eyed him too, "see, mom? I told you," Suraionee grumbled.

"It's okay, we're almost there, and see, the line is moving fast," Milly said, pointing to the food.

"Yeah, it is okay, because we're going up with Teag," Suraionee said, bolting toward her brother with John by her side. They shoved each other playfully.

"Mmm…it smells so good," Suraionee said licking her lips, "this is my favorite."

"Mine, too," John echoed.

Teag, John and Suraionee sat in a large booth near the door eating their food like they hadn't eaten in days. The buffet was against the wall in the far right corner. The wooden panels that were on the walls at each of the booths looked as though they came off easily. The floor was old and worn even rotting. Several large tears in the linoleum could be seen in random places all over the floor.

Now watching the people and how they interacted with one another, he could tell who were friends and who were family, not just by the obvious, but also by their body language. Teags eyes went across the room when he stopped at an old woman sitting by herself. She didn't look like she could handle a journey like this. Her skin was old and leathered, as if she had been in the sun for too long. She had long blonde hair that appeared dyed. Her jaw line was almost non-existent, her body appeared frail. Curiously the more he watched the old woman, the more he began to feel the old woman was watching him, except, it was strange, her eyes never left the table. Shaken for a moment, he searched the room for someone looking at him, but found no one. His family stood up to go back to their rooms, and Teag slowly followed behind them. Glancing back to the old woman, he waited, searching to see what would happen, only to be disappointed.

After lunch the family made their way to the lower levels, "the bowling alley is somewhere down here," claimed Milly as she looked at every sign they came to trying to find their way.

Suraionee lead the way skipping and twirling before she found a sign that read, *"Bowling this way,"* she repeated it and pointed down the hall the same direction they were already heading. "Here it is!" She exclaimed Suraionee before she bolted into the room making sure she was the first one inside.

There were four lanes, the room was dimly lit and had a few flickering lights here and there. All the lanes were in use except the one in the far left corner.

"It's our lucky day, looks like one is left," Jacob remarked after he asked for a size twelve shoe. Suraionee and John had run over to pick out their bowling balls. Teag stayed and waited for his shoes then went to pick out his bowling ball.

Milly, Suraionee, John and Teag were busy tying their shoes while Jacob put their names on the scoreboard.

"Your first Sura," Jacob informed her while adding the last name, his name, to the list.

Suraionee stood up and stuck her fingers in all the black bowling balls trying to find the one she picked as her own. When she found it she stepped up and did a little dance step before she sent her ball gliding down the lane. She laughed and giggled as it looked like the ball was staying in the center, but then gasped a little as the ball slowly rolled into the gutter.

"No!" Suraionee whined, then mopped back to her seat.

Though Teag enjoyed bowling, he felt silly sitting there with his family. 'Family time is for baby's,' he thought, 'but it's better than the bead making my mom wanted me to do for Suraionee,' he thought. Teag glanced over to the family in the lane next to them. There was a boy that looked about his age. 'Finally someone I can talk too, someone my age, maybe this trip wont me a waste of time,' he wondered. He sat there and watched as the little girl bowled a spare and swore while she walked back to her seat.

The boy laughed at her, "you didn't do it, you didn't get the turkey, poor little Pepper." The girl looked like she was going to cry but she shook it off and stuck her nose into the air and ignored him.

Their mother gave the boy a dirty look as if she thought that would make him stop laughing, "Don't tease your sister, and stop calling her Pepper, I hate that nickname," the mother growled trying to be discreet.

Teag looked up at their scoreboard and noticed they were all playing a great game, better than himself. He was surprised that the girl was playing so well, she only looked to be about four or five-years-old.

The more he watched the more he thought they looked very out of place on a ship like this. They wore expensive clothing and glowered at everyone as if they were beneath theor own upstanding background.

The father wore stylish thin silver glasses, had reddish blonde hair, and he had a stalky build to him.

The mother had light brown hair and dark blue eyes and was very thin. Though she was cordial she seemed to hold disdain for the people around her. She held her head high and smirked as though laughing at everyone around her.

The boy looked about his age and just about his hight. He wore a short military cut flattop on his darker blonde hair and appeared to have gray eyes. He laughed at his little sister every time she made a mistake and missed a pin.

The little girl had red hair and freckles; she looked very young but acted much older and proper, though she seemed just as dissatisfied with the company they seemed forced to keep.

Teag started thinking about introducing himself, 'maybe they aren't as bad as they appear,' Teag thought, 'maybe I can actually make a friend.'

"Teag it's your turn," Jacob informed him, interrupting Teag's thoughts.

"Oh," he stood up and picked up his ball, he hadn't paid attention to what Suraionee and John had done so far so he looked at the screen. Suraionee hit only five pins, but John got a strike. Teag walked up and with his feet together and took aim. To his right the other boy walked up and took aim in his lane. They both started moving at the same time and gracefully slid their balls down the lanes. The boy next to him started swearing when his ball started rolling into the gutter.

"Don't you know it's common courtesy to wait while the person next to you bowls first? Woow...Freaky eyes!" He sneered glaring at Teag noticing the light blue star in his left eye.

"Yeah, but I was up here first, so that means it was you who should have waited," Teag smartly replied. The boys glared at one another for a few moments and Teag decided he didn't want to be friends with this kid. After all there was just something about him that really irked him more than just his snobby tone.

"Okay, Okay. Sorry, lets have a good game and be courteous to the other players," Jacob remarked stepping in trying to calm things down a little between the boys. When Teag and the boy kept staring at one another almost nose to nose, Jacob grabbed Teags arm and pulled him away. He looked over at the other father who sat there smiling, like nothing was wrong.

"Dad, it wasn't...,"

Jacob looked back at Teag and cut him off, "I don't care Teag, you be the better man about it, besides, you got a strike out of it, nothing to complain about."

Teag didn't care though, he looked over at the boy who was still swearing about the whole thing. He watched as his father gave him a high five. It was infuriating. These people didn't even know him and they hated him. The boy called him *freaky eyes*, and his father just wanted him to leave it alone? Be the better person for it? He didn't want to be the better person anymore, he wanted revenge for all the horrible things all the kids over they years had done to him. He was fed up. He knew that there was nothing he could do at the moment so he sat in his seat and steamed. The feeling of great injustice hung over his head. He wanted to make the boy see things his way.

* * *

At the end of the third game John boasted of his triumphant win, though Suraionee won the first round and Jacob won the second. Teags' mind hadn't been on any of the games. He only bowled one hundred and ten points on all three games. He didn't play often but he normally at least made two hundred and twenty-five points.

"Are you feeling alright? You haven't really been playing. Are you still upset about that boy?" Milly asked.

"Yeah, I think I just want to get some fresh air," Teag said. He excised himself, stood up and walked out weaving his way through the narrow tunnels of the corridor until he found himself outside standing by the pool. He sat down on one of the deck chairs. The rain had stopped and the sun peeked through the dark clouds above him warming him from the chilly breeze. The fresh air smelled sweet and was relaxing. He sat back in his chair and closed his eyes enjoying the warm sun. A shadow blocked the nice warm rays and Teag opened his eyes.

"Where's your daddy now to fight your battles?" The boy from the bowling alley was standing above him smirking at him trying to pick a fight.

"What?" Teag asked trying to figure out how his dad's comment became fighting his battle. "Oh was that a fight? I didn't realize that the insignificant comment you made was meant as *fighting words*," Teag made quotation marks with his fingers and gave him a dirty look.

"Where I come from I always win the fight."

"Fight a lot do ya?" Teag laughed looking him up and down. "Whado ya do, hand them a check and tell them to go away and never come back?" Teag imitated handing someone a check and then shooing the invisible person away with his hands. He knew the boy was bigger than him but he couldn't help himself.

"Come say that to my face, you freaky-eyed punk."

Teag was angry that this boy kept calling him *freaky-eyes* and even more that he sought him out to start a fight. He wanted to fight, but all that kept going through his mind was his father telling him to *walk away*, and *be the better man*. His father would be outraged if he was caught fighting and Teag couldn't take disappointing his father.

"You're not worth my time," Teag blurted out. That wasn't what he wanted to say but thinking about his father made the words, just come out. Once it was out there he couldn't take it back so he stood up out of the pool chair. He started to walk away but was suddenly yanked back and shoved into the nearby pool. Furious Teag struggled to swim to the side, the weight of his clothing weighing him down making it much more difficult. The water was freezing and his teeth began to chatter. When he made it to the ladder he climbed out with water splashing everywhere making a huge puddle where he stood. Spectators were starting to appear, the boy watched with delight and laughed as he ran away. Teag's clothing stuck to his body and made the chilly wind feel like ice to his already shivering body. Rage and embarrassment burned his face and ears. He was so angry he wanted to rip the boy apart and throw him overboard. Teag glanced around to find him in the crowd and shook his head in anger when he was no where to be seen.

Teag was left with the snickers and chattering of the onlookers. Once again he was made a fool, his eyes narrowed as he swore to himself, angry that he was even in this situation. He quickly walked past the spectators, embarrassed he kept his head down and made his way back to his room. 'I have to do something, but my parents will kill me if I do, but I can't be made the fool anymore. I need to make sure these people know they can't hurt me anymore.' He made it to his room where he was happy to find that no one was there. He changed into some warm clothing and then sat on his bed on the floor, steaming about what had happened at the pool. 'The stupid jerk,' Teag thought as he laid there trying to figure out why he always got picked on everywhere he went. 'What am I doing wrong? Am I wearing some kind of kick me sign on my forehead? I can't really be that much of a loser.' Teag thought as he laid there on the floor, "I've go to do something about this, I've got to stand up for myself, but how?"

The next morning was beautiful, not a cloud in the sky. The day was warm and inviting. While the rest of the family lazily lay in bed, Milly and Teag got ready for the day, then headed outside to take in the morning air. Teag wandered away from Milly and ended up at the bow of the ship, thinking about his dream. The cool small gusts of wind that swiftly passed by, smelled clean and refreshing making Teag feel relaxed and subdued. 'I'm so glad it was just a dream,' he thought as he looked out over the ocean. The water was glistening in the sun. It was so calm and there was no sign of land. The sky was a deep blue. Not having any clouds out made the crisp morning air warm up quickly. On his way to the dining hall, Teag saw Suraionee, John and his dad walking towards the dining hall. He caught up with them, and they all walked in to play cards with Milly. Playing cards was something his family loved to do when they were able to spend time together. Many hours would go by so quickly while they would laugh, play, and just have a good time. Together they ate breakfast and then played till lunch. After they ate, they went back to playing cards. A few short minutes later, Teag became bored and asked, "Is there anything else to do in this place?"

"Oh, I'm sorry, are we boring you?" Jacob asked teasing.

"No…well, yes…No! I mean, No. It's just that we have played the same game over and over for hours, and I think I need to stretch my legs," Teag replied, trying to be truthful, but also trying to be nice. He got up and walked out to the deck. Suraionee wanted to go out too, so she and John ran out, teasing and picking at each other as usual and running the opposite direction of Teag. There were two little kids playing hide-and-go-seek on the bow. Spurts of laughter were heard, making Teag smile. The lunch bell rang, but Teag was enjoying the nice, hot sun. He thought it strange that the weather was oddly warm for this part of the country. He held onto the railing and looked over the side, watching the water break on the bow. It was refreshing to take in all the fresh sea air. Just as soon as he started enjoying himself, he felt eyes on him again, like the night before. Looking around, Teag found the little old woman sitting in a chair in the shade, watching the ocean.

"It's time I find out what's going on," he told himself out loud. He walked over and took the seat next to the woman.

"Hi," he said as he approached her.

The woman peered up at him with her cool blue sagging eyes and wrinkly, leathered skin with a smile on her face. Her blonde hair was up in a tight bun. Her lips were almost a dry pale pink that made Teag want to take a drink of water to soften them, as if they were his own. Her khaki capris, Hawaiian dress shirt and keds with ankle socks made her appear as a tourist. The only thing missing was a camera and a friend.

"Ah, hello there. I wondered when you would come over to talk to me."

"You were expecting me?" Teag asked surprised.

"Oh yes, but its taken you much less time than the others."

"Others?" he asked out loud, 'She must be out of her mind,' Teag thought to himself.

"Yes, there have been others before you," the woman said.

"Before me? What are you talking about? Who are you?" Teag asked even more confused.

The woman's eyes seemed to be sizing him up. "You are much more intelligent than them though."

"Okay, I give. What are you talking about?" Teag asked, not really sure whether he wanted to know the answer now. He sat in the chair next to her.

"Can you keep a secret?" asked the woman, looking him straight in the eye and playing with what looked to be an exquisite, purple crystal necklace that was hanging around her neck.

"I live on a secluded island kingdom, and every five years I choose a few families to come and live…" she stopped, seeing the confusion in his eyes. Then after a short pause she continued, "you're not ready for the whole secret. You'll see soon enough. My name is ZaBeth. I'll be around when you need me," she then got up to walk away.

"When I need you? Why would I need you? Where did you say you were from?" Teag asked quickly still perplexed. She smiled and gave him a look that made him feel like she was withholding something important. She started to walk away. "Wait, why do I get the feeling that there is something important that you need to tell me, but aren't?"

"My dear Teag Trager, there are a great many things that I know about you that you don't even know for yourself yet. I'm sorry, I must be going now, but I'll see you soon," she smiled again, then stood up and started walking away again.

"Hey, how did you know my name? I didn't tell you my name…," he yelled after her but she didn't turn around. Her walk showed nothing of her age. Her pace was quick and swift. The frailty that he had seen in her wasn't real. Teag suddenly leaped up and ran to find his family.

Back in their room, Milly and Jacob were talking about current events when Teag stormed in a little out of breath.

"Oh there you are, where have you been?" Milly asked slightly concerned.

Teag looked over his shoulder surprised that his mother seemed concerned. He hadn't been gone long. "I was just out for a walk on deck," he said. He decided against telling them about his encounter with the old lady.

"Hmm, that means you took three steps and a twist of the head, and you're out of breath? Humph, boy, do we have work to do," Jacob teased while laughing.

"First of all, dad...your shoe's untied," he smartly replied back, knowing his father wasn't wearing any shoes at the moment. Jacob's cheeks went red when he looked anyway. "I just wanted to see if anyone wanted to go to lunch. When I walked by there was a line already starting," he started, "where's John and Suraionee?" Before Milly could answer Suraionee opened the door and walked in. She had just been out making jewelry for herself. John followed her in. He was playing a bit of basketball and just happened to come back the same time as Suraionee.

"Back so soon?" Jacob asked John surprised to see him.

"Yeah, well we lost the only two basketballs when that guy from the bowling alley tried to show-off with a three pointer. The ball smacked the edged of the backboard and bounced over board."

Teag laughed a little at hearing this but then shut his mouth when John gave him a dirty look.

"Who's *we*?" Milly asked.

"Me and some girls, they were twins," John answered and then went back to his story, "we told him it was no big deal that we could still keep playing, but he insisted that he could make the shot and tried it again with the last ball," John shook his head.

"Let me guess that one went over too," Teag laughed feeling a little justice.

"Yeah, so the game was over and I came back, besides I smelled food," John licked his lips.

Teag smiled, "yeah, lets go eat," he John and Suraionee raced out the door.

When lunch was over they walked back to their room. Jacob had beat them back and was sitting on the couch reading the paper trying to soak up every last word before he went stir crazy. John stepped over to the cozy looking couch to sit down, "excuse me, Dad. I would like to lay down," John motioned with his hands for him to scoot off the couch.

"Tell you what, how about you lay down on the bed and let me sit here for a while?"

"Really? I get the bed? Greatest day ever!" John exclaimed.

"Don't get too excited there, turbo. You get your cushy of a couch back when it's time for bed."

"Awe, dad. Just one night?" John pleaded, all the while knowing the answer was going to be no.

"Well John, how do you suggest I lay down…like this?" He stood up and flopped himself over the arm of the chair, his face planted right into the seat cushion and his feet touching the floor over the other side. As everyone started chuckling, he stood up to try another position, "or how about this?" He put his head up on one arm of the chair, his belly facing down touching the seat cushion, and his feet in the air on the other arm. The family started laughing harder.

"Yes, dad. Just like that. You'll see…it's actually pretty comfortable after a little while. I tried it last night. I heard it's really good for your back. In fact they say that everyone should start sleeping like that, and then all their back problems will be gone. They especially say that if you take a cruise like this one to look for the rooms just like this so you have the best couch for a bed," John joked, trying not to laugh.

"That last one looked like it hurt," Milly said as she reached out to help Jacob sit the right way on the couch, and to see if he was all right.

"Yeah, it did," he started in agony, "if anyone sleeps that way and they think it's better for their back, they'd better have their heads examined," smiling, Jacob finished, "I know how thorough your investigation was on the matter Johnny."

"Oh yes," John chuckled, "years of research," he remarked with a smile.

Milly stood up and went over to her bags in her room. She unzipped her large suitcase and rifled through it. She pulled out a small wooden chest she had been keeping for Suraionee's birthday. She walked back into the room everyone was sitting in, and her eyes met Jacob's.

"Oh...now? Okay," Jacob said as he put the paper away and sat up straight, "Suraionee, why don't you sit right there," Jacob pointed to the edge of the bed across from him.

"What's going on?" John asked.

"We are going to have an early birthday for Sura," Milly replied.

"But mom, what are we going to do on my actual birthday then?" Suraionee asked, concerned.

"Don't worry, we have more planned," Milly smiled, walking over and sitting on the couch with Jacob. Teag and John sat at the end of the bed with Suraionee facing Jacob and Milly, "besides," she added, "this is a special gift," she held the small box in her hand, unlatched the front, and opened it to show the three kids. As the lid slowly lifted and light lightly shown on the object inside, it sparkled. The jewel inside was a one of a kind necklace. It was a diamond-shaped black onyx gem about the size of a silver dollar. In the center was a glowing golden yellow circle with flames like the sun surrounding only half the circle. Attached to the sun was a waxing crescent moon that glowed a deep blue. Set on each of the four corners of the diamond shape were tiny silver shimmering stars.

The black onyx was fashioned in a twenty-four carat gold frame. At each of the four corners of the golden frame sat a snail shell-like swirl design that sat on each side of the point so that it swirled outward. At the very top between the two swirls sat a small diamond. Under the two swirls on the top sat three diamonds. On the other three points at the very tips between the swirls sat one small diamond to match the top point. Dangling from the two side points and the bottom point was a glittery, sparkling, onyx teardrop. It was different from a regular onyx stone because it was a rare deep blue color and had what appeared to be silver shiny flecks of glitter spotted and swirled around in each of the stones. There placed carefully next to the necklace was a set of teardrop earrings that matched the teardrops dangling from the necklace, with a diamond on top.

"A necklace and earrings? Oh, how pretty!" Suraionee reached over, and Milly shut the lid quickly and pulled away.

"Wait...there is a story about it I want you to hear before you put it on."

"A story…aw, mom. Do we really need to listen to another story?" Teag asked, weary of all the stories his mother loved to share about everything.

"This isn't just some story or just some necklace. This necklace has a background. Many, many years ago, there was a good king and queen who ruled over a large island kingdom. Their castle was on an island called "KobiKobis," somewhere between Australia and Hawaii. The people loved their king and queen, and were all happy and prosperous.

They had two daughters. Princess Alura was the eldest and most beautiful. Her fair skin, long golden-blonde hair and purplish blue eyes always glittered in the sunlight. She was kind and generous and always wanted to help others. Princess Desdemona was Alura's opposite. She looked just like her mother with her light olive complexion and dark brown hair. Her light brown eyes were also beautiful, but not more so then her sister Alura's.

Desdemona was jealous of everything Alura had. Every time anyone was in the room, they would fall all over Alura, and regardless of her obvious beauty, she seemed to be invisible to everyone. Being the youngest by eighteen months made living in the castle hard because she knew, when her parents died, Alura would be crowned Queen, and she would be left living in a castle with her sister as ruler.

Soon after Alura turned twenty, her parents suddenly died. Old age is what was thought to have taken them, though Alura was never convinced. It was strange to her that they both went at the same time. With the King and Queen gone, Alura was about to be crowned Queen.

Green with envy, and determined to not be overshadowed by her sister again, Desdemona stood up in the middle of the ceremony and yelled, "you will never be my Queen!" Then looking at the congregation that was witnessing the ceremony, she lied. "She killed the King and Queen to get to the crown. Can't you see? She's fooling you. She poisoned them, and you're letting her get away with it," at the same moment, General Flann (a young new commander) and a few of his Militia made their way over to her. They grabbed her by the arms and escorted her out of the room.

"You'll all be sorry you let her be your queen!" she yelled as she was dragged out of the room.

Standing in the hall, General Flann informed her, "you are a danger to our new Queen, and you are no longer welcome here," he stood there until she walked away.

Desdemona's eyes narrowed and burned with rage, her face convulsed with anger. "You'll pay," she spit out, as she whirled around and stalked off.

Alura held her head high while the congregation rumbled with commotion. The lies her sister told cut her to the core, but her good nature made her realize it was her sister's pain. That thought made it hard to hold back the tears, but she couldn't show her emotion here. Being a Queen meant that she had to show her strength. Holding back the tears made her throat and head throb.

Melanion the Wizard turned his attention to Alura. "Have no fear, I know that she wasn't being truthful," he turned to the congregation that was still rumbling with conversation.

"Wait, mom, there's a wizard in your story? Now I know it's not real," Teag said with skepticism and a little irritation that he was wasting his time listening to a made up story. On the other hand it wasn't like he had a lot to do.

"Who says?" Milly asked.

"Wizards and witches don't exist. They're figments of someone's imagination," Teag said with disdain.

"You shouldn't be so quick to judge," Milly said calmly, "Things are not always what they seem."

"Besides, Teag, you're ruining the story, be quiet," Suraionee added, upset about the break.

"Go ahead with the story, sorry for the interruption," Teag said feeling a little stupid for listening to such a silly story, he swished his hand to move on.

"Silence!" Melanion growled. Everyone in the room grew silent and turned their attention back to Melanion and Alura. "We have a ceremony to finish," he spoke calmly, smiling at Alura.

After Alura was crowned, she ruled with love and honor. She was kind and honest in all of her dealings, and the people of the islands loved her just as they loved her parents.

* * *

Two years later...Queen Alura stood gazing in the mirror. Her long, golden-blonde hair was neatly arranged on her head. Her unusual, purplish-blue eyes were bright with life, but her usually attractive face was afflicted with worry. She had been pacing the room for nearly an hour, reading over the letter she received two weeks earlier again and again, hoping to find an answer that would never be found. It read:

Dear Queen Alura,

I am so grieved that we haven't spoken in a few years.

I truly wish to apologize for my bad behavior when you were chosen for the crown. Please allow me to come in person to beg your forgiveness and allow us to start anew. I miss you so dearly and wish to make amends. I will be there the second Monday in May.

With Love,

Desdemona

After reading the letter Queen Alura took a walk through the castle garden of thick shrubbery, flowers, and trees. She was thinking about the letter and what it meant.

Looking in the mirror she was reminded again of the day she read the letter. Her concern wasn't about forgiving her sister for the troubles she caused, but rather the gossip she overheard while her house maiden and gardener were unaware she was there...

"Everyone knows she is ripe with envy and wants the crown," the housemaid said with concern in a heavy Australian dialect.

"And I assure you, she'll do anything to get it. I heard from the grocer who heard from the blacksmith that she still desires the crown and is attempting to take it. No, if you ask me, this visit isn't just for pleasure. I hope the Queen doesn't turn her back on that imp Desdemona for one second," the woman gardener agreed more than delighted to gossip.

Queen Alura wasn't shocked to hear such rumors, but she had hoped that it was different. Something in her heart told her the rumors were all true.

She glanced in the mirror again and straightened her beautiful lavender gown, 'Is she really coming to see me because she misses me, or does she have another motive?' She thought with dismay.

There was a knock at the door, and Queen Alura snapped out of her trance. "Come in," she commanded.

The door opened, and one of the Queen's most trusted servants walked in and curtsied. She was a beautiful well-dressed handmaiden, "Desdemona is here, your majesty, shall I show her to the parlor room?"

"Yes, please, and inform her I will be in, in a moment," she said with her head held high, showing her strength.

"Yes 'em," the handmaiden said, then she curtsied before leaving the room.

It was lunchtime, and the heat from outside was already warming up the castle. Queen Alura walked gracefully down the stairs and into the parlor room.

Desdemona quickly stood up and curtsied. She was wearing a worn-out, red, party gown that styled a classic puffy skirt and sleeves with a red velvet hat. Her dark brown hair was fixed up under the hat. Her light brown eyes looked directly into Queen Alura's as the queen walked around to her royal chair. Desdemona's face wasn't as pleasing as her sister's, but she was by no means ugly.

"Desdemona, how good to see you, please have a seat," Queen Alura said pointing to the elegant beige sofa behind her sister.

"Oh, thank you for seeing me, I'm only too sorry it has taken me so long to come," Desdemona said while taking her seat asked, "will you ever forgive me?"

"Of course, all is forgotten, think of it no more," the Queen answered eger to forgive, then asked, "would you care for some tea?" She motioned for the tea to be brought in before she heard an answer.

"Yes, please, but let me get it for you as a gesture of thanks," Desdemona's demeanor seemed to put Queen Alura at ease.

'Look at her, she's changed, she really means it. The rumors were wrong, and I worried myself for the past week for nothing,' she thought. "Oh, it's fine, they already have it. Please sit down, and let us cater to you. It's the least I can do," Queen Alura smiled, happy to have her sister back.

The same handmaiden that announced Desdemona's arrival was carefully walking the silver tray of tea over. She set it on the portable serving table and put it between them. She made eye contact with The Queen and curtsied. The Queen motioned her hand to the handmaiden, and young girl knew to leave the room at once, leaving The Queen and Desdemona alone.

The parlor door opened, and the General of the Royal Militia also known as the Queen's fiancée, stepped just inside the door. "Your majesty, I beg your pardon," he said bowing before his Queen, "but there is an urgent matter I must discuss with you."

Knowing that he only appeared in this type of situation with real purpose, she stood up. "Please excuse me for a moment, Desdemona. I'll only be a moment. In the mean time, please enjoy the tea," the Queen stood up, and gracefully walked out of the room. She joined General Flann, who was standing right outside the door dressed in his handsome black and royal blue uniform. Her words with him were short and to the point.

"Your Majesty, I have reason to believe that your sister is planning to take the crown," he said in a firm tone.

"Yes, I've heard that rumor as well, but she has not threatened me here and has been checked for weapons. I don't believe her to be a threat," she pointed out.

"Perhaps that may be true, your highness, but please, for your safety, allow my men to be in the room to keep watch, as a precaution," he asked, but was really insisting on the matter. His light hazel eyes had splashes of brown, light yellow and green. It wasn't hard to see that he had feelings for her and was making this attempt to protect her because of his love, not just because of his job.

Queen Alura shared his feelings but couldn't express them at the time. She paused, glancing at the closed door that held her sister inside. She truly felt that she was in no danger and called him by his first name, "No, Scott, I will show her that I have forgiven her and trust her. I must give her this much," she kindly demanded, then nodded at him as if to kindly say thank you before she turned and walked back into the room.

Desdemona was calmly sitting on the sofa sipping her tea when Queen Alura sauntered back in. She stood up and smiled to politely welcome the Queen back into the room. Her light brown eyes were glistening as if she were happy to see her sister.

"Please forgive the interruption, it won't happen again," Queen Alura said as she sat down across from Desdemona.

"I hope everything is alright?" She asked inquisitively.

"Oh yes, quite," Queen Alura picked up her tea, which was sitting on the coffee table in front of her and took a sip.

"I hope that my being here isn't causing any trouble," Desdemona asked, as if she had heard the Queen's conversation with General Flann.

"No, of course not, nothing of the kind," Queen Alura smiled hiding the truth of the conversation.

The rest of the visit, the sisters shared pleasantries while eating a wonderful lunch. It wasn't long before Desdemona said her goodbyes and left the castle. General Flann was standing at the parlor door when the queen stepped out.

"I'm fine, Scott," she addressed him unformerly and touched his arm, "nothing happened, just as I had suspected, however, I am tired now and would like a rest. Would you be so good as to inform my handmaiden that I would like to finish my tea in my room?"

"Of course, my lady," General Flann was pleased to find her well. He bowed to excuse himself and went to find the handmaiden.

Queen Alura walked up to her room and closed the door behind her. She was glad that the visit was over, but happy to have her sister back in her life. Moments later the handmaiden knocked on the door and awaited her answer.

"Please, come in," she nicely commanded. Once again the handmaiden entered the room. She gently placed the tea tray on the bedside table. "Will there be anything else, your highness?"

"No, thank you," she politely nodded again, telling the handmaiden she could leave the room.

The queen picked up her tea, then sat on her bed and began to sip it slowly. She pondered about the visit with her sister. Then her eyes grew heavy. She quickly finished the rest of the tea, then laid down to sleep.

That evening the well-dressed handmaiden knocked on the door holding the Queen's breakfast. There was no answer, so she tried again. Yet still no answer came, making her concerned. She opened the door and peeked inside. The Queen was still in bed. "Oh, your highness. I'm so sorry for intruding," she started while walking in, "I brought you your dinner, I hope you're hungry," She looked over at the Queen still lying in bed. It was unusual for her to sleep for so long. Before leaving the room she went to pull the covers over the Queen. Upon closer examination, she noticed the queen was pale. She touched her face to see if she was ill. Her forehead was cold as ice. The Queen she loved and admired was gone.

"I bet it was that Desdemona. I bet she did it," John said with anger, really into the story.

"What about General Flann? She was going to marry him and live happily ever after. Did he get Desdemona?" Suraionee asked, concerned about the injustice.

"Well, you need to listen to the rest of the story to find out," Milly said, glad that they were enjoying it.

"General Flann and others of the kingdom believed it was Desdemona's doing, while others claimed it was just her time because she died alone in her room. The kingdom was in an uproar. General Flann had Desdemona arrested for the death of the Queen but could never prove it, so she was released. Knowing she could now never inherit the crown because of being suspected of murder, Desdemona left and was never heard to be seen on KobiKobis Island again."

"Then who got the Kingdom?" Suraionee asked.

"Just wait. I'm getting to that part," Milly said, smiling.

Teag was still unconvinced of the truthfulness of the story and asked, "if this story is true, how come there is no such place named KobiKobis Island?"

"Good question, Teag. I'll get to that in a minute," Milly patted his knee and then went back to her story.

* * *

"ZaBeth was named Queen soon after Queen Alura's death. ZaBeth was Aluras' cousin and the next heir to the kingdom. She was a good queen and ruled as Alura and her parents before her had done.

Teag immediately recognized the name but just thought it was a coincidence.

"It has been said that in her search for power, Desdemona was lead to a jeweler named Hans on Koki Island. His reputation for making fine jewelry and casting magical spells made him her new best friend. He was an old man with grayish, silvery hair. His desire for riches made him willing to do anything for anyone if the price was right. Desdemona promised to give all the money he desired, to give him a place in the castle, and that he would be made the Queen's royal jeweler."

"You are not Queen Desdemona, how can you promise me these things?" Hans asked inquisitively.

"You fool! I am the Queen's cousin, and I have her ear. She will keep any promise I make you," Desdemona snapped.

"Okay," he said, taking her word for it, "there is one jewel I can make you, your highness, that will ensure total power over the universe. It's called the *'Universitas Dominium Monile'*," Hans said, with a strong excited tone, "It won't be easy to find the materials and so between the time it will take to find the items and actually making it, could take months."

**Universitas
Dominum
Monile**

"You may have anything you wish, just make that jewel," she demanded. Her greed filled her bosom, "you must also keep this conversation between us, or you will lose everything," she warned. Desdemona was abiding her time, playing nice until she had this new power, 'my enemies will rue the day they crossed me,' she thought.

Months went by, and finally the "*Universitas Dominium Monile*" was finished. The jeweler wrapped it in a black satin cloth, then placed it in a small wooden chest, locking it up. Then he put the key in his pocket for safekeeping. He locked up his shop and climbed into a horse-drawn carriage to deliver the jewel he had made into a necklace. The jeweler was daydreaming of all the wonderful new things he would have once he moved into the castle when the carriage stopped suddenly, "oh, are we there already?" the jeweler said with delight, placing the box in his jacket pocket, his other hand reaching for the door. Before he could open it, the door swung open, and a common thief jumped in, commanding him to hand over all of his jewels and money with a sword to his throat. Being the coward he was, the jeweler gave him everything except the box, hoping the thief hadn't noticed it.

"What's that?" the thief asked, pointing to the bulge in Hans's pocket.

"Oh, it's nothing…, just my bottle of medication…, nothing that would interest you," Hans said nervously.

The thief, sensing his nervousness, called his bluff and instructed, "pull it out."

Hans didn't dare hold back any longer and gave him the box. As soon as he did, someone from outside the carriage yelled, "come on, someone's coming!" The thief jumped out and took off, leaving no trail to follow. The Universitas Dominium Monile was gone, and Hans, afraid of the wrath of Desdemona, went into hiding.

When rumors of the jewel, Desdemona's actions, and the robbing of the jewel circulated, Queen ZaBeth had Melanion put a spell on the Islands making them invisible. "If Desdemona can't see the islands, she can't take control of them," Queen ZaBeth had said. It has also been said that the invisibility spell will last until Desdemona is caught and put away, and in a place where she can't take control.

Milly looked at Suraionee, then said, "This jewel is a replica of the Universitas Dominium Monile. It has been passed down with the story from generation to generation. My grandfather gave it to my grandmother when they were young and first married, she gave it to my mother who then gave it to me, and now I'm giving it to you. Grandpa said it's good luck," Milly was pleased.

"Well, if it was such good luck, why haven't we seen you wear it?" Teag asked curiously.

"I did a few times, but I just felt like it was for dressy occasions. Your father and I don't go out that much. I'm giving it to you Suraionee, because I just feel it's time to pass it on. Take good care of it, and it will take good care of you," Milly put it around Suraionee's neck.

"Thanks, mom," Suraionee said, pleased about the beautiful jewel around her neck.

"Everything on this necklace is a symbol that stands for something. The sun, moon and stars symbolize the universe. The four stars represent North, South, East and West. See how they are pointing in each direction?" Milly enjoyed seeing Suraionee's interest, "see here," Milly pointed, as if to count the diamonds on each of the corners, "there are twelve diamonds that represent the twelve months in the year. Put all of these things together, and it gives you control over the Universe."

"Cool," Suraionee said, getting up and walking to her room while gazing at her new treasure.

Chapter 3

The next morning came quickly. The last and final day on board the *Treasure*. After packing and preparing to leave the ship the family went to the dining hall to eat and play cards until they docked in Alaska. Upon going outside everyone noticed that there was no land in sight. The sun was brightly shining and the air was hot and humid."Has Alaska's weather changed?" Teag asked curiously.

"Not to my knowledge," Jacob answered. By now everyone was out and noticing that the weather wasn't right. Seeing a crewman walking by, Jacob asked, "sir, what time are we to be in Alaska?"

The man gave him a funny look and then looked around like he was hoping the answer would be in the air or someone would answer it for him, "uh, sh...should be within the uh...day sir, why don't you uh, go and eat an...and enjoy the rest of the t...t...trip until then," The man seemed to stumble over his words then walked away quickly.

Confident that the crew knew more than he did about navigating on the ocean, Jacob smiled and did as he was told, "this way, you heard the man, lets go, we'll be there soon. Just odd weather that's all, happens all the time at home."

Inside after lunch, the family pulled out their cards and began to play another game of cards. Before they knew it the day was over and the sun started going down. Half way through their fourteenth game Milly looked up from her cards and casually glanced out the small window beside her. Dark clouds were swirling around quickly closing out the last colors of the beautiful sunset.

"I don't believe it! It's raining again. What happened to our sunny, beautiful day?" she questioned. She looked over at Teag and saw apprehension in his eyes, "it's okay, Teag. It's just rain. The weather out here in the ocean is so unpredictable," she said, trying to give him some comfort and feeling silly for the comments she made moments earlier.

'That's what I'm afraid of,' he thought to himself. He stood up and walked over to the door. When he opened it, he noticed that the waves were a little higher and the wind was picking up. He looked at Suraionee, who was enjoying herself.

"We should have been there hours ago, where are we?" Jacob asked mostly talking to himself.

"We might actually get to be in the middle of a real typhoon," Suraionee said in excitement, watching the weather get worse, but not really realizing the danger and damage a storm like that could do.

John looked like he was going to be sick. His face turned a little pale from all the up and down motion.

Suddenly there was a loud noise and bells began ringing. The crew started running with haste in different directions yelling instructions to one another. One of them came to the dining hall and said, "the Captain asks that everyone stays in here. It's for your safety, not to worry though, everything is okay…it's just a precaution," then he disappeared into the darkness of the storm.

Suraionee was excited, "we really are, we really are."

"Stuff it, Sura!" Teag said, mad that she wasn't taking it more serious.

All the passengers were being rounded up and sent to the dining hall. Everyone was nervous about what was happening.

Teag stood up just outside the booth they were in to see out the window.

"Teag, sit down," Milly instructed, tugging at his shirt.

"Mom, I want to see," he started in frustration, "do you think they'll come in and tell us what is going on?" He asked as he sat back down.

"I'm sure they will," Milly replied, beginning to feel a little sea sick from all the movement of the ship.

Everyone sat in the room, some talking to family and friends and others with their heads between their legs, getting sicker by the minute. Many of the small children were crying, people were talking, and the storm was getting louder.

All the noise started giving Teag a headache. Covering his ears with his hands, he closed his eyes and tried to pretend he was at home playing his video games. His daydream was interrupted when the dining hall door opened. The Captain walked in with the door slamming behind him from a strong gust of wind. The Captain was a tall, bulky man. His gray hair was short on the sides, but a little longer on the top, and wild from the winds of the storm. He looked like a strong, capable man. In any room, his presence would have demanded attention. Strangely, everyone seemed to feel safer with him there.

"As all of you know, we are asking that you stay in here because it's the safest place during such a storm. Things are a little rough out there and, from the looks of it, will probably stay that way for a while," he calmly explained with his deep voice, "now, the sea is a little rough and might get a little worse, but all should be well in a few hours. If any of you are seasick, the best way to deal with it is to sleep through it. If you can fall asleep now, it may not get worse. If you remove the table and pull on the benches, they turn into beds," he said pointing to the four tables in the middle of the room, "also if you take a look at the panels around the room, they pull down and turn into beds as well. There are extra cushions in the cabinets inside the benches. Everyone should have a place to lie down should you feel like doing so. I will be on the bridge, but I'm only a call away. One of my best men will be in here with you during the remainder of the storm," with a blink of an eye, he disappeared into the blackness.

Frightened and unable to keep his dream a secret from his parents he began to tell them what had happened, "Mom, dad, remember that bad dream I had the night before we left on our trip?"

"Yes," Milly said interested. Jacob nodded and paid attention. John and Suraionee were listening in too.

"Well, it was a dream about a shipwreck and I drowned in it and now here we are in a similar situation."

"Oh, no, this is just a precaution, nothing is going to happen to the ship. It'll be alright," Milly comforted him.

"Remember deja vu dad?" Teag asked feeling like his fears were just dismissed by his mother.

Jacob nodded, looking as though he was in deep thought, "It's possible, but the likely hood of us sinking is not that great," he tried to convince himself.

Frustrated that they seemed so unconcerned about what was happening he reminded them, "Dad, Mom, are you not paying attention to what is going on out there? It's a hurricane, that can easily sink the ship."

"Well there's nothing we can do about it now, so sit down and try to relax. Everything will be alright, you'll see," Milly instructed him.

Everyone found an area and pulled out the beds. Some people played cards, while others went to sleep. John's stomach hurt, so he decided to try to sleep. Within an hour, the waves had grown. The winds were strong enough to carry anyone outside off into the sea, if the waves didn't pull you under first. John curled up next too Milly, who was laying next to him for comfort, still unable to sleep. One of the passengers was walking across the room taking a pitcher of water to her bed area. John watched her as she got closer and closer. She had blonde straggly hair, her clothing looked damp from the rain outside. She was thin and homely looking. It was hard for her to keep the water in the pitcher because of all the movement. The young lady had an impressively steady hand, wet, but steady. She had to pass by John and Milly to get to her bed. Just as she passed Milly, a huge wave hit and threw a nearby man off balance, he bumped into the lady causing the pitcher of water to fly out of her hand and straight for John's head.

Teag saw it and tried to catch it, throwing himself into a wall and knocking himself out cold.

It was hard to breath. Teag's chest was tight, and sharp pains flowed through his body. He opened his eyes and found them burning. Suddenly aware he was underwater, he started kicking himself to the top. When he reached the top, he took in several deep breaths, gasping for air. His lungs were still tight and in pain. As he was coughing out water, he saw something coming closer. The sky was so dark that his attention was drawn to what looked like a flashlight that illuminated a lifeboat. The people on the lifeboat were calling his name. The voices coming from the boat weren't his parents, 'maybe mom and dad told them to find me,' he thought to himself, 'but where are they, then? What happened? Why aren't they looking for me?' Teag's thoughts became fearful.

"Help! I'm over here," he yelled, choking on seawater as the waves went up and down. "I'm over here," he went on, waving his arms. It seemed that they were coming right for him.

A large wave crashed over his head. Teag was once again fighting for his life. He didn't take a breath before the wave hit. His lungs were burning with pain for the need of air. His will to fight was diminishing. He couldn't hold on any longer. He breathed in, and seawater filled his lungs. 'That's it for me? Oh please, not yet,' he thought to himself. The pain was so intense, and then it was no more.

Teag saw himself pull out of his sinking body. He watched as a strange figure jumped in and grabbed him, pulling him to the surface, 'is there hope?' He thought, as he watched the man push him into the lifeboat he had seen earlier. John and Suraionee were there too. The man was giving him CPR, trying to bring him back. Teag was above the boat, floating in the air. The feeling of tranquility rushed over him. When he looked around, he could see the ocean in its calmest state. The beauty of nature and life was showing itself to him. The night sky seemed different, too. It was lighter than before. In the distance, he could see dolphins gracefully jumping and twisting in the air. It seemed as if they were dancing just for him. There were beautiful birds in flight above his head, singing and soaring through the sweet-smelling air. His attention went back to the man who had now stopped trying to revive him. When he looked up, he saw a bright light coming for him. A man was standing in the middle of the light as he floated down to greet him.

"Teag, my dear boy, its time for you to return," said the man.

"Who are you?" he asked, looking into his deep green eyes, "you're...you're..." he started to think back. His firm jaw line, light brown skin and short dark hair brought back memories of being a little boy, "Grandpa Great?" Teag asked in astonishment, "but you're dead," he said, remembering his great grandfather's funeral.

"You will be, too, if you don't get back to your body fast."

"But I want to talk to you. I'm not ready to go yet."

"Teag," he said firmly, "get back there, or you'll be brain-dead...and that's no way to live."

Teag obeyed his grandfather. As he slipped back into his body, the swift feeling of pain came back to him in massive waves. He turned over and coughed, while spitting up the remaining ocean water that still lingered in his lungs, then took several gasps of air. With his heart pounding, he tried to sit up. Trying to look around in the darkness, he started to panic, "where's my mom and dad?" The wind was blowing and the waves were crashing again. He could hear Suraionee and John sobbing next to him.

"Your alright mate. Just relax, you've been through a lot," came an Australian-accented voice from above him. The shape of his body wasn't normal. Teag tried to figure out what it was he was looking at, but the darkness surrounding them was too thick. The strain of trying was hurting his eyes. The man wrapped a thick, warm blanket around him and said, "Sleep now, rest your eyes," then he heard the man speak to Suraionee and John, "it's okay, he's alright now, you're all safe. Go on and rest your eyes too. Go on, now, both of you," Suraionee turned the flashlight on again and aimed it at the stars.

The feeling of safety overwhelmed Teag. He felt safe like when he was with his mother and father. Although he felt protected and tried for a while to sleep, he was no longer tired. Perhaps it was the adrenaline flowing through him, or maybe it was the many thoughts that were racing through his head. Unable to settle his mind, he sat up and watched as the man searched for others. Teag looked over at Suraionee and John, who were sitting right next to him. They had managed to calm themselves down long enough to fall asleep. From what he could make out in the darkness they looked so calm and peaceful. Hours they were a drift in the raging sea, and eventually Teag fell asleep next to his siblings.

Teag awoke when the dark sky started to turn light. He could now see the ocean, once raging with anger, now only small rolling hills. The lifeboat slightly roll from side to side as it glided across the ocean. The man that saved him and his siblings was standing at the bow of the boat, looking out. He was still searching the deep water for survivors. As Teag watched him from behind, he couldn't help but notice that something was different about him. The sky grew lighter as dawn approached. The shadowy outline of this man was slowly becoming clearer. But it still didn't make sense. He had a lot of hair that flowed wildly in the wind. His shape was large and broad, but he didn't look human. As Teag glanced down at his feet, he saw giant paws, 'but that's impossible,' he thought as he took a deep breath. Terrified now, he wondered if he was dreaming again, 'yes that's it...I'm dreaming! A creature with large paws that also talks...that isn't real,' yet ready to face his dream, he questioned the man.

"Who are you?" He asked, still weary from the pain in his chest.

The man turned abruptly to the sudden break of silence. Teag gasped as he looked into the eyes of his strange floating companion, "I'm sorry!" Teag exclaimed, pulling himself backwards to get as far away from him as he could. While pulling himself backwards, he climbed over John and Suraionee, who awoke to his panic.

"You don't need to fear, son," came the Australian-accent. "I'm not going to hurt you. You're safe with me," he added calmly.

Then, getting a good look for the first time at the man Teag had just disturbed, John and Suraionee screamed in horror. The man had thick, flowing hair, deep orange/yellow eyes, and big thick strong paws' for hands and feet. They looked like a lion's paws. With nowhere to go, Teag searched the sea for another boat or someone to whom he could yell for help. It was to no avail.

"Please, children…I am not what I seem. I know I look bad, but, well, it's hard to explain," the man said back to them, "I'm Maddox Pembroke. We were far off when the storm hit. A giant wave turned your ship over. My sons and I came to help. From the looks of it, they must've gone back already," Maddox explained.

"Back where? There isn't anything around," Teag said, searching for land or even a ship in the landscape of ocean surrounding them.

"Things aren't what they seem," Maddox told him. Just then the boat hit something that pushed it up just above the ripping water.

Looking down, it appeared that they were floating above the deep blue ocean. Maddox started to step over the side to climb out of the boat.

"Where are you going?" Suraionee exclaimed, "don't leave us here all alone," she added with fear of being alone on the ocean.

"Not to worry, you're coming with me," Maddox said, jumping out of the boat. When he touched the ground below him, he disappeared.

"Maddox?…,Where are you?" Questioned John.

"What? I'm right here," Maddox said a little confused, "we're here on KobiKobis Island."

"What? No we're in the middle of the ocean and we're floating above the sea. Are you *crazy*?" Teag asked. The mention of KobiKobis Island reminded him of his mother's story. 'This must be where it all happened, but how did we…this is impossible, it was just a story,' his thoughts were cut off by Maddox's reply.

Suddenly remembering that he was no longer visible, but he could see them, "oh...forgive me...I forgot." Maddox searched in his pocket and handed the three of them a purple crystal-like rock. Its color reminded him of the crystal ZaBeth wore around her neck. Looking into it was like falling into a deep hole. He could see forever. It glittered in the small bursts of sunlight that were trying to peek out of the lightly gray clouds. It was on a long attached to a golden clasp that held it to a one millimeter black leather cord. The workmanship of the clasp was unlike any he had ever seen. Though it reminded him of jewelry found on the Egyptians in ancient times. Gold clasps wrapped around elegantly on both ends of the rock creating a necklace. Suraionee's only had one clasp that was attached to a thick gold chain, so it could dangle on its side.

"What kind of rock is this?" Teag asked in curiosity, still staring at it.

"It's called Diamante Púrpura. It means Purple Diamond. It comes from our island," Maddox replied as if they should have known it.

"What's it for?" Suraionee asked, growing more and more curious.

"It helps us see our island. It only works if we have it around our necks; that makes it close to our hearts, watch." Maddox took the Diamante from Suraionee and put it around her neck while Teag and John put their own on at the same time. Unexpectedly, the ground they were standing on changed to beach, and in front of them, they could see miles of land and beautiful lush plants and vegetation. There were other lifeboats along the shore all tied up to a small dock to the right of them. To the left of them, they saw tents and people gathered around campfires. There was a sign about ten feet ahead of them that read North Beach.

Teag searched all the faces and couldn't see them, "Suraionee, do you see mom and dad?"

"No, but let's go look around," Suraionee said, jumping out of the boat. John, Suraionee and Teag walked around the camp and looked at all the families, but there were no sign of their parents.

Worried, Teag went back to Maddox, who was talking to two other lion-like men and asked urgently, "are there any other lifeboats out?"

"I'm afraid not." Maddox turned to the lion-men standing next to him, "this is Ronan and this is Rylee, they're my boys. They were out there pulling out survivors, too," Maddox tried to introduce them, but Teag was filled with dismay.

In shock Teag asked again, "you're sure there are no others?" Hoping that somehow this time the answer would be different. Suraionee and John joined him with hope in their eyes, but were soon disappointed when they learned the truth.

"That's not acceptable!" Teag yelled as he shook his head, there had to be something he could do. He had to see it for himself. His parents were the only good thing in his life. They had struggled to eat and live all their lives, they had moved eleven times in six years and because of it, could never keep or make friends, no one cared about him. Now that they didn't even have the one thing he could count on in his life, what were they to do. The thought was unbearable, the feeling overwhelming. He had to do something or he felt he would explode, so out of nowhere he ran over to one of the lifeboats, trying to push it out. John and Suraionee saw what he was trying to do and for a moment their rush of helplessness dissipated. They ran over, John helped push after Suraionee climbed in. Suraionee was still weeping and sniffling softly. Her eyes were red and swollen and her nose was lightly running.

"Where do you think you're going?" Maddox asked, trying to stop them.

"They're out there somewhere, and we have to go help them," Teag's eyes filled with tears, but he quickly choked them back.

"They aren't out there, son," Maddox gently pulled Teag over to him, trying to comfort him. But Teag pushed him away. "When I was looking for survivors, I saw your father push your sister and brother to the surface. But the current of the ship pulled him back down when it went under. When I pulled them in, I jumped in to try and save him, but he was gone I couldn't find him. I never saw your mum."

Suraionee howled with sorrow again, "what about my mom?" Teag said, trying to calm himself down in hope that one parent might be left to save.

Suraionee cried harder remembering the events that took place and was unable to talk.

"Teag, you got knocked out, and mom and dad ran over to you. Mom tried to help you out after the ship had suddenly turned over and water started flooding in. Dad was trying to help Suraionee and me, so mom had you. The next thing I knew I was being helped into the boat," John sniveled.

"Mom wasn't with me, I was underwater when I came to," Teag said in a panic, "I was all alone."

"We all searched those waters thoroughly," Ronan's said trying to help, his Australian-accent was strong, "we would never leave if we knew someone was there and needed help."

"But it was so dark out last night. How could you know if you got everyone?" Teag asked, now angry about the entire situation.

"We are lion men, we can see in the dark like you see in the day," Rylee remarked with a light Australian-accent, frustrated about his own misfortunes.

John and Suraionee, now believing that there was nothing left for them to do, climbed out of the boat and stood hugging each other and sobbing hard.

"I'm so sorry," Maddox said, wishing he could have done more to save their parents. "Why don't you go choose a tent and rest for a while?"

"No, I'm going out to search some more," Teag said, trying to push the boat off the beach. Maddox decided to help them. He picked up Suraionee and put her back in the lifeboat. Teag and John jumped in after them, and then Maddox pushed off. They searched for hours with nothing to show for it.

When they returned to the Island, the three of them were in shock. No one cried. No one even whimpered. They stayed straight-faced, not really sure how to feel, like it was all a bad dream.

When the three of them walked toward the tents, they saw that everyone's eyes were on them. No one made a sound not even the babies. They picked a tent and closed the flaps. They laid down next to each other and cried as softly as they could. None of them wanted anyone to know what had happened.

After they got a long rest and their eyes were out of tears, they began talking about what they remember and what had happened to each of them.

"I thought you were dead, Teag," John said when he recalled Maddox diving in to get him and then watching as Maddox tried to bring him back, "Maddox gave Suraionee a flashlight and was waving it around looking for people. Maddox gave it to her for something to do, not because she needed it."

"I thought I was dead, too. I watched my body from above, oh, and I saw Grandpa Great," Teag said in excitement, remembering what had happened to him.

"What? Grandpa Great is gone, Teag," Suraionee said, reminding him, "maybe you have one of those concussions or something," she added, trying to look at his head and eyes like a doctor would.

Pushing her hand aside and ignoring her comments, he went on, "he told me to come back. He said we would talk soon. Everything around me was so cool. Grandpa Great came in a bright light," he stopped and thought for a moment. Then in wonderment asked, "What happened to the ship?"

"Well everything happened too fast. When the lady fell, you tried to save me from getting hit with the pitcher of water, and you ended up hitting your head on the wall. We all tried to wake you, but then the ship turned over and water flooded in the dining hall. We had to swim out before the whole ship met the ocean floor. Dad was pulling Suraionee and me with him, and mom took you. That's about all I know," John explained as best he could. He was shaking from the knowledge of losing his parents. Then remembering more he added, "Dad pushed Sura to the top, but he lost his grip on me just after we swam from the boat. I didn't see where dad went. I thought he was already at the top, so I swam up," John boasted of his accomplishment of not needing help.

Teag stepped outside to the smell of food. He looked at the people that were walking around. He was angry that they all survived with their families in tact. He was jealous that they still had time to spend with one another. Holding back the emotion was hard. He swallowed and then took a deep breath. John and Suraionee followed Teag out and were no longer at each others' throats. They were kind and thoughtful to one another, trying to help each other get through it all. Each one of them trying to be tough for the other, they stuffed their true feelings and their sadness into a corner and stifled it at every opportunity.

Chapter 4

North Beach was a wide-open for about a mile all around. About twenty-five feet from shore was a thick, wild, green grass. In random places as far as the grass touched, there were scorch marks. The ocean touched three sides of the large, circled beach. The fourth side (southwest of them) appeared to be luscious, green, rolling hills. Teag, John and Suraionee were facing the island. To the left of them were millions of tall trees up on a high dirt cliff. All of the trees were somber leaving them all a sense of uneasiness, "I don't want to go there," Suraionee said to Teag and John, who were looking around with her. On the right of them were tall mountains. It was so steep from the water that it appeared that no one could climb it.

Glancing back at the camp, Teag noticed the old woman he had seen on the ship. She was now sitting by the door of a tent talking to Maddox.

"I don't believe it...LOOK!" He pointed to the old woman, "that's the woman I was talking too on the ship. She said she lived on a remote island," Teag said as he started walking over to talk to her. John and Suraionee followed close behind.

"Really? When was this?" Suraionee asked as they walked, but before Teag could say more they were there.

"Hi...uh...uh..." Teag started, not remembering her name. Maddox stopped talking, smiled then turned and walked over to Ronan and Rylee, who were standing by the dock talking and drinking something out of their own large water bottles.

"Just call me ZaBeth," she jumped in and then smiled back at him, "are you alright?" she asked, peering into Teag's eyes searching for something.

"Fine, I guess," he said, trying to hide his sadness from her, "but I have a lot of questions."

"Like what, dear?" she asked trying to sound concerned.

"Did you bring us here?" Teag questioned.

"Yes, for reasons you wouldn't understand even if I told you," ZaBeth gazed upon Teag's face and then turned and looked at the other children, "you're all part of an amazing plan. I'm sorry you had to experience the storm, but it was the only way to get you here."

Surprised and a little unsure of what she was talking about, Teag tilted his head slightly and gave her a confused look. John and Suraionee looked at each other, confused.

"And who might you two be?" ZaBeth asked as she looked right at John and Suraionee. "I don't remember there being two more," she said, starting to look frazzled.

The other survivors started gathering around to listen to what was being said.

John and Suraionee looked at each other, thinking that the old woman was crazy. Their eyes met Teag's, and he shrugged his shoulders. Suraionee whispered, 'This woman is really creepy,' and at every attempt they made to understand what she was talking about, ZaBeth avoided the conversation not wanting to give them too much information about why they were there.

"You are simply not ready for that kind of information," ZaBeth said, tired of the subject.

"Well then, ZaBeth, is it?" A tall and large man said in a discouraged tone while putting all the emphasis on her name, "maybe you can tell us how we get off this island and back home?"

The realization of their situation hit Teag like a brick. He hadn't even thought of that. 'What about home?' he thought, 'I have to take care of Suraionee and John from now on,' he suddenly felt a large weight cover his body, knowing he needed to take charge and make sure his younger sister and brother had everything they needed.

"Where can I get a job?" Teag suddenly blurted out.

Everyone looked at each other, "a job? What do you need a job for?" asked ZaBeth.

"Well, my mother and father are dead now, and someone needs to take care of my sister and brother. Looks like I'm just the guy," he spit the words out, trying to keep the pain out of his voice. The rumbling of talk filled his ears, "so, is there anything for me to do on this island?" he asked, more serious now. He felt everyone's eyes on him and wanted to shrink away.

"Let's not talk about that now. There will be plenty of time to talk about that later. Tonight we will sleep in these tents, and tomorrow the journey begins," ZaBeth seemed to perk up. The excitement of the journey brought a light to her eyes, "we leave just before dawn. Get your rest, because the journey is precarious. It will demand all of our attention."

The same man from before rose his voice with disapproval, "What are you talking about? We aren't staying, and we're most certainly not going on a journey of any kind," he insisted. The other families who were already gathered around and listening to the conversation agreed with the man. All the voices in the group started chattering, discussing what was going on. Maddox, Ronan and Rylee walked up to ZaBeth's side.

Maddox whistled so loudly, strange looking birds took flight out of the trees in that frightening forest that was still a great distance away. "Now listen up!" he demanded, "There is no ship to take you out of here, and there certainly won't be any ship that makes it to this Island. The Diamante Púrpura is the only way that *You*, know you're here," Teag looked down and gripped his Diamante that hung around his neck.

"This will be your home now. I assure you that once you see Makoto City, you will desire to stay." ZaBeth assured them trying to be firm but kind.

"You can't do that! We have lives and homes, Family to go back to," yelled a man with two young twin daughters.

"Every Five years I choose a few small families to join our world. I only choose the particular families that are revealed to me to be the ones that will grow to be the strongest in magic. Your children will develop special abilities that you do not understand. All things have a purpose and you will understand them in time."

"Who are you lady?" The large man asked, "what makes you so special that you could rip us from our lives and tell us that we're going to live somewhere else and expect us to be fine with that?"

"She is Queen ZaBeth, Queen of these Islands," Rylee spoke up as if defending her honor.

"Islands? Meaning more than one?" Asked the man from the bowling alley.

"Yes, there are Seven Islands that surround this one," Ronan informed them with his Australian accent.

"So, we should be calling you Queen ZaBeth?" Suraionee asked.

"Why? I didn't vote for her," Said the large man slyly. Several of the adults laughed.

"No, you may call me ZaBeth, I never did care for the full formal name," she smiled then changed the subject back to the journey, "There will be challenges getting to Makoto City, but we will do it together. No one will be left behind, As you can see this is the only place we could bring you that is safe. There is another beach that is much closer to the City entrance, but there are creatures there that…, well it's too dangerous to go there," ZaBeth replied giving in and telling them a little more then she wanted too.

"So that's it? Nothing we can say to get back to our lives?" asked the large man red with fury.

"You may think that you are held captive here, but if you like you may leave. Give your Diamante Púrpura to Maddox and you may swim out to sea with the creatures of the deep, wait in the hopes that a ship may come by and find you, or you can come with us and give this life a try. If you are still unhappy we will build you a ship and you may leave." ZaBeth explained. "Think of it as a vacation. You were all leaving for a vacation in the first place so, you have nothing to lose and everything to gain. The calmness in her face was reassuring to all who looked upon it.

The men and women chatted amongst themselves for a moment. The men were angry and started plotting to take leave in the middle of the night when their captures were sleeping. But to not give them a clue to what they were thinking they all agreed and accepted the terms.

"Now, we shall eat dinner and then off to bed with you all. Morning comes early and we mustn't stay till dawn." ZaBeth told them before disappearing behind a tent.

Dinner wasn't as pleasant as it was on the ship. Teag didn't like fish but knowing that they were going to travel in the morning he needed his strength. John and Suraionee were eating like they hadn't seen food in ten days.

"Slow down, you don't want to choke do you?" Teag said embarrassed because others were watching.

"Sowee," John tried to apologize with a mouth full of fish, "I juff wuv fiff."

"Nee tu," Suraionee agreed, then started coughing. Then she swallowed and said, "I'm okay."

"I told you," Teag said keeping his head down now. He didn't like all the attention the others paid them. They were all watching and making him uncomfortable.

After dinner everyone sat around the campfire. The sun was going down and the air was starting to become crisp. The chatter of voices and laughter were all about. Everyone seemed happy except the Trager kids. Teag wanted to live up to his father's expectations of being a man and caring for his siblings, but everything was so fresh he had no idea what he wanted to do or even what was going to happen. He sat there and listened to the conversations around him and tried not to think too much more than that. A deep voice broke up the chatter.

"Since we are going to be traveling together perhaps we should all introduce ourselves," Maddox suggested. "Why don't you start?" He pointed to a man sitting next to him.

"Well…yes, umm…I'm Kory Dayton," he started then pointing to his wife who was tending to the two youngest children outside the circle, "that over there is my wife Farah, our oldest son Seven who is four years old, our other son Ramsey, two years old, and Natalie is one." He put his hand down while his wife and Seven smiled and waved. Ramsey was too busy playing in the sand to notice what was going on.

Kory had a stocky build, short sandy brown hair and a large bulgy nose that often took the focus off his eyes. Farah had a little extra meat on her as she had just had a baby a year ago. Her dark black hair made her green eyes stand out. She had a pretty face that seemed to be worn out form all the sleepless nights. Seven was a well-mannered little boy. Sitting in the sand with legs crossed and his arms folded his long brown hair twisted in the wind. He had dark brown eyes that seemed to understand everything that was going on around him. Ramsey and Natalie both had the same features. They looked like twins if it wasn't for the height difference. It was the same all around black hair, green eyes, and a button nose.

"I'm Tracy Miles," She started because she was sitting right next to Seven Dayton, "This is my husband, Dan, our daughter Elana who is five years old and our son Kyle is three," She stopped and looked over at the next family.

Tracy was thin and her features were plain with her blond straggly hair and hazel eyes. Dan was the opposite. He was a big boy in every direction. He was fully bald and he had blue eyes. He looked like a tough strong guy. Elana and Kyle looked just like him only they were petite little things.

"Hello everyone," he waved, "I'm Gabriel Esteban, this is my wife Becky, our son Oran who is ten, and our twins Amara and Baylee who are twelve-years old."

Gabriel's black hair was graying; he was a nice looking man with dark brown eyes and a medium build. Becky was an attractive woman. Even after the storm she was graceful in everything she did. She was still striking with her black hair straggling in her face. She reminded Teag of his mother. Oran was a well-behaved boy. He was polite and often seen giving up his spot in line for an adult. He had black hair and wore thin glasses.

"Hello all, Willem Karik, My wife Hailey, our son Preston is sixteen, and our daughter Piper is four."

Willem demanded everything, from his choice of tents (even if it meant kicking someone else out) to his family being first in line to eat but would never pay a high price, "only the best for my family," he was heard saying in a snobby tone earlier in the day. He wore glasses and had reddish blond hair. Hailey had light brown hair and dark blue eyes and was very thin. She always held her head high and didn't speak much to the others. Preston was as tall and well built. He had blonde hair and gray eyes. Preston was heard talking about himself and all the millions of dollars his family had. As if that was going to make him a load of good friends. Piper had red hair and freckles and though she was a little girl she seemed just as snooty as the rest of the family.

"And here we have," spouted Maddox, "Teag Trager who is…"

"Sixteen," Teag added to help him.

"Then we have Suraionee Trager who is…"

"I'll be ten day after tomorrow," Suraionee blurted out following Teag's lead. There were a lot of voices wishing her a happy birthday.

"And John Trager is…,"

"Thirteen," Teag jumped in because John stopped paying attention and was fidgeting in the sand.

"Where are their parents?" Asked Willem knowing they weren't there but wanting to make a scene because of his distain for anyone not related to himself.

Maddox saw the Trager kids faces and became upset, "they aren't with us anymore," he snapped, angry that Willem would make the poor kids relive it. Tears filled John and Suraionee's eyes. They both fought it back not wanting to make a bigger display of themselves. Teag was angry but remained undisturbed. After a few minutes of silence everyone went on talking amongst themselves.

After the introductions everyone started talking about tomorrow and what might happen: "How far do you think we will need to go to get to the Makoto City?" Gabriel Esteban asked Kory Dayton.

"What do you think the City looks like?" Hailey Karik asked, now dreaming of what beauties they might get to live in.

"I'll bet it's a crystal city that sparkles in the sun," Said Becky Esteban to her twins.

Teag had mixed emotions. On one hand he was sad and wanted to hide forever because of his parents, on the other hand he was starting to get excited about what might be coming. It is every kids dream to find a new world (in this case an Island) and be able to explore it. 'What abilities might I have? What was ZaBeth talking about? Teag wanted to be alone so he crawled into their tent laid himself down by Suraionee who had fallen fast to sleep already. The sounds of the ocean washing up on the beach and then going back to sea, was so calming. 'Why was all of this happening? What is going to happen and how am I going to get us all through this alone? Is this real, or is it just another dream. I hope it's a dream, I'll see mom and dad when I wake up and all will be well,' Teag wondered. Before he knew it, the calming sounds stopped any further thoughts and he fell asleep.

Gabriel was the first to wake up. He quietly started waking up all the men. After they were all awake they quietly woke their families and started walking to the boats. Baby Natalie Dayton was trying to get out of her mothers arms because she wanted to play. When Farah wouldn't let her down Natalie let out a loud scream. Quickly, Farah put her hand over Natalie's mouth and set her down. Everyone turned around to see what the problem was, than they all looked at the tent that the Pembroke's were sleeping in hoping that they didn't hear. After a moment of silence and seeing no movement they all started walking again. When they were just about to reach the lifeboats they all heard a sound come from the Trager tent. Teag appeared and ran towards them.

"Where are you going? Why didn't you wake us?" He asked loud enough to wake everyone still asleep.

Whispering, "I'm sorry, um, we are going to leave this place, we all have families and jobs," Willem started, "you have no family now so it is best that you stay here with these…, things," Willem motioned towards the Pembroke tent, "I'm sure they'll take good care of you. Now be a good boy and go back to bed," Willem said with a patronizing tone.

"Willem, you didn't need to do that," Dan stepped in feeling sorry for the boy, "do you have any relatives back home?"

"Yes, there is my Grandma and Grandpa Phoenix, but they don't live in Washington they live in Texas."

"Well then why don't you get your family and come with us," Dan told him.

"No thank you, I think we will stay, just in case my parents did make it and just got on another part of the island."

"Okay well, then let us leave before the Pembroke's wake up," Willem said shooing him away.

Everyone was paying so much attention to Teag and the conversation no one was watching behind them. When they turned around the lifeboats were gone. They all looked at each other and then in every direction, but the boats were nowhere in sight.

"Where'd the boats go?" Willem asked.

Everyone looked and waited for an answer but no one spoke. The plan was dead and Willem was angry about it.

"No one wants to hear it Willem," Dan whispered loudly before he had the chance to make any comments. "As I see it we have no choice now but to go along."

"No Choice? No Choice?" Willem started, "Sure we have a choice, I'm sure if we just get out there and stick together that a ship will come along."

"Are you dumb or just stupid?" Gabriel said staring at Willem, "who knows how far off course the hurricane pushed us, I mean I've never heard of KobiKobis Island have you? Besides, think of the sharks, don't even get me started on that one…no, go if you want, but I'm not risking my family on it. I would rather take my chances with the lion people," Gabriel whispered loudly.

Kory and Dan agreed and they started walking back to their tents.

"I want out of here damn it, if I have to carry my family on my back or build a ship myself I'm getting out of here," Willem went on not caring who heard him at this point. Hailey pulled him closer and whispered in his ear then he went on, "that's what I said, lets get back to our tents, morning comes early," he finished as though it was all his idea.

The group laughed as they walked back and crawled into their tents and went back to sleep.

The early morning air was crisp. Teag awoke to the sounds of the others moving around outside the tent, "hurry quickly," he heard Maddox say. The flap of their tent was flipped open and Maddox was in the doorway. "It's time to get up, we need to move quickly," he said then went out to help the others pack up their tents. John and Suraionee sat up and stretched their arms while yawning.

"Is it time already?" Suraionee asked laying her head back down and wanting to go back to sleep.

"Sura, I think they are in a hurry. We better not make anyone mad," Teag remarked while he and John hurried to fold up their sleeping bags. When Teag was done with his own he helped Suraionee fold up her bag. When they stepped outside of the tent, they noticed in the darkness of the morning that, they were the last ones up. Everyone else was almost finished packing up their tents. "Suraionee, John!" Teag called with urgency in his voice, "they're almost ready to go, and we haven't even packed up our tent yet."

John and Suraionee stepped out of the tent realizing they really had to get a move on. When they pulled their sleeping bags out, all the men came over to pack up the tent. It only took them two minutes to pack it up and attach it onto a hiking pack. Teag started to place the heavy pack over his shoulders when Maddox came and took it from him.

"Please allow me, this thing can get really heavy and it will hurt your back," Maddox started to put it on his back when Teag interjected.

"I'm a man Maddox, I can do it," Teag protested.

"I know you are son, but you'll be needing to take care of your sister and make sure she doesn't fall behind," Maddox insisted softly.

"I can do both," Teag kept on.

"Teag, you are a man I have no doubt about it, but you also have a family that needs looking after. All the men here have wives too look after the children, please, just trust me, let me help where I can," Maddox didn't sway in his tone, he remained calm but firm on the matter. Though Teag didn't like looking like a wimp he was really happy that he didn't have to lug that heavy pack on his back.

"What time is it?" Suraionee asked John because it was still really dark out. He looked at his watch. The dim light that came from the flashlights still made it hard to see. Stopping in his tracks to look more closely he saw that it had stopped.

"Sorry Sura, I think the water broke it..." He was interrupted when Rylee had bumped into him from behind knocking him to the ground.

"Oh, sorry John," he said in surprise helping him to his feet. Rylee had been watching the ground, but was also at the end of the line to make sure no one was left behind. "Please John, please don't stop, we must hurry on, it's much to dangerous to stay any longer," he added looking around in every direction.

"Why is it so dangerous out here?" Suraionee asked glancing around as well, not really feeling unsafe.

"The dragon likes to hunt just after dawn out on the beach. There always seems to be millions of fish that flock to the shore at that time," Rylee held his hands out and kept walking trying to push them along.

"Dragon?" they said softly to themselves. Suraionee, John, and Teag took another look around, this time a little more concerned for their safety.

"I gather it isn't a kind dragon," John commented trying to joke.

Rylee didn't smile, "no. No one has ever been able to get close enough to try to tame her."

"Well if they don't get close enough then how do you know it's a girl?" Teag asked with curiosity.

"Just keep walking we have a lot of ground to cover," Rylee said with hesitation not really wanting to talk about it at the moment.

"Not much for talking people are they," Suraionee point out to Teag.

By the time the sun started peaking over the Island they were at the rolling hills, "quickly, everyone under here," Maddox hurried them. They all stopped at the first hill they came too and stood in front of it. Everyone looked at one another trying to figure out what they were doing just standing there. Maddox said a loud, "pañuelo azul," and the hill started to open. It didn't look like a door it looked just like the rest of the grassy hill, like they wanted to conceal its existence. Maddox waited until everyone was in before he walked in and shut the hillside behind him. "Sit and relax a little, were not done yet."

The room was rather large. It had everything the group would need to survive for several days. It looked like the inside of a house with drywall and tile on the floors. There were only two other rooms from where they were, the kitchen and a bathroom. Teag took a momentary look in the bathroom. It was a medium size, with a large shower. There was a sink and mirror, and the hand towels hung nicely on the wall. Everything in this place looked like someone had prepared for the group to be there, maybe even for long-term. "We will wait here for the dragon to pass and then we will be on our way," Maddox had said explaining why they had stopped.

"Dragon?" Dan said. Then chatter filled the room as everyone discussed a dragon.

"I thought dragons were a myth," Gabriel said with disbelief.

"I'll bet you don't recall a place called KobiKobis Island or ever seeing lion men before either. Just because no one has ever been known to see something, doesn't make it untrue or unreal. I assure you the dragons on this island are real. If you don't believe me, by all means find your own way, but don't say I didn't warn you," Maddox cautioned.

"Dragons? There are more then one?" Kory asked concerned.

"Oh yes, there are several different types through out the island kingdom. Though on this Island there is only one Dragon, but there are several types of Dorgoggin's," Maddox smiled at the look on all the faces of everyone in the room as they realized what kind of world they were in.

"What's a Dorabogin?" Dan asked, thinking they were all crazy.

"It's, Dorgoggin, and it's a creature so fowl, that even dragons fear them. It's has a head, tail an scales like a dragon, but it's body and legs are like that of a horse," Ronan corrected and informed them all.

"Okay so there's several types you say? Like what?" Becky Esteban asked with a semi-interested look on her face.

"Well, there's the Makotice Dorgoggin that roams the base of the Polar Hawk Mountains. Its face is snakelike and has seaweed like hair down the spine of it's back to the end of it's long tail, on it's chin, and around it's hooves. It has black shiny scales all over its body has black bat like wings, and it spits poison from its mouth. It's the fiercest Dorgoggin because it will hunt you down after it smells you. You become its prey. If you find a place to hide where it can't follow, it will lurk in the shadows until you come out. The room was filled with shocked faces, fear etched in their eyes.

"We don't have to go to the Polar Hawk Mountains do we?" asked a frightened Amara Esteban who was clinging to her twin Baylee.

"No," Maddox replied getting a kick out of the first time frights they were all showing.

"Then there's the Spitniker Dorgoggin that lives in these parts. It has a parrot type beak that can crack bones in half. It has bone like spikes all over its face, down it's spine to its tail, and around its hooves. It has a scaly thick work horse body and the worst part is before it attacks it makes a horrible heaving sound like its coughing up a hairball, then it spits sharp bones from previous kills at it's prey," Maddox warned them. There was a gasp, as everyone was now afraid to leave the room at all.

"Not to mention the Hoarfrost Dorgoggin, that spits water that freezes when it touches something. It's a metallic blue color with large bat like wings. It has large crescent moon pointed horns that point forward at its prey and sharp pointed scaly spikes all the way down its spine to the end of its long tail. It lives in the Polar Hawk Mountains where it hunts, it can smell flesh up to four miles away," Ronan added like he was giving a lesson in class.

"There are too many different kinds to tell you about, but those are the deadliest ones."

"I still don't believe, why haven't we heard of these types of creatures before? If they can fly why haven't they left and made their way to other lands?" Gabriel said questioning.

"Because, why leave when you have plenty of food here on the Islands?" Rylee commented.

"No, It's because Melanion cast a spell to make sure they couldn't leave the surrounding area," Maddox corrected.

"What kind of Dragon is it that we're waiting for to pass?" John asked, "is it Dragon or Dorgoggin?"

"Fernospurt Dragon. She may kill everyone that crosses her path, but she doesn't do it as often as the Dorgoggin's I mentioned. Dorgoggin's can smell their prey and they hunt them out, you don't have to just cross their path."

"Oh, do we really have to go out there again?" Farah Dayton asked now really concerned for their safety, "isn't there another way?"

Changing the subject, "If we are here for only a short time why so many supplies?" Asked Willem Karik sitting in one of the chairs at the table.

"If the dragon sees us, she will wait us out. It has happened before, and the people before were not so lucky," Maddox replied in concentration. Moments before he had pulled out a periscope, the kind you would find in a submarine, and was watching intently, "she knows that we have to travel through the Orange Dragon Field, and that is where she lives, so she doesn't take too kindly to it."

"Here is what is going to happen," Ronan took over, "as soon as Maddox tells us the path is clear we're going to run. I know that the packs are heavy, so we can leave them here. There's a spot about a mile and a half from here that we can rest for a short time. There we will eat and take naps, if you need them. There will also be a ride waiting for us to take us the rest of the way. Does everyone understand?" Ronan asked feeling important.

"I don't know if we can make it that far running with our children. They can't run fast and they are so little," Farah commented from the center of the room concerned about all the little ones in the room.

"We will all work together. If you need help with your children, Maddox, Ronan and I will help you carry them. We can handle four at a time each, well, except Maddox, he can usually carry more," Ronan stated.

No one said anything else for a long time. Teag sat in a chair against the large circular wall. He felt a slight breeze from behind him. He turned and looked at the wall and observed a small crack in it, "what's this?" He asked following it all the way around, "it looks like a hidden door," he added in surprise, "Where does it go?"

Rylee jumped to his feet and walked over to hold it closed. "Going down there is a last resort. It's just as risky, if not more, and it's the long way around," he said sitting in the seat next to him.

"There she is. Right...On...Time," Maddox commented slowly pronouncing each word carefully while watching the Dragon fly by. "Alright everyone get ready. Just a minute more..."he said still watching. Swiftly he let go of the periscope and while looking at Ronan and Rylee said, "GO!"

One by one everyone raced out the door glancing around trying to spot the Dragon. Not watching where they were going, every once in a while someone would fall down. Rylee being at the back of the line grabbed whom ever it was up helping him/her to their feet again, as he was still running and carrying Elana Miles, Kyle Miles, and Seven Dayton on his back.

Tracy Miles stopped and tried to catch her breath, "please," she started panting, "can we stop? I can't go any further."

Ronan came up from behind her and grabbed her, throwing her on his back, to sit with Baylee Esteban, Suraionee Trager and John Trager. *"No Stopping,"* he roared in a deep voice.

Maddox was the largest and was able to hold the most people. He had Piper Karik, Ramsey Dayton, Amara Esteban, Oran Esteban and Farah Dayton who hung on to her small infant Natalie. All three of the Lion men ran like animals. It was curious that they talked and walked like humans, but had the looks and abilities of a lion.

Dan Miles fell hurting his ankle making him unable to walk. Rylee came up and grabbed him throwing him on his back with the children.

"Watch out!" Rylee roared as he glanced behind him and found the Dragon flying their way, *"she's coming!"*

With nowhere to hide all they could do was run as fast as their legs could take them. The Dragon was hot on their tails now. Teag took a quick look behind him to see where it was causing him to trip on a rock. He fell rolling three times hurting his ankle.

Preston jumped over Teag as he rolled and then stopped to help him up.

Ronan tried to grab his arm to help him up, but missed, accidentally bumping Preston and knocking him to the ground with a thud. Knowing that Rylee was at the end he kept running "Don't stop!" He roared at Preston egging him back to his feet.

Teag tried to get up, but couldn't get his footing. His ankle was hurting horribly. Preston stumbled over to him and then helped Teag onto his foot, while the other was carefully cradled off the ground.

"Come on freaky eyes, you don't want to be dragon meat do you?" Preston snapped as he threw Teag's arm over his shoulder trying to help him run, but Teag couldn't hop fast enough. Teag could hear Rylee coming from behind and knew he could help him go faster. As Rylee ran past him, he grabbed at Teags arm trying to throw him on his back, but the amount of weight he was carrying already made him have to let go or fall himself. Not wanting to let Teag and Preston stay behind, he dropped Dan and the children and told them to *"Run!"* Dan limped as fast as he could only taking him as fast as the children. Rylee returned to Teag but was too late, the Dragon kicked him out of the way while grabbing a hold of Teag and Preston. Everyone stopped running when they saw the dragon fly overhead. They all noticed she was carrying two people though no one knew who at first. Maddox glared at Rylee for his mistake. Rylee lowered his face in shame.

Chapter 5

The Dragon flew for a while then landed in a large patch of tall orange grass that hid her well. There was a large hole in the ground leading to a large open cavern with a long tunnel attached. The Dragon carried them in dropping them both in a nest full of three eggs that were as large as they were. Teag's' heart was pounding with fear trying not to make any noise that might aggravate the dragon who walked deeper into the dark tunnel. "That's why they know it's a she," Teag whispered to Preston looking at the eggs.

"Who cares if it's a girl or not, were dead because you couldn't stay on your feet," Preston quietly snapped.

"It's not my fault you hate me so much. Why did you even bother stopping to help me?" Teag asked.

"I felt sorry for you just losing your parents and all, but a lot of good, helping you did me." Preston whined.

The dragon returned and then glanced over at them in the nest snorting and looking angry.

"Please, Don't eat us," Teag requested gazing into the Dragons eyes.

"Right, like that's going to work you idiot, lets just ask her not to eat us," Preston raged at Teag.

The Dragon looked deep into Teags bright blue eyes snorting and snarling. The light blue star in Teags left eye started glowing light blue. With a jerk the dragon pulled away and laid herself down next to the nest. Calm and serine she gave Teag the sense that she wasn't going to hurt them. He sat there for a moment trying to figure out if they were safe or not. When he tried to stand up, his ankle throbbed and shot sharp pains up his leg, "Aargh."

"Serves you right freaky eyes," Preston muttered as he lazily sat back and pulled pieces of the nest up and threw them.

"Will you stop calling me that you looser. Can't you find something else to nag about?" Teag snapped with contempt. He then very carefully pulled himself to the edge of the nest and looked over at the huge dragon. Her head was down on the ground as if she were sulking.

"What's the matter girl?" He asked wondering if she too could talk like the Pembroke's. No answer came.

"What you're going to talk to her? Do you have a death wish?"

"Didn't you just tell me that we're dead because of me? So what if I make that happen sooner than later."

"Just leave me out of it, she can eat you first that'll give me time to get away," Preston snarled then returned to sit down on the opposite side of the nest.

"Why did you take us if you didn't want to eat us?" He asked her. The Dragon looked up at him and then quickly looked away as if ashamed of what she had done. He carefully climbed out of the nest using only his good leg, but every bump and scrape made him feverish with pain. He pulled himself toward her head and then petted her beautiful metallic yellowish orange toned scales.

'You are different,' came a voice.

Startled Teag looked at her and asked, "was that you?" He watched her mouth for movement.

'Yes,' she thought. Her lips never moved but Teag could hear her just fine.

"How do you do that?" He asked.

"Do what? Who are you talking too?" Preston asked as he peeked over the nest and down at Teag and the dragon.

"Myself okay, why don't you go find a way out or something while I sit here and try to get eaten," Teag snapped back.

"You're crazy you know that?" Preston said shaking his head.

'I'm not doing it, you are,' She smiled back at him. Then noticing his pain, "are you hurt?"

"Yeah, I think I've broken my ankle," he said with pain in his voice. He carefully took off his shoe and sock to look at the damage. His whole foot was black and blue and was starting to swell very badly.

Preston sat back down inside the nest trying to think of a way out, "what does it matter anyway? She's going to eat us and then you wont notice your leg anymore," he said to himself.

The dragon carefully looked at Teags wound and then pulled in her tail close to him.

'Take a scale from my tail,' she instructed him.

"Won't that hurt? I don't want to hurt you," Teag whispered hoping that Preston couldn't hear him.

'How does it feel when you pinch your skin or pull out a hair from your head?' She asked.

"Well, it hurts a little for a second and then it's fine," he replied still whispering, trying to understand why she was asking such a strange question.

'Well, that's just the same as me. Now hurry before your foot becomes too big. There wont be enough fluid to get to the bone if your ankle gets too swollen,' She cautioned. Teag leaned over and found a small scale and wiggled it a little, 'oh come now, you can do better than that, pull hard.'

"Okay," he pulled as hard as he could and the scale came out with a slight, "crunch," sound. "Okay, now what do I do with it?" The scale was a metallic yellowish/orange tone that appeared to look as if there was liquid inside making it twinkle.

'Break it open,' she guided him, trying to help. Teag tugged and pulled and twisted trying to snap it open or crack it, then he tried using a nearby rock to break it open, but nothing worked.

"What are you doing down there?" Preston asked once again looking over the side.

"Mind your own business, I'm just playing with a rock," Teag snapped back loudly. Preston went back inside the nest and started walking around the eggs.

"How do I break it open? Is there a trick to it?" He asked her dumfounded.

'I've never had to use it before, so I don't know,' She said thinking really hard at what might work. 'I know, set it on the ground over there,' She instructed pointing to an area not too far away. Teag tossed it over and then watched her. She looked at him and smiled. Then she breathed fire and scorched it.

Fearful Preston looked over again at Teag and the dragon. He felt they were distracted enough and then decided to sneak past them and ran down the tunnel, deeper into the hole.

"Can he get out that way?" Teag asked watching him run away.

"No, he'll be back later. It's just a dark hole and then a dead end where I store my extra food," like it was no big deal. When she was done she said, 'quickly while it's still hot, see if you can snap it in half. Teag inched his way over as quickly as he could and grabbed the scale. It was still so hot he tossed it from hand to hand so he didn't burn himself. He quickly wrapped his hands in his shirt and then took the scale in both hands snapping it in half.

"It worked,' he said with a smile, "now what should I do?"

'Put the gel on your ankle, it will help,' she said nodding to him. Teag did as he was told. The gel inside was a metallic silver color. It was thick and smooth to touch. When it touched his skin, it dissolved and disappeared into his ankle, his pain instantly went away and before his very eyes the black and blue swelling went away, and his bones healed.

"Wow, that was amazing. I never knew that magic existed. I thought places like this were all just stories, and I've certainly never been able to talk to animals before, how am I suddenly able to do it now?" He asked with wonder. Then looking back at her and before she could answer asked, "You're not mean at all are you?"

There was a cracking sound in the nest. Startled, and now able to use his leg he climbed back into the nest to see what was happening. One of the dragon eggs was hatching. The mother Dragon lifted her head to watch with enjoyment. Soon the baby's head peeked out of the shell. It was beautiful. Not knowing if it was a boy or girl Teag watched in awe. The sweet little head popped out, it hiccupped small flames out of its mouth, and the stunning blue and green scales made him beam with pleasure. When the baby had come completely out of its shell he could tell it was a boy at once. The baby laid his head down tired from all the work. Teag went down wanting to touch him, "is it okay?" he asked the mother who was watching his every move. Teag looked up at her and smiled. He had his hand facing the baby about to pat him, yet waiting for a response. The baby's mother replied, 'sure.'

The baby dragon was his height. He jumped to his feet and rumbled a tiny squeak as Teag got closer. Then he coughed, spitting out flames. Teag jumped back, but flames singed the hair on his arms. The baby again tried to growl only this time he roared then advanced to bite him.

"Aaah!" Teag screamed in panic.

The mother Dragon was watching, and snarled back telling the baby to stop. Teag decided he had better climb out and hide before he became the baby dragon's first meal.

The Mother Dragon climbed out of the hole, "hey!" Teag called to her, "where are you going?" He asked in fear of the baby dragon. Looking back up at the top of the nest, hoping that he wasn't going to come down to get him. Teag hid and waited. Soon the sounds of cracking again filled his ears. It sounded like the other two were now out of their shells. The small Dragons were making gargling noises as they played about. It seemed like hours had passed before the Mother Dragon appeared descending back into the layer. She dumped something out of her mouth into the nest. The smells of dead fish rapidly fill the air. The mother Dragon leaned over and picked up a fish out of the nest and dropped it at Teag's feet. With it was Suraionee's teddy bear she had lost in the sea.

"Teddy? Oh thank you. Suraionee will be missing this," Teag wrung out as much of the wet that he could then set it down to dry out. The Dragon was watching him.

'Who is Suraionee?' She asked Teag

"My sister," he replied then decided to tell her all about the shipwreck and losing his parents and that his dad had given Suraionee the bear so it was extra special now. He told her about Maddox and all the people they were traveling with and about his younger brother he was worried about.

'I'm so sorry all that happened to you,' she said, 'don't let you're fish get cold hurry and eat.'

Teag looked at the fish with disgust, not wanting to offend her he said, "well you don't mind if I cook it first do you? I can't eat raw fish."

In reality he couldn't eat any, but there was nothing else and he was hungry. She nodded to agree so he looked around for sticks to build a fire. He found a few close to the entrance of the hole. Once he put the sticks together to burn, he looked around for some rocks to contain the fire. 'How am I going to light it?' He wondered trying to rub two sticks together like they taught him at scout camp. After several minutes of trying and failing he threw the sticks he had in his hands in frustration. The overwhelming smell of fish was starting to make him nauseous.

The Dragon pushed him aside and then blew a little fire out of her mouth lighting the sticks. "Thanks," Teag said petting her nose, "you know Rylee told me you weren't nice," he said while placing the fish on a stick and putting it in the fire to cook, "why would he tell me that when you are?"

'Well, you're the only human that has lived after I've taken them. I don't take prisoners. Too many humans come to get my toenails or want my liver. Some try to take my eggs, but I show them,' she said, anger in her tone.

"Well that isn't very nice of them," Teag agreed with her.

'The thing is I used to love people. I was raised by a man. I thought he loved me, but then one day, he tried to kill me, he wanted all my parts for potions, said all I was meant for was to help his wizarding career. I promised myself I would never trust another human again…and then you came along,' She paused. 'I've never been able to communicate with a human before. You're nice,' After Several minutes the Fish was ready to eat. Teag choked it down trying to make himself believe that he was eating Tacos.

"I don't trust Preston, I think it might be better if he thinks you still might want to eat us."

'Well, what are you suggesting, I could, you know keep him here and let the babies have him. That would rid you of your problem.'

Teag laughed for a moment tempted by the offer, but could never do that to someone, "Thanks, but I think that maybe, I can run after him and say that you're after us and then we can somehow escape. That way, he wont think he could just come back to kill you someday."

'You may have something there, how about I take the babies out and then you go get him, I'll let you get out and then I'll chase you a little and scare him, but you have to act scared too.'

"Good plan," Teag smiled, "so, do you have a name?" He asked changing the subject.

'Yes, it's Nyla,' She replied.

"Nyla, that's a pretty name," Teag said, 'how could it be that this large and scary creature chose to befriend me? This is the coolest pet ever,' Teag thought, 'I've gotta tell John and Suraionee about this if I can find them.'

"We need to name your babies…how about Bosco for the boy?" He asked laughing a little. Nyla winced at the thought, "Okay how about Blaze?" Teag asked liking the name himself. Nyla agreed with enjoyment, "lets see…umm…how about Alaura for the yellowish/ red girl, and Moya for the purplish/green girl."

'I Love those names,' Nyla said pleased.

"So, in the morning, I would really like to get back to my Brother and Sister. It's Suraionee's birthday tomorrow and I'm sure they are really worried about me," Teag told her.

'Of course, and you are always welcome here as long as you don't try to kill me or my children,' Nyla smiled.

"Thanks."

Meanwhile, the traveling group made it to safety. Hailey stood there crying inconsolably while Willem held her and tried to comfort her, though he was just as emotional about it. Piper stood hanging on her mothers leg trying to comfort her crying mother not understanding why she was so upset. Suraionee looked around for Teag, not knowing that the Dragon had caught him. After a moment of searching Suraionee became panicked, "where is Teag?" She asked John hoping that she may have overlooked him in the crowd of people.

John looked up and searched the huge room; it was another hill just like the previous one, only there were other rooms attached by large arched doorways, "has anyone seen Teag?" he asked.

Rylee pulled John and Suraionee aside and told him what had happened, "I fear the worst for him. I'm so sorry I couldn't do more."

"Where did she take him? He is still alive I know it, and I'm going to get him. I'm not losing another family member," John insisted.

"It would be suicide, you cannot go where they are," Maddox insisted calmly, "The Dragon would eat you before you even got there. The grass is too tall, and the field is too large. Besides, the Dragon blends in," Maddox sat on a bed to lie down, "I'm so sorry.

This is not what was in the plan," he added in sorrow a little worried about what ZaBeth would say when she found out.

"So that's it then? Are we supposed to just forget about him?" Suraionee jumped in, anger filling her eyes, "that's NOT good enough! You brought us here...for what? To die?" Suraionee exclaimed, now more beside herself then ever.

Willem agreed, "She's right, what are you planning to do now? Will we be sending out a search party for the boys?"

"We can't help them now. It's too late," Maddox paused for a moment trying to gain some composure but the longer he tried the angrier he felt. Though there was nothing he could have done to stop what had happened to Teag and Preston he felt guilty beyond measure.

"No that's not it, it can't be, we need to get out there and search for them," Willem looked around the room then asked. "Who's with me?" everyone's heads went down, no one would look him in the eye. "You're all giving up?" He was outraged, "get out there and find my son," he pointed at the door yelling at Maddox, but Maddox didn't move.

"Willem I want to find them too, but even if we ever found the dragons home, the boys will have been dead, then we will die for just trying, and then who would get the rest of you out of here? You would be stuck here forever."

"No, we kill the dragon," Willem said optimistic.

Maddox laughed a little, "you have no idea how many men have died trying to do what you are asking us to do. Let's say we get lucky and we do kill her, we will surly be killed in the attempt, we would all be dead and then what happens? More lives lost for a dead attempt? And then we have to try to get through the other dangerous creatures, if we go we'll all end up dead."

"So when you said no one will be left behind, you really meant that you don't really care. And where is all the "*happiness*" you promised. It seems that if we even attempt to enjoy any of this beautiful country that we're crossing, we will be eaten alive," Willem sneered furious that they weren't out there searching for them right now.

"I do care, but what good will it do if everyone ends up killed Willem? Now, I'm done talking about this," Maddox shook his head in frustration with the whole thing. He glared over at Rylee who wasn't paying attention to any of the conversation.

"Great, then it's settled, we leave in five minutes," Willem motioned toward the door.

"*No*, Willem, your not listening to me, We're, not, going," Maddox said careful to pronounce each word so that he might better understand, his Australian accent was very prominent. As he sat back on the bed he tried to be calm, but instead sounded cold. "Now, lay there and get some rest while lunch is being made," Maddox sat in silence for a few moments.

"If you wont help us, then we'll go on our own," Suraionee insisted standing up and storming out the door.

John jumped up and chased after her, "Stop Sura, Wait a second."

Suraionee was in tears, "John, why did we come on this trip? Why didn't we talk mom and dad out of it?" Suraionee cried mournfully, "Oh Johnny! We are all that's left in our family."

John, not wanting to show her how scared he was for their brother tried to calm her. Looking up he saw something coming toward them, "hurry back to the hill!" he yelled shoving her toward the door, "it's the Dragon."

With a slam of the door they both backed up against it panting.

"Back so soon?" They heard a woman's voice, "I wouldn't want to be out there alone either," she added. They looked where the voice was coming from and found her. It was ZaBeth. She stood there in her elegant old robes staring at them like she had been there the whole time.

"Where have you been? I don't remember seeing you at camp this morning. Come to think of it I don't remember seeing you at all today, until now," John said in disgust.

"I just came to check on you all and see how you were doing."

"Well, we aren't fine, our brother's been taken by the dragon, and these oafs refuse to help us find him," Suraionee said in the frustration of not being able to do anything about it.

"*What!*" ZaBeth exclaimed glairing at Maddox and then over at Rylee with thin eyes. Then quickly composing herself, "oh, I'm so sorry. I'm sure the boys did all they could to help him. I am sorry. It is quite impossible to go after him."

"My sons been taken too, what are you going to do about it?" Willem demanded.

ZabBeth glared at him and then continued with what she was saying, "However," She said loudly, "we do have to travel through the Orange Dragon Field on the way…" she paused and acted as though she had a sudden astounding thought, "so we could look for him, but I cannot promise anything. We will not leave the path, but, if we should come across him…" ZaBeth's voice trailed off. It seemed as though she went into some kind of trance.

ZaBeth then pulled Maddox, Ronan, and Rylee aside and started a discussion that no one could hear. Though it appeared it was a heated conversation, all three lion men seamed very sad and ZaBeth seemed to be outraged.

Suraionee and John found a discrete place and Suraionee started to cry for the loss of her brother while John held her in a hug and tried to comfort her while feeling the pain of the loss himself. It was all too much for their little hearts to bare. They both felt despair and that nothing could possibly get better.

Maddox went over to them and tried to console them, "please, I'm so sorry, Suraionee, look at me please," Maddox coaxed.

"I'd rather not, please just go away," Suraionee sobbed with her face buried in her left hand and her right hand waving him to go away.

"John, please, I just want to apologize for being so cold, it was wrong of me. Even if you wont look at me, I'm sorry," Maddox felt even more miserable than he did before.

"Just leave us alone, we just need to be alone," John didn't know what to say or do. He kept his head down and refused to look at anyone.

Everyone was so worn out and tired. Maddox walked back to his bedside sat back down and then decided out loud, "we will eat lunch and rest a little longer and then we will move on," Then he started telling everyone what would happen. "We have a ride so it will be easy, however, we must stay quiet while in the field. That is the home of the Dragon and we don't want to disturb her. It will take us about five hours to go thirty miles so plan on having dinner at the Great Oak. We will stay there for the night and leave our ride behind," he looked around the room, "Any questions?" No one answered or even seemed to be paying too much attention. Dan Miles had already fallen asleep and was snoring. Maddox grunted out a small chuckle as if he wasn't surprised then fell asleep himself.

ZaBeth had disappeared again. Though no one seemed to notice. The food was ready but no one had seen anyone working on it or putting it on the table. No one really seemed to care either as everyone that was awake crowded around to get something to eat.

Back at the Dragons Lair...

Nyla, Blaze, Moya, and Alaura, left to hide in the grass, while Teag took a large torch he pulled from the fire and went in search of Preston. Calling out for him every few feet, Teag found him about half way down the tunnel sitting on the ground and playing with the dirt. When he saw the light he jumped up and walked towards Teag.

"I thought you would have been eaten by now," Preston said in an arrogant tone.

"Yeah well she's saving us for her babies."

"Did ya figure that one out, all on your own when she didn't eat you, or when she put us in the nest with the eggs?" He snarled, "What do you want?"

"Well I thought you wanted to get out of here, she took off and the coast is clear, I could have left you here but I thought you might not want to be tonight's dinner. But if you like I'll leave you here, by yourself and you can find another way out," Teags tone was sarcastic.

"What are you waiting for, if I didn't come back for you you'd be dinner, so stop dragging your feet, here we have a chance to get out of here and your wasting my time talking, lets go," Preston said acting like it was him trying to help Teag all along. Teag simply shook his head and started running to catch up with Preston who took off right after his comment.

When they made it to the opening they both stopped to catch their breath. The crickets were chirping and the birds were singing softly in the distance. But when they suddenly stopped the boys looked at each other knowing it only meant one thing.

"The dragon," they both repeated as they both took off running into the thick grass. The grass towered over them like they were ants. Unable to tell which way to go they just picked a direction and went with it. They could now both hear the dragon over head roaring loudly.

"I guess she found that we were gone," Preston commented laughing a little.

"Yeah," Teag said as he tried to keep a smile off his face.

The dragon's roar was becoming louder as she got closer. The sound of rustling grass filled their ears while the dragon ran towards them. They continued running and screaming for their lives as her giant jaws of sharp teeth snapped several times behind them.

Back at Pony Hills...

Suraionee laid on a bed sleeping when John woke her quietly, "Shh," he said looking around to see if anyone had noticed them. He then held up to her view a full backpack. Her eyes grew large as she knew what he was planning.

"Where did you get that?" She whispered in excitement.

"I found it and other supplies laying around, no one saw me taking them."

"How are we going to get out of here everyone will notice us if we just walk out the front door."

"We'll be leaving with the rides soon and Maddox, Ronan, and Rylee will be busy with the other families, we can sneak off then," John informed her of his amazing plan.

A short time later Maddox stood up and announced to everyone it was time to move on. There were moans and groans as people were woken up and told to get moving. When the door opened to the outside John put on the back pack then he and Suraionee made their move.

When they walked outside they saw five Giraffes. The saddle was an orange leather carriage that was able to seat five people inside comfortably. Attached to the carriage was an orange canopy top that had thousands of the tips of the orange grass on top to help camouflage them inside the field. Dangling from the inside of the canopy hung four lanterns brightly lit with hundreds of moving fireflies. There was a ladder hanging down behind the giraffe and a door to the carriage for safety while traveling. While his attention was turned the two kids made their way under the giraffe legs trying to stay hidden and then when the coast was clear they ran for the tall orange grass and disappeared inside it.

Maddox Showed Gabriel Esteban and Kory Dayton how to guide their Giraffes, "Your Giraffes know the way. Gabriel, your Giraffe will follow mine, and Kory yours will follow Ronan's, however, should they start to wonder off course, just take the reigns and lead them back to the group," when Gabriel and Kory were confident, Maddox left them and climbed aboard the giraffe carriage that should have contained the remaining Trager kids. He froze when he realized that they weren't there. He jumped down and searched each carriage, wondering if they had gotten on the wrong one. Calling to Ronan and Rylee they huddled into a tiny group and talked about what might have happened to them. One last attempt to find them Maddox sent Ronan into the hill to see if they were there. Ronan went in and searched but came out shaking his head.

"They went into the field to find their brother. I should have been watching them better," Maddox said angry at himself for not taking better care, "I have to go in after them."

"What? No dad, you'll be killed," Ronan pleaded.

"What kind of man am I if I don't protect the young children who need me. I'm ashamed of myself, for being too afraid of facing death to save any one of them," pausing for a moment he took a deep breath. "Go, get them all to safety, I'll meet you later when I have found them," Maddox commanded. He climbed up into the carriage, pulled up the ladder and closed the door. Maddox waited as the other carriages started on their way and then followed the last carriage into the tall orange grass. The grass was so tall that the giraffes heads could just barely see over the top of it. Once inside he pulled away from the other carriages and disappeared in search of the kids.

Chapter 6

Several minutes of running passed before Teag and Preston Realized they weren't being followed anymore, "Where is she?" Preston asked looking and listening for anything that might tell him she was still there.

"I don't know, I think we lost her."

"How much further do we have to go?" Preston asked.

"It can't be much further," Teag said as they kept walking in and out of the thick blades of grass. It was so thick and heavy that sometimes they had to walk around the worst parts. Though tired and hungry, Teag kept pushing himself to go further.

"The sun is starting to go down and we need a place to sleep," Preston demanded.

"Where would you like to sleep Preston? There is clearly no place here or any food. Stay if you like, but I'm going to keep going."

"Teag, why do you think they had a ride to go the rest of the way? It's too far and for all we know we're going in circles. We can't see anything," Preston whined.

Teag thought about what he said and he was right. As he looked up at the tips of the grass he could see the sky was just a little darker. Then he got an idea, "lets climb the grass."

"How are ya gonna do that?" Preston asked with a heavy sigh.

Teag didn't bother to explain he started taking his shoes off. First his right shoe and sock. Once the sock was off he stepped on his shoe so that his feet didn't touch the dirt. Then his left foot, being careful not to touch any of the dirt on the ground. When his feet were bare he started climbing the closest thick orange blade. Teag's feet were sticky just enough to climb, inching his way to the top. Preston watched and laughed a little until Teag actually started making headway, Instantly Preston decided to try and beat him to the top. Quickly he tore off his shoes and socks then grabbed a hold of the closest blade, "almost there," Teag yelled down to Preston as he looked down to find him.

"Yeah, me too," Preston yelled closer than Teag had expected. Preston clearly had the advantage as he was a lot stronger than Teag, but Teag still beat him to the top by just seconds.

Their heads peeked over the tops of the blades that swayed slightly from the breeze. The sun was setting, leaving a colorful sunset. Birds were flying in and out of the grass. Teag had hoped to find something close by but everything appeared to be miles away from them in every direction.

"Great, you brought us to the middle of the field you idiot," Preston snapped at Teag.

"I'd like to see you do better, you're just as blind as I am down there," Teag defended. "Looks like we were headed for the ugly trees in that forest. We need to go back to the hills, look," Teag pointed to his left, "there they are. We are going to have to just stay here tonight." Teag slid down and started to look for anything that could mark the direction they wanted to go. Unable to find much of anything he used his finger to mark the way in the dirt.

The sun was down and the moon was full, but inside the tall dark grass no light remained. Teag and Preston didn't speak. They sat on opposite sides of the small area and propped themselves up on the grass blades and soon fell asleep.

Meanwhile, John and Suraionee were also fighting their way through the blades of grass. After a few hours they both began to get tired, "Can we sit and rest for a while?" Suraionee asked as she huffed.

"Sura, we can't stop, Teag might need us," John motioned her on, but she refused.

"Just for a minute, let me catch my breath."

"Fine, but only a minute, we have to hurry, Maddox will have noticed that we were gone just a few minutes after we left and he might be right behind us, and he'll force us to stop. I don't want to stop looking for him do you?"

"No," a deep Australian voice came from behind them, "I wont stop ya, lets find him together."

John and Suraionee jumped and ran for Maddox, who was walking the giraffe by the reins, they both hugged him tightly.

"Really? You're going to help us?" Suraionee asked excited.

"Yes, but you must agree that if we find the dragon lair and he isn't there that you'll come with me to the Great Oak, we wont be searching for him any further. Agreed?" Maddox asked seriously.

John and Suraionee looked at one another and then said simultaneously, "agreed."

"Quickly get up here and lets get going, it'll be dark in a few short hours," Maddox helped them up the ladder and then climbed up after them closing the door. John and Suraionee each took a seat next to one another with two empty seats left directly across from them. Maddox sat in the single seat that was at first facing them at the front of the carriage. He flipped a switch and his seat swivelled away from them facing the back of the giraffe's neck. He then pumped a lever that made his low sitting seat get higher and higher so that he could guide the giraffe. John and Suraionee relaxed in the seats that were squashy and lined with soft black animal fir. There was a small circular hole on the center of the floor. At the back of the carriage was the door and rolled up ladder.

"Maddox?" asked Suraionee as he was watching the ground, "if the dragon lives in this field, how come it isn't all burned down? I would have thought that a fire breathing dragon would have burned everything up."

"She would have, but Vidor Lysander, he's a wizard in the Black Wizard Forest, well, he enchanted it many years ago. He didn't want anyone getting close to him because of all the Magical experiments he was working on," he answered.

"Well if the Dragon is so bad why didn't you just undo the enchantment and let her burn it all down?" Suraionee asked more interested.

"We've tried, but we don't know what kind of magic he used and we can't find a spell to change it. Vidor and Melanion were the only real wizards in the City. They helped us build the city to be safe from the large and brutal beasts on the island. Vidor became paranoid that someone in the City was planning to kill him with his own magic to gain greater power. So, One day he left Makoto City and took everything he knew to the Black Wizard Forest and Melanion just disappeared," Maddox explained.

John had been listening, but decided to join in, "has anyone tried to talk to Vidor about it? Reason with him?"

"Yes, like I told you when we first met, *we aren't what we seem*. My sons and I traveled to the Black Wizard Forest a year ago. We told him we would protect him and that he was safe, but the Forest got to Vidor's mind, he was crazy, he talked gibberish. Oh, he would talk normal for a short time, but then out of the blue he would go berserk. Somewhere in the conversation he got the notion that we were the ones who'd come to kill him. Then he, he..." Maddox stopped and looked at his hands, then looked back at the ground.

John understood, "he changed you into human lions?"

Maddox nodded then went on, "Vidor refused to change us back, he said that if we ever came back he would kill us. I don't care about me, but my boys, I can't have that," he stopped and glanced off into the distance, then he looked back at Suraionee and John. "Don't worry, we'll be alright."

Maddox had a good idea of where to look for the dragon lair, from years of reports of where the dragon always seemed to first be seen when she took flight. They were almost there. The sun was beginning to set when they arrived. Stay here, I'll call you if it's safe. He opened the door and slid the rope ladder out the back and then stepped out. It wasn't long before he came back. Quickly you can look and then we must be going, before the dragon comes back," Maddox said motioning them to jump to him. John went first. He jumped into Maddox's arms and then was set on the ground. Then Suraionee leaped out to him. Then they quickly ran inside, to look around. It was dark, but the light that still shone from the entrance lit the room just enough to tell that Teag and Preston were no longer there.

Suraionee cried into her hands, "she ate him bones and everything."

John bowed his head but he could no longer cry as he had cried it all out earlier in the day.

"Quickly we have to leave. She'll be back soon," Maddox whispered.

"How do you know that?" John asked, looking at Maddox who was looking inside the nest.

"Shhh," Maddox put his finger in front of his lips to quiet him, "because her babies are in here sleeping," he whispered as he ran pushing them out of the lair as quickly as he could. He helped them up into the carriage and then set off towards the Great Oak. Just as they had disappeared into the grass he heard the flapping of large wings and heard the dragons large body land. John and Suraionee held their breath as they waited to see if they had been spotted. But after a few moments let out a sigh of relief as they had just had a close encounter.

Back in the Orange Dragon Field...

The next morning was warm and humid; Preston woke up first and took off a shoe then dangled his smelly sock covered toes under Teags nose, waking him up with a snort, "real mature, spike," Teag snapped making a comment about his hair and even more angry that he didn't think of it first.

Preston laughed, "yeah, well I'm sure my father is out there looking for me, so lets go," with nothing to carry they started to walk in the direction Teag had marked on the ground. After about an hour, Teag wondered how much further they had to go. He took off his shoes and socks and made his way up another tall blade of grass. Again they were off course only this time they were heading away from the ugly spooky trees and headed for a large lake. The morning sun was getting high. The fresh humid breeze blew in Teag face making him want to go swimming for a while, but his stomach just wanted food. Knowing the only way to food was to find the hills and make it there as quickly as possible, Teag found the hills now on the right of them and pointed to Preston, who was standing on the ground, the right direction. Three more times they had to check and make adjustments to their direction.

Teags stomach was growling loudly he was so hungry and even thirstier. His body was growing week from the heat and lack of food and water. He sat down for a few minutes. Preston crashed on the ground not too far away, feeling the same way as Teag. They were both drenched in sweat. The tall grass kept the wind out, though he wished it was cool, he would take any wind at this point. Too weak and tired to climb the grass and find their direction Teag laid on the ground smacking his dry tongue in his mouth he wished for water.

He looked at the grass in the direction they were headed and thought he saw, a ray of sun light just between a few blades of grass.

"Preston," Teag rolled over to him, and warily tried to get him to his feet, "I see the sun, we're almost there." Teag said tiredly.

"It's a mirage Teag, we're never getting out of here," Preston said giving up, "just leave me alone," he then pulled his arm away from Teag and rolled to his side.

"Get up, I know we don't have far to go," Teag started, but when Preston just ignored him, he said, "there's food and water inside," though he really had no idea.

Preston jumped up like he had just had a fresh bowl of cold water thrown on him, "which way is it?" The fast rush of energy quickly faded.

"This way," Teag pointed, it took his last bit of strength to stand up. Pushing themselves, he and Preston stumbled through the last bit of grass, "I never want to see another blade of grass as long as I live," Teag swore as they staggered towards the nearest hill. At once Teag yelled, "*pañuelo azul,*" remembering the word Maddox had used, but nothing happened. "This must not be it," he went to the hill next to it on the left and yelled it again, but still nothing.

"Maybe it's a different password," Preston guessed before he yelled, "*open says me,*" with no luck.

"No it's the same, we just have to find the right hill," Teag demanded. Teag called out to John and Suraionee, hoping that maybe they could hear him and would run out, if they were even still there. 'I hope they're here,' he thought looking around. There was a sudden chomping sound way off in the distance but it seemed to be getting closer. He wasn't sure what the noise was but just wanted to get inside fast so he started calling out again but stopped suddenly when he heard a snap of a branch behind him.

Preston was standing there with a smirk on his face, "what?, Did I scare you?" he chuckled.

"No," Teag lied, but was relieved it wasn't a creature of some kind. Alternating between calling out the password and John or Suraionee's names, he started walking all the way around the hills, making sure he didn't miss the door on the other side. As he came around his third hill, Preston was calling out his own family names and random words behind him, Teag stopped abruptly. A strange looking creature stood before him. It had a bony looking parrot type beak that looked like it was strong enough to bust through rocks. It had bone like spikes all over its face, a brown scaly workhorse body, and a long tale with sharp bony spikes all the way down its spine and around it's hooves. Teag stood there looking the beast in the eyes. Preston not watching where he was going bumped into Teag making him stumble a little closer.

"What's your problem loser? Why'd ya stop," Preston snarled, before he looked at what Teag was looking at, "is that the Spudacre, or whatever Maddox called it?"

"I think so," Teag whispered, "slowly back away maybe it wont follow us," Teag instructed. It was close enough that he could hear it's heavy breathing. It started clicking it's beak like mouth together and making a horrible heaving sound. Teag and Preston slowly backed away taking a second to glance over at another nearby hill when suddenly something whizzed past his ear just missing Preston and hit the hill behind him. He looked at what it was and was terrified when he saw the sharp bones wedged into the hillside. The beast started clicking its beak together and making that awful heaving noise again. Teag and Preston took the opportunity to start running. They were stumbling, pushing and shoving each other out of the way. The beast followed, it's heavy hooves clopping on the ground, he knew it wasn't too far away. Weaving in and out of the hills Teag and Preston kept calling out *pañuelo azul* in hopes that they might find safety in a hill. Preston wasn't making up words any more, he was calling out the same words Teag used and was very serious about it. The beast cut them off and they both slipped to a skid, kicked themselves backward and back to their feet running away, once again toppling over each other trying to get away. They rounded a corner, but were forced to stop when a second Spitniker Dorgoggin appeared. With one now on each side of them they both glanced from one to the other. The dreadful heaving noise started from both sides, echoing so loudly it hurt their ears.

"Their gonna spit," Teag warned Preston, "get ready to drop to the ground," the heaving stopped and both creatures began to make the chomping sounds as if they were cracking bones in half. "Now," Teag yelled as both boys dropped covering their heads, several sharp bones flew through the air and spread out, one hit Teag in the arm while Preston seemed to make out with no injuries. The other bones flew with such force that both beasts ended up with a few bones in them. Angry now they both charged each other, giving Teag and Preston a chance to escape.

Teag had lost track of which hills they had tried to open, short on time, he quickly looked around. They were a few hills in, the light sounds of the battling beasts still ringing in their ears, Teag picked a hill and yelled *"pañuelo azul,"* to their great surprise the door opened and they entered the deserted room, closeing the door behind themselves. It showed signs of having recent guests. The cleaning hadn't been done. There was left over food on the tables and the beds had been slept-in, "when do you think they left?" He asked Preston who seemed stunned that his parents weren't waiting with open arms.

"I can't believe they left me," Preston whined for a moment. When he remembered Teag was there he straightened up, "what do you want?" He grumbled when Teag looked at him. Preston sulked as he kicked the trash around the floor and slammed cupboards as he walked by them just to show he was angry.

Teag felt a bit uneasy, 'why would they leave us,' he thought to himself as he searched the bathroom cupboards for a first aid kit. When he found one he pulled out the bandage tape and tore off four large pieces, and stuck them to the edge of the sink. The bone was still in his arm, wedged in deep. Teag grabbed the bone with his free hand and then yanked it out as fast as he could, "Aargh," he screamed through his clinched teeth as the bone left his bleeding arm. The sharp end was slightly curved, while the end he grabbed was shaped like a bulb and had divots all over it. He dropped the bone in the sink as it dripped blood all over everything. The wound in his arm was deep, blood it drizzled down his arm. Trying to work as fast as he could, Teag put the tape on the gauze pad so it was ready to stick on. He grabbed a cloth and cleaned up the blood as best he could. Every move he made with his arm was agony. He held the cloth there and applied pressure for a few minutes, and then he pulled it away looking at the wound. It was starting to clot and had just a little blood still creeping out of it. He quickly grabbed the thick gauze pad with tape on it, and placed it on his arm again holding the pressure. After a few more minutes he pulled out the tape and with his teeth tore off a few more long pieces, then he tried to make it a little stronger. When he was done he tried to clean up his mess, but didn't know what to do with the dirty laundry, so he threw it in the bathtub.

Teag walked out of the bathroom and headed to the kitchen. Preston was sitting at the table eating a sandwich that was left in the refrigerator. Seeing the sandwich made his mouth water. He was so hungry his stomach cramped and growled. He opened the fridge and found a turkey sandwich all wrapped nicely in plastic wrap. He took the only soda that sat there nice and cold. Without sitting down, pulling out a plate, or even breathing he scarfed the sandwich down. Then he opened the fizzy soda and slurped it while still chewing his food, making it go down faster. The boys didn't speak; they just stuffed their faces with anything eatable they could find. When Teag was full he sat down at the table then asked, "so, why do you think they left us?"

"Probably, because they thought we were dead," Preston answered in an angry tone, "no one cared to find out for sure, just leave him to die."

"You mean them?"

"What?" Preston asked ornery.

"You mean "them" just leave them to die?" Teag corrected him.

"No I meant him, who cares about you, your parent's are dead, you have nothing going for you, you're certainly more than your share of trouble. None of this would have happened if it weren't for you and your stupid, clumsy mistakes," Preston needled, standing up and standing over Teags chair egging him on.

Teag felt the steam rise in his body. He stood up to challenge him, 'I can't believe that I saved this jerks life more than once. Nyla would have let the baby dragons eat him for sure if it wasn't for me, and if she didn't, the Dorgoggin's would have killed him if I hadn't remembered the password to the hill. The tripping and breaking my ankle that set all of these events in motion, well that was an accident. But to say that it's all my fault and to bring up my parents deaths,' the thoughts just threw him over the top. "How dare you say anything about my parents, you didn't know them, you have no idea what your talking about. Say whatever you want about me, but never speak about my parents again," Teag yelled. All of the torture, and mental anguish he had lived with over the past several years came flooding out. All he wanted to do was 'beat the living daylights out of egotistic, uncaring Preston Karik.'

Knowing he was bigger he felt he had the advantage over Teag, he wasn't scared, in fact all he wanted to do since the first time he met him was fight him. His own father had told him to let it go, "we fight with our money not with our fists. You can win any battle if the price is right," his father had told him on the ship.

At his-own limit and not caring what his father said Preston went for the jugular, "What did you forget? Your stupid daddy trying to save face, saving his little son from the embarrassment he is. He had to fight your little problem for you, and you being the sissy you are, let him." Preston imitated a little girl with fury standing nose to nose with Teag. Teag gave him a dirty look.

Not willing to wait for a comeback from Teag and unable to contain himself any longer Preston punched Teag in the nose knocking him to the ground and making his nosebleed. Teag took a second to realize what had happened and with all his rage he jumped up raced at Preston and body slammed him into the ground, where they began to wrestle around hitting one another and knocking over any furniture that happened to be in their path. Around the room they went taking turns picking each other up and knocking the other to the ground again. Until Preston hit Teag so hard it knocked him through a wall. Breaking for a moment they both stood up. Teag slowly stood up and wiped the blood that still flowed from his nose. When he looked at Preston he saw his expression of awe and had to turn around. Realizing he had actually gone through a wall he looked at the hole he had left behind. It was actually a tall and wide round top door that was placed there to look like a wall. On the other side sat the largest cavern he had ever seen. It smelled of dirt and misty stale air. There was a ramp of dirt that leads to the lower level below them. The center of the room was a deep black pit that he couldn't see the bottom of. There was what appeared to be a five foot wide walkway of dirt on the bottom level, before the drop off, all the way around the circular floor. Along the dirt walls of the very large circular room there were rickety old wooden stairs that led up to wobbly old wooden scaffolding with railings that lead up five stories high. There were twelve doors evenly spaced on each of the five levels. Going all the way around the room. At each level of the stairs sat lanterns that were lit like someone had been there recently or was still in fact there somewhere watching them. Along the scaffolding every three feet hung another lantern, on each level, all the way around the room. The dim light that the lanterns emitted together showed some of the details to the large room.

Teag ran out of the room he searched for a bag or backpack of some kind. It wasn't hard to find as everyone had left their packs from camping on the beach the first night laying about. He searched through the bag and made sure he had plenty of supplies. He then went to the kitchen and grabbed dry food out of the pantry, and then threw it in the backpack. Trying to put the pack on he noticed his arm was bloody again. He ran to the bathroom and added the large first aid kit in the mix. Not wanting Preston to make further fun of him because he couldn't carry the backpack. He forced it on over his hurt arm and then pulled it on over the other shoulder.

Preston had already entered the room and was at the bottom of the ramp when Teag appeared again through the broken wall. He walked down and both of them went their different directions looking around the cavern. Teag first started to follow the path that took him around the large cavern on the bottom floor. As he walked by he placed his hand on the side of the dirt wall. Little flicks of dirt fell as he skimmed his hand over it. He walked half way around the room and then almost fell towards the dirt wall when his hand went through it like air. He could clearly see, it was clearly still there but his hand would vanish within it. He backed up and felt where the wall actually began again. Stepping forward he faced the wall. Then feeling brave he put his face in and opened his eyes. Blackness surrounded him, so he stepped forward and disappeared inside it.

Inside the wall was a dazzling room of treasures. Beautiful lanterns all around the room instantly lit as soon as he walked inside. There were large round marble pillars carefully placed along the sides of the room reaching the high cathedral ceilings. He couldn't see the floor through all the treasures he had to step on. All over the large room laid large piles of Jewels, gold and silver. Treasure chests randomly placed all over the room held beautiful necklaces, bracelets, golden goblets and colorful gems. Teag walked around and picked up as much as he could, placing the beautiful treasures quickly in his pockets. He turned to the right to walk around a large hill of gold coins and saw, against the beautiful marble walls, stood four short old looking armor suites. They looked like they might have belonged to little people. Behind the armor, hung on the walls, swords, javelins and weapons of all kinds placed nicely for display.

Teag turned to the left to walk to the back of the room walking between the armor and the pillars. Towards the back and covered by a large white cloth laid two maps. The first showed the way out of the cavern and the other showed a map of KobiKobis Island. Sitting right next to that was a compass and a necklace the size of a silver dollar, a necklace that Teag knew as the Universitas Dominium Monile. He took it and placed it in his shirt pocket. Then being as heavy as he could stand to travel with all the treasures he had picked up he turned to leave the room.

As he stepped out of the hidden doorway he saw Preston looking around like he was looking for something. Teag called to him.

"Hey Preston look what I found," He turned to put his hand back through the opening, but the wall was solid. He moved his hands along the wall to find the door but it was gone. He then checked his pockets and found that he still had all the treasures he had picked up. Relieved he walked back towards the ramp to the Hill room. Preston was standing there glowering at him.

"So what were you going to show me?" He demanded, like Teag was wasting his time.

"Nothing I lost it," Teag answered walking past him up the ramp of dirt. He stopped at the broken door and put up his hand like he heard something. There was a loud thud against the hillside. Then again and again the sound came only getting louder. When something that appeared to be a bone, broke through creating a tiny hole in the hill. Teag realized the Dorgoggin was trying to break through. "It's coming after us, we've gotta get out of here," Teag pulled out the map of the cavern and opened it up. The once small hole was now getting bigger.

"Where did you get that?"

"I found it, look this is the way out, follow me," Teag ran down the map and started climbing the rickety old stairs that lead to the scaffolding's above. "We've gotta get to the fifth floor," Teag informed Preston as they climbed floor after floor. There was a loud crash sound that came from the hillside. The Dorgoggin had broken through and was now glaring at them from the broken wall. They were halfway up the third floor staircase when the creature walked slowly down the ramp making his horrible heaving noises. Preston took another step, there was a crack and a snap and his weight caused him to fall, grabbing a hold of the railing just before he fell all the way through. He hung there dangling.

"Teag!" Preston called out.

Teag was still moving up the steps just hearing the snapping sound and the crash of the broken board hitting the ground. He turned around and ran back down the steps grabbing Preston's hand pulling him up. The Dorgoggin made the chomping sound with its beak and then spit bones out. Teag managed to pull Preston up just before the bones dug into the dirt wall where he was hanging.

"Quickly!" Teag yelled racing up to the top again Preston right behind him. The Spitniker knew it had to get them down so it backed up. Teag and Preston were a little more than halfway up the forth set of stairs when the Spitniker charged, "here he comes, he's gonna take the whole thing down, hurry!" Once at the top Teag and Preston ran down the scaffolding, praying that they would make it to the door.

"It's door number seven," Teag called out. The Spitniker had hit the staircase causing it to crumble and creating a domino effect. Right behind them the floor was collapsing and falling to the dirt ground five levels below. Teag found the door and opened it running in. They had both just stepped inside when the scaffolding they were just on, fell to the ground. "That was too close," Teag knelt to the ground trying to calm his breathing.

"You said it," Preston huffed standing against the wall and trying to catch his breath.

The room they had entered smelled like something died inside. The only light, was the light that came from the open door. It was dim and hard to see where they were. It appeared to be a small living room. The room was large enough but the furniture was tiny. There was a little couch in the middle of the room. Next to it stood a small side table with an unlit lantern upon it, and bookshelves lined the walls.

"There has to be over a thousand books in here," Preston remarked, trying to get a look at the titles, "I can't read it...It looks gibberish to me."

"I wonder what kind of language this is," Teag commented as he pulled out a book, blew the dust off of it and looked at the writings inside.

"I told you, it's gibberish."

"Oh, you're a master of gibberish are you?" Teag laughed.

Preston shot him a dirty look. "How'd I get stuck in this situation with you?" Preston started, "oh yeah, you tripped and fell," He sarcastically answered his own question. Teag sat on the small couch and surprisingly it held his weight. Preston left the room through the open arch doorway that lead down the hall to the rooms in the back. Teag studied the book he had pulled out. The writing appeared to be in a foreign language of symbols he had never seen before.

'What does it say?' Teag thought to himself staring harder as if it would help him decipher it. There was loud crash in the other room. Preston came running out and tried to hide behind the small couch. Teag stood up fast and looked at what was slowly walking into the room. It was short and well rounded in the mid section he looked like a dwarf. It had a long silvery beard and pointed ears. It wore animal skins and had ratty old socks on its feet. The small man had an axe in its hands raised high above ready to swing at Teag.

"No, wait!" Teag yelled as he jumped out of the way of the falling axe that came crashing down and split the couch in half barley missing Preston. Preston's eyes grew big at the axe next to him. He stood up and ran for cover. The Dwarf said nothing but kept going for the first person in his way. Raising the axe again in a war like fashion he grunted as he swung it again, landing it in his wall. Teag and Preston took another second to find another place to hide,

"Wait, we aren't here to hurt you or steal your things. We just needed to find our way out and the map showed me..." Teag begged, his left eye again began to glow light blue. The Dwarf spotted it and then spoke.

"Toeh nah?" The dwarf said in a deep loud voice.

"What? What did he say?" Preston asked worried for his life.

"I thought you understood gibberish?" Teag mocked him.

"Lo hoi toeh nah?" The dwarf lowered the sword. Looking at Teag with curiosity.

Teag looked into his eyes and suddenly the words became crystal clear. "The map, he wants know if we found the map."

"I didn't, you did, he can kill you for it," Preston shrunk.

"Whoo dai lo ho toeh tunt koium? La ki mahitong od u zunigrie," The dwarf stared at Teag waiting for an answer.

"What did he say? Is he going to kill you instead?" Preston asked.

"No," he said ignoring his negative comments, "he said, How did you find the lost room? It's been missing for a century." Teag repeated for Preston again.

"I didn't find the lost room, I didn't," Preston said frightened.

"Look at him you idiot, he isn't swinging the axe right now," Teag rolled his eyes.

"I was just walking around the wall. I had my hand up and, there it was," Teag explained. The Dwarf looked at him carefully.

"Daini ehk lo?" He asked keeping a careful eye on him.

"Did she send me? Who" Teag asked confused.

"Desdemona," The dwarf said carefully. Teag thought back to his mothers story.

"Why would Desdemona, I mean, she isn't real, how do you know that name."

Raising his axe the dwarf asked angrily, "Ta ni agak ehk lo, whoo da lo now gie wamoo?"

"Wha'd e say? Wha'd e say?" Preston asked fearfully, seeing the anger in the dwarf's eyes.

Whispering back to Preston but still keeping eye contact with the Dwarf Teag said, "If she didn't send you, how do you know her name?"

"My mother told me a story on the ship, and it happened to have her name, I'm sure it isn't the same person. The one my mother told us was just a story," Teag assured the Dwarf.

"Qo!" The Dwarf Yelled loudly, "monee gie lood faknive toe romee toeh tunt koium lo gono see lood. Ni gono whooda met lo od toeh Universitas Dominion Monile."

"Blood? But how can that be?" Teag also recognized the name of the Monile, but he didn't want to further incriminate himself so he didn't mention it.

"What about blood?" Preston asked terrified.

Whispering to Preston again Teag said, "only her blood relatives can access the lost room so "I" must be blood. He also said that she must have sent me for the Universitas Dominium Monile."

Preston was puzzled, "What's that?"

"Preston, I'm a little busy at the moment trying to save us, so can you save the questions for later?" Teag tried to smile, knowing that the dwarf could understand everything he was saying.

"Wahioo lo da mot now sho lo erh."

"Maybe I don't know who I am? I know who I am! And I'm not related to Desdemona I assure you."

"Toehn whoo dai lo be noot utay koium?"

"Then how did I get into that room? I told you already," Teag became irritated.

"Toehn lo frith lood pa Desdemona!"

"No, I'm not her blood, you can't kill us, Maddox Pembroke is looking for us and we need to get to Makoto City, Please, just let us pass," Teag began to plead.

"Maddox?" The dwarf repeated, "La now pa Maddox?"

"Yes we know of Maddox. Will you allow us to pass through?"

The Dwarf nodded *yes* and lowered his axe, then turned and started to walk away. After a few steps he noticed that Teag and Preston hadn't moved, "coon dobin za toehn, utz falla lo toeh tay."

"He said, well come on then, I'll show you the way," Teag repeated for Preston.

Through the long dark hallway they walked. Cobwebs were hanging from the ceiling edges. The smell of death still lingered. They walked for only a moment before they entered into the back bedroom. The bed was made but the sheets appeared old and tattered. Several old patches in the old quilt were falling off. The headboard was solid wood and hand carved. Wooden carved beehives sat on top of the posts.

"What can we call you?" Teag asked feeling like introductions should happen now.

"LoRock." The Dwarf replied with his back turned, walking further into the medium sized room.

"I'm Teag and this is Preston," Teag told him. LoRock nodded with his back still turned. He walked over to a large mirror that was hanging on the wall. It was tall and wide. He pointed to it.

"Bog joe toehra xad ma kit la gor toeh Bakada, lo toe ho lor tay hav toehra."

"He says he wants us to go in there, it will take us to the Great Oak and we can find our way home from there," Teag translated.

"How? You want us to walk through that mirror? When was the last time you walked through a mirror?" Preston said in disbelief.

"Preston, I thought we've been through this we're on a magical island. If you haven't noticed, things are never what they seem," Teag glared gaining more and more confidence the more he struggled to stay alive in all of the situations he had faced in the past few days. He walked up to the huge mirror and placed his hand lightly on the surface of the mirror. Like the lost room his hand just floated past. He placed his face through, holding his breath. He then stepped through and instantly he was in a small little room that had several buttons in it like an elevator. He stepped out into the beautiful hallway and looked up and down the corridor. There seemed to be a large room not too far away that had several people mingling. Preston appeared behind him and stepped out into the hall. Without waiting Preston ran to see the people in the large room leaving Teag in his dust.

Chapter 7

Screaming and cheering could be heard down the hall as Teag slowly walked towards it. His whole body ached, more specifically his arm and face. Teag walked through the arched doorway into the large room and found himself in a foyer. The main entrance to the Great Oak was straight in front of him. It was large and open and had three large arched doorways.

The first door fifty-feet forward on his the left, was an amusement park with huge indoor rides and a massive room with tubes, slides, ropes, netting, ladders. All of it large enough for even adults to play on. There were several kids inside playing tag and running around. He could hear laughter, fun screams, and the chatter of people talking seeping through into the entry way he was standing in.

The second door in the room was on his right. It lead to a restaurant and bar. There was a hostess standing near the door with a smile waiting to greet and seat the next guest. It was full of busy chatter and families eating and enjoying their conversation. No one seemed to notice him as he made his way through the packed foyer. They were all ogling Preston and listening to his tall tail of how he made it past the terrible fire breathing dragon and then ran into the Spitniker Dorgoggin and had it out with the beast only to find himself in the presence of a Dwarf who he managed to kill and found his way to the Great oak all by himself.

Too the left of him was a large counter with a man standing behind it waiting to greet anyone new. The third door was behind him. It has a wooden sign above the door that read, 'Hotel'.

'The mirror brought me to the Hotel hallway,' Teag made a mental note. He then walked over to look in the Restaurant. He saw Maddox, John, Suraionee, Ronan, and Rylee sitting there solemnly at a nearby table. He walked up and asked, "is the food here any good? I'm starved."

When Suraionee looked up from her plate of spaghetti, she screamed, jumped up and hugged him tightly. John got up and joined in. Maddox, Ronan, and Rylee started clapping and smiling joyously.

"Good to see ya boy," Maddox smiled brightly, "thought you became the Dragons lunch."

"I almost did," Teag started. They all sat down and Teag then retold how he got away from the dragon, Spitniker, and Dwarf while saving Preston, careful not to let anyone in on Nyla being a good Dragon or his ability to speak to her. He also managed to leave out his fight with Preston though his appearance was more then a testament.

"Wow, to escape a Dragon that no one has ever before gotten away from is one thing, but dodging the Spitniker, and a dwarf, that was a harder feat. Those creatures don't mess around; they're dead on aim. You managed to escape two real predators that even the natives in this land don't go near and you've only been here how many hours?" Maddox looked at his wrist like a watch should have been there.

"Oh I'm so glad your okay," Suraionee said with tears streaming down her cheeks.

"Here Sura," Teag handed her the beat up teddy bear.

"Oh, my bear, where did you get it? Oh thank you Teag," Suraionee said so full of emotion, she didn't even seem to care how much more beat up and ratty the bear had become. All she cared about was that her father had given it to her and it was back and so was Teag. It suddenly reminded her of the necklace her mother had just given her. Feeling around her neck she panicked, "Mom's necklace, I lost it."

"So, how did you get away again?" Rylee asked with wonder changing the subject, "No one has ever..."

"Well it's a long story but, uh, she dropped me and I hid in the orange grass. I managed to find my way out, though, it took me all night," Teag lied trying not to tell too much, because he was worried for Nyla's new family.

Teag turned and looked at Suraionee, "Happy Birthday sis," he then gave her a big side hug as he was sitting right next to her.

* * *

When they were finished eating, Maddox lead them all to their room. Walking back down the hall he had come out of after walking through the mirror, there were even numbers on the doors to the right and odd numbers on the left. The hallway was beautifully lit and was like they were walking through a Palace. The walls were a cream and gold marbled granite stone and had such beautifully detailed workmanship on the top and bottom borders. It was smooth and shiny and it made the hall warm and inviting. There were beautiful Ivy plants along the top of the walls hanging loosely like a border and a dark red carpet under their feet. It appeared as if they were the first ones to walk on it, it was so clean and free of stains and debris. When they reached the end of the hall there was the elevator or what looked like an elevator. When the Dayton family was ahead of them and walked into the elevator they turned around and pressed a number and suddenly they disappeared.

Teag gasped when he suddenly found that the Dayton's were gone without a door closing. "Where did they go?" He asked.

"Just to their floor," John informed Teag as though they had been there all their lives.

The Tragers' walked inside with Maddox and pressed the button number four. At the blink of an eye they were on their floor. Teag never felt the elevator move at all. Walking down the hall to room four hundred and twenty six, the hallway was just as beautiful as the one that lead to the main lobby, in fact if he didn't know better he would have thought that he was in the same hall. Maddox walked them into their room. It was large and roomy. The paint on the top half of the walls was sandy speckled cream and half way up the wall from the floor was navy blue. A navy blue sofa and love seat sat nicely placed in the middle of the room, a big plasma television was hanging on a custom free standing wall built just for the television. It was there so that the sound would not permeate any of the outside walls, therefore bothering any of the surrounding guests. Board games, books, and video games of all kinds lined the shelves that sat against the right wall. Against the back wall were three doors each leading to a large bedroom with king sized beds and each their own bathrooms.

Just as they stepped inside the room Teag noticed a large window on the wall next to the door. It was open and a cool breeze was flowing peacefully in the room. Curious Teag stepped back outside into the hall, 'I don't remember any windows in the hallway.' He thought. He found it bizarre that the hallway was empty except for the doors to the rooms. He stepped back in the room and looked back at the window on the inside. The view was like he was on a mountaintop. He and had a beautiful view of the Island and one of the surrounding Islands. He could see birds flying and the trees swaying from the wind.

"Is this real?"

"Yes, it is what is going on right now outside. It's enchanted to show you a view when there is no view from this spot. See?" Maddox pointed to the Great Oak, "This is where we are right now," Teag nodded his head with enjoyment staring at the breathtaking window.

"Can the Dorgoggin's ever get in here?" Teag asked looking at the hills in the window and seeing a Spitniker wandering the hills and remembering how all it had to do was ram the walls of the hill a few times and it was inside.

"No, first of all, to anyone standing outside, the Great Oak looks just like that, a Great Oak Tree, nothing more nothing less. Secondly we are protected with magic. No creatures are aloud inside the building. If that rule is broken, the poor creature gets a horrible jolting zap, and is then tossed outside, to a random spot on any of the islands in our kingdom. So your perfectly safe here."

"Are the hills protected?"

"Yes, you're perfectly safe indoors." Maddox responded.

"Well then how did the Spitniker ram the hill wall until it busted it down?"

Maddox looked shocked. "When did this happen?"

"Just before we found the dwarf."

"This is so strange, it's never happened before. Maybe, well...I don't know how it was able to get in. I'll check it out. Thanks for telling me."

"Yeah, well if it can get into a protected space like that, it can get in here."

"No, Dirt is one thing to bust down, but wood? No, not to mention that the Spitniker saw you and Preston go inside so it was waiting you out, but then I guess it decided it would come in and get you instead. None of the creatures saw anyone come in here through the Great Oak entrance."

Teag smiled, "That still doesn't re-assure me."

"Well think of it this way. Were on the fourth floor, if a Dorgoggin breaks in, you'll have plenty of time to get away."

"Yeah Teag, it'll get the Karik's first because their room is on the first floor." Suraionee laughed.

Suraionee ran, jumped, and rolled onto her bed. It was just the way she liked it, squishy soft and the sheets weren't scratchy, they were smooth and silky to the touch. Back in the front room on the beautiful oak coffee table was a large basket of fruit and snacks.

Maddox walked in the room shutting the door behind him. He sat down on the love seat. "Come sit down we need to talk about some other things," Teag did as he was told, "I'm glad that your alright, we went to find you, but you weren't in the dragons lair."

"No, we had already escaped I guess," Teag quietly nodded.

"ZaBeth would have my head if I told you this but I think you need to know," he paused for a moment trying to find the right way to tell them, "Teag, have you ever dreamed something awake or asleep that ended up coming true?"

Teag looked at him thinking back. His eyes widened as he remembered the most recent. "Well there was the shipwreck. I've had a few others but they mostly just started happening recently. I never thought about it until now."

"You're here because you have a special gift. When you hone that gift. ZaBeth believes that you will be telepathic. We are hoping that you will be able to get close enough to read Vidor's mind to get the antidote," Maddox informed Teag.

"*No way*! You want him to get close to that...that...Vidor, to put him in harms way again? No, no, no..."Suraionee said angry at the thought of something bad happening to her brother again. She looked at her brothers, "NO! It isn't going to happen," she said firmly

"Who's Vidor?" Teag asked looking at everyone.

"Oh yeah you didn't hear that conversation," Maddox started, "Vidor Lysander was a wizard in the palace a few centuries ago until..." Maddox explained the whole story to Teag. Teag's curiosity grew. After hearing all that Maddox had to say Teag was intrigued.

"No, he can't do it," Suraionee insisted again.

"It isn't up to you Suraionee," Teag said feeling up to the challenge because of his conversation with Nyla and because he really liked the

Pembrokes'. He glanced over to Maddox, "Would I have to talk to him at all?" Teag asked thinking it over some more.

"No, I would be with you. I plan to confront him myself. That way he'll be thinking about the antidote. You're our only hope. Keep in mind that this is later down the line and *please* don't tell ZaBeth that I told you."

Suraionee and John were furious, "how could you do this after the pain that we went through when we thought you were dead, In the Ocean and then with the dragon?" John asked hurt that he was even considering it.

"Think about it, if it were mom and dad you wouldn't even think twice about it. We wouldn't be having this discussion. Mom and dad would want us to do this," Teag persuaded them.

John and Suraionee thought about it for a few minutes then looked at Maddox. Seeing the emotion in his eyes, which he hardly ever showed to anyone, and knowing that they would never persuade Teag otherwise, they decided together that they were okay with it as long as they could help. Then there was silence. Maddox knew that they couldn't help because they didn't have any powers. ZaBeth only saw one not three. But he kept his thoughts and comments to himself but Teag heard them; he now knew what Maddox knew. But not wanting to upset his brother and sister any further, kept it to himself.

"I have a confession to make," Teag broke the silence, "what if I heard the dragon talk, what if she really isn't bad, but she's only misunderstood?"

"You're mad. That Dragon has killed anyone that has tried to get in her way," Maddox said skeptical.

"You're wrong, I got away..."

Maddox interrupted him, "yeah you got away, she didn't let you go."

"Actually, she did. She went and hid herself and her babies in the orange grass while I went to get Preston and pretended to get away. She let us live because I could talk to her and I meant her no harm. See after she took me I realized my ankle was broken, she healed me and then I named her babies," Teag said with confidence and his head held high.

Maddox, John and Suraionee stared at him their mouths wide open.

"How?" Maddox asked with deep interest.

"We just looked at each other and words came out, and she, well she was nice. Blaze wanted to eat me and she stopped him then brought back fish for us all to eat. She even helped me start a fire to cook my food."

"You named them and you ate fish? I don't believe it," John insisted.

"Yeah and Nyla, the mother, liked the names I picked out. The bluish green one is Blaze, the yellowish red one is Alaura, and the purplish green one is Moya."

"She talked to you?" Maddox asked but was more skeptical and unbelieving.

"Well no, but I could hear her thoughts and she spoke to me that way, and she understood every word I said."

"This is strange, usually for your powers to start you would have to drink ZaBeth's Keno Tea," Maddox said in deep thought.

"Keno Tea?" Suraionee asked, "What's that?"

"It's an herbal tea that starts your Powers. They start your powers up slowly so you can learn to control them," There was a short pause, "See, it's already starting. There have been so many attempts to catch that dragon and tame her, even kill her. She has never understood anyone before even when they tried to talk to her begging for their lives..." Maddox hesitated, "Teag do not speak of this to anyone. I believe that everyone in Makoto City is a friend, but we must be careful with who we give our information," he looked over at John and Suraionee asking for their silence. They nodded in agreement, "I will talk to ZaBeth and see what she thinks about it," Maddox stood up to leave. Just as he was walking out the door he stopped and turned around, "I almost forgot, this is my pager should you need me for anything," he tossed John a smooth clear crystal rock.

"It's a rock." John said laughing like Maddox had tossed him the wrong thing.

"Yes, I know John, if any of you should need me, toss it on the ground and I will be transported to you as long as I have mine with me.

"That's a cool trick," Suraionee said taking it from John to get a closer look.

"Thanks Maddox, for everything," Teag appreciated just before Maddox walked out closing the door behind him.

On the coffee table in front of him with the basket of fruits and snacks were three stickers for the amusement park.

"Stickers? Wont they fall off to easily?" Suraionee asked.

John picked up the stickers and looked at the back of them. "Their from the Everlasting Sticker Company. It says here, the hypoallergenic special blend of glue and pixie dust make the stickers stick until you pull it off. It's guaranteed to stay on or you get a free yearly pass to the Great Oak Amusement Park."

"Cool," Suraionee smiled I hope mine falls off.

"Wait, there's more, in super small print is says the side effects are minimal but may include, random hair color change, frog voice, random mastered magic spells spontaneously emitting, and or temporary flying…those aren't side effects, I hope I get the flying one," John smiled and put on the sticker.

Teag quickly ran to his room and found clean clothes in the drawers that fit him just right. He took a five minute shower and got dressed. Teag and Suraionee took their stickers and put them on their arms, then walked out of the room.

They quickly found their way back down to the foyer, then into the large Amusement Park. There were so many kids. Teag could see a couple of the other families had made it there too.

Running up a slide Suraionee almost knocked down a girl at the top, "oh sorry," she apologized, "I didn't see you there."

"That's alright," the girl smiled back, "my name is Analeigh Darshnan, what's yours?" She held out her hand to shake Suraionee's.

"Suraionee Trager," she replied as she reached out and shook the young girls hand. She had blonde hair and a pretty smile that made her light blue eyes dance. She was wearing a red t-shirt with blue jeans and a baseball cap on with her hair in a ponytail hanging out the back of the cap. The girls chatted for a few minutes and became fast friends.

"Suraionee, we're going over to the rides, okay?" Teag told her.

"Bye," She waved to them then went back to talking to her friend.

Teag and John ran over to a ride called the 'Halo'. The ride looked big and had six loops in a row, several twisty turns, and four, two hundred foot, high drops. The boys looked at each other and smiled.

They waited in line behind a few other boys they didn't recognize and watched as the cars went zipping around. When the riders came to a stop they all had smiles permanently engraved in their faces. It was their turn to ride. One of the workers walked over with a scanner and scanned all the stickers for entry. Each sticker blipped as the scanner read it and accepted it. John ran over and climbed into the three-man seat first, followed by Teag and then they waited. Before the over-the-shoulder bar came down to lock them in another boy came over and sat next to Teag.

"Hi I'm Zared Theron, you don't mind that I sit here do you?" He asked but didn't really care for an answer as he was already sitting down. The boy was tall and round. He pushed back a patch of dirty blonde hair that fell into his face. He had a bowl haircut, but he seemed to be well groomed. He turned and smiled at his new friends then sat and waited for the ride to be off. The over-the-shoulder bar came down and locked them all into place and after a few beeping sounds from the controls they were off like a rocket. They went straight up into the air, made a fast right, then a two hundred foot drop into a dark hole in the ground, which actually looked like they were in outer space. They felt weightless while the blackness surrounded them. Bright shining stars were everywhere and a few moments later, they were headed for a huge cluster of glowing matter and glittering stars that were swirling all about. The track wasn't visible and the weightlessness made them all feel like they were no longer on a controlled path, but then suddenly they flew straight through the cluster, and up out of the ground for what felt like a mile. A quick turn then a straight drop down. Just before they hit the bottom they hit a three-loop swoop then back up in the air about two hundred feet only to race down a spiral spin. Faster and faster the car shot around and around down the spiral. When they reached the bottom they shot around in squiggly circles all over the place and then back too the top, the third of the two hundred foot drops. They hung over the top for a moment and then straight down and into the six loops, a right turn and then the car took them back home. When the ride stopped the boys climbed out and gave the ride a standing ovation. Soon everyone was clapping and laughing. Teag, John and Zared ran around for another run. While in line the second time Zared was standing next to Teag.

"Teag Trager," he held out his hand, "Nice to meet you."

"John," he also held out his hand to shake Zared's.

"You two are new here," Zared commented, "I've never seen you before."

"Yeah, we got here two days ago, well to the island I mean," Teag mentioned.

"Cool, I came five years ago, it's an awesome place don't' ya think?" Zared pointed to the rides.

"Yeah sweet, we couldn't have even dreamed of a place like this at home," Teag remarked.

After riding the ride three more times the three of them went off in search of another exciting ride. Hours of fun passed before the boys decided they were hungry enough to stop and get something to eat. As they started toward the playground where Suraionee was playing the three friends turned a corner not paying attention to where they were going and Teag bumped into Preston Karik, but before he could stand up straight and see who he bumped into Preston knocked him back down. "Star light star bright first star I see tonight," Preston teased.

"Hey!" Teag yelled, "What's your problem? It was an accident."

"Oh I'm terribly sorry, I never heard you say you were sorry," Preston scowled and puffed out his chest trying to egg on a fight.

"Because you didn't even give me a chance to stand up," Teag protested.

"So lets hear it," Preston stood there with his nose in the air. Little did Teag know that he purposefully made sure that he bumped into him.

"I'm sorry, okay? It was an accident, I don't want to fight about it," Teag said trying hard not to cause a bigger problem. When he looked into Preston's eyes he heard his thoughts.

'You think your so great. You're lucky I was there to help you get away from the dragon, the Spitniker and the dwarf. You're so stupid! (he laughed in his mind) I made you fall down and now your sitting here like a big baby apologizing for it and everyone here knows it."

Teag became angry, "Who do you think you are?"

"I'm the guy you're going to apologize to for purposefully running into me," Preston snickered looking back at the new posy of friends he had behind him.

"I'm not telling you sorry, you ran into me and I helped *you* get away from the dragon, if it wasn't for me you would have been minced meat," Teag scowled standing up for himself.

"You liar!" Preston screamed. He didn't want his new friends to think he was a sissy, so he antagonized Teag more, "from the first day I met you, all you did was lie and whine, you're the biggest little girl I ever met and back home we would have hung you out to dry, quite literally."

Stepping a little closer so that they were almost nose to nose and their chests puffed up, Teag let it out, "you're an idiot, everyone can see through your stupidity, besides who are you to complain about me whining when in the dead mans pit you sniveled like the little girl when the Dorgoggin came at us, I'm the one that pulled *you* out," Teag started. Then he turned to Prestons' new friends and lied a little, "he has a little problem keeping his pants dry."

Preston was furious. His new friends were laughing at him and Teag had a slight smile on his face. Infuriated, Preston lunged at Teag and hit him in the jaw. Instinctively Teag swung back hitting Preston in the chest. Preston was a little winded, but pretended it didn't hurt, "what's the matter the little girl, can't hit? That felt like a mosquito bite, can't you do any better than that?" Preston egged Teag on to hit him again, trying to look cool in front of his friends. The boys behind Preston laughed. Teag was even more furious than before, you could almost see his rage steaming out of his ears. He tried to hit Preston in the face, but Preston beat him to the punch and shoved Teag hard causing him to fall down, "you ignorant baboon," Preston, hollered. John stepped forward as though he was about to step in to help Teag, but Zared whom was standing next to John put out his arm and shook his head to stop him from trying.

"At least I don't have to resort to name calling to get my point across," Teag derided. Preston swung at Teag again this time hitting him in the stomach, knocking the wind out of him. Teag fell to the ground in pain. Preston kicked him in the ribs and then turned to look at his friends laughing. Teag jumped up while Preston's back was turned and with his full body tackled him to the ground, pounding on his face with all of his strength. Preston tried to wrestle him off and they went rolling around hitting and kicking one another bumping into benches and people in the way. Preston's friends were cheering and laughing while John and Zared were concerned.

A large group of people started gathering to see what was going on, but no one was stopping them. Some of the adults and kids could actually be seen making bets on who would win. Suddenly the crowd went silent and stepped back when Maddox appeared. The boys didn't stop fighting even after everything went silent. Maddox reached in and pulled Preston off of Teag, but without caring Teag kept going at Preston trying to hit him.

"*Teag*! That's quite enough," Maddox roared. Teag stopped in his tracks and looked at Maddox who was now glaring at him. Ashamed as though his parents were reprimanding him he looked down and put his hands in his pockets. His nose was bleeding again, he had a fresh black eye, and his nice new shirt was now torn. Preston took off running while Maddox pulled Teag aside and started to reprimand him. "I expected more from you. I'm very disappointed. You know if your parent's were here…"

"Well their not!" Teag shot out angry that Maddox was trying to take over as his parent.

"Yes, their not, but that means that you need to be a better example for your bother and sister. Now you are like their parent, they look up to you and watch everything you do. What would you have done if it was John fighting just now?"

"I would have stopped him and yelled at him for fighting."

"Why would you have done that?"

Teag took a deep breath and then answered, "because my mom and dad taught us better, but he started it, Preston knocked me down and then laughed at me with all of his friends."

"Teag, you should have walked away."

"But if I walk away, he's always going to make fun of me and torment me like the kids back home. I always walked away and then I was pegged as the looser that was too afraid to stand up for himself. Do you know how hard it is for a guy to make friends when everyone thinks you're a looser and has no respect for you?"

"I'm sure it wasn't that bad. I was in school, and I didn't have any problems."

"Maddox, the nerds and other guys marked as *losers* wouldn't even talk to me because they had no respect for me."

"Well that is bad, but none the less, I don't want to see you fighting anymore. I expect you'll be a better example for your brother and sister from now on," Maddox scolded. Teag nodded in agreement and then walked off and joined John and Zared. The three of them walked on to look for Suraionee.

Teag and John found Suraionee and used sign language to tell her that they were hungry. Then Teag pointed to the restaurant and motioned for her to come with them. Suraionee got down and said goodbye to Analeigh. Teag introduced Zared to Suraionee and the four of them walked over to the Restaurant together rehashing all of the rides and fun things that they did.

Teag walked into the restroom to clean up his face. When he came back out they all wnet to be seated. The formally dressed hostess greeted them and looked around for their parents. Before she could say anything Maddox, Ronan and Rylee entered the room. Maddox took charge and said, "the Tragers' will dine with us this evening," acting as though nothing had happened.

The hostess nodded and began to lead them to a seat.

"Hi Zared," Maddox said when he noticed there was one extra person, "where are your parents?"

"Oh, they are doing their own thing with my little sister, they said to meet them in our room at midnight," Zared started, "you don't mind if I join you do you?"

"Of course not, it's a pleasure," Maddox smiled.

All the woodwork was dark redwood. The Restaurant had an elegant style too it. The seats were comfortable and all the employees were dressed nicely. Everyone smiled and seemed to be very happy to be there. All the tables were full, so they were escorted to a separate dining room. The six of them sat down and looked at the menus.

"What strange names. What is a 'Port of Wassle with baked chip, rabbit food and shrink?" Teag asked Maddox.

Smiling Maddox tried not to laugh, "my wife Sarah came up with the names wanting it to be original. 'Port of Wassle with Baked Chip, Rabbit Food and Shrink' is fried calamari with baked potato, salad, and steamed veggies. It's really good you should try it.

"What's Calamari?" Suraionee asked.

"Squid."

"Eeew, I like fish, but squid? I don't think so," Suraionee winced.

"You should try it. You'd be surprised," Ronan urged her smiling.

"I don't know, let me think about it," Suraionee looked over to John who was licking his lips.

"Which one was the Hamburgers and French Fries again?" John asked worried about the names and getting something yucky.

"You'll want to order the "Moo and Chips" Maddox smiled when John laugh. His laugh was so infectious that everyone around had to laugh too.

"Okay, I'm looking for three cheese ravioli covered in Alfredo sauce, do you have anything like that?" Teag asked.

"Ha ha ha, you kids don't mess around, you aren't much for looking are you?" Maddox looked at the menu, "let me see it isn't the 'Fluff Dog & Chips' that's a Corndog with Fries, and it isn't the 'String & Moo with a side of Rabbit food and seasoned Dry Bread' that's Spaghetti and meatballs with a side salad and Garlic toast. His finger pointed a little further down, it isn't 'Triangle Pie & Trough' that's Pizza and a soda, where is it, I thought I saw it here somewhere," He turned the page of the menu then read. "Ah ha, here it is 'Three Mold Pocket with White Sauce, fluff sticks and side Rabbit food' that's what you want.

"Three Mold Pocket? I don't know if I want it now," Teag said with disgust.

"Oh it's just a name Teag. Though it seems we don't sell a lot of that item, maybe the name has something to do with it?" Maddox tried to coax him.

"Triangle Pie and Trough' sounds good. Yeah, I think that is what I'll order," Teag put the menu down in front of him happy with his choice.

"Are you sure you won't try the 'Port of Wassle with Baked Chip, Rabbit Food and Shrink'?" Maddox started in again.

"No I've got it thanks," Teag smiled.

"I will Maddox," Suraionee decided, "I'll try it."

"All right. You won't be sorry" Ronan said with approval.

When the waitress came over Maddox placed the orders, "well have the Port of Wassle with Baked Chip, Rabbit Food and Shrink for the girl there, Moo and Chips for the young man over there," Maddox looked over at John to make sure he was happy with that choice still then went on, "Triangle Pie and Trough for the boy there," He looked over at Teag and then over at Zared who he hadn't asked yet.

"String & Moo with a side of Rabbit Food and Seasoned Dry Bread." Zared smiled.

"String & Moo with a side of Rabbit Food and Seasoned Dry Bread" Maddox repeated nodding his head, "another Port of Wassle with Baked Chip, Rabbit Food and Shrink for Ronan, and 2 Flat Moo, Fish Flutter, with Baked Chip, and side of Rabbit food for Rylee and myself," there was a short pause and then he said, "oh and Ocean Spritz to go around, did I miss anything?"

"No, but what's a Flat Moo, Fish Flutter, with Baked Chip, and side of Rabbit food?" Suraionee asked.

"All you can eat Steak and Shrimp with a baked potato and side salad. Rylee and I get that every time we come in here," Maddox grinned.

"Oh I should've gotten that," Teag said upset he didn't listen to more of the items, "oh well next time."

While they were waiting for their food the Karik Family came in celebrating the return of their dead son. They were seated a few tables over. Shortly after the food came, everyone enjoyed it and lighthearted conversation. Suraionee loved the Calamari so much she ordered a side of just the fried Calamari. She gave John a taste and he soon was ordering more of it for himself. Teag refused to taste it having had enough seafood in the dragon's lair and the day before that on the beach. When their plates were almost clean Teag noticed the waitress taking food over to the Karik table Teag couldn't see through the lady but everyone that was located in the separate dining area of the restaurant turned their attention over to the Karik table when Willem started yelling at the waitress.

"What is this?" He demanded watching the octopus before him squirm with its tentacles flipping and flapping all over the place.

"Sentient Oc, sir, it's what you asked for," She smoothly answered.

"I didn't order that!"

"Yes you did sir, but if you would rather have something else I'll gladly get it for you," She smiled.

"No, you don't understand, we did, *not*, order this squirmy octopus. Besides even if we did, shouldn't you have cooked it first?" Willem screamed.

Maddox started laughing under his breath and so was the rest of the table. Soon everyone in the Restaurant was laughing.

"We didn't order this!" Willem demanded to all the people watching him. Preston shrunk in his seat embarrassed about the whole thing.

Maddox stood up and walked over.

"Sit down everyone, nothing more here to see," he instructed, "sorry about the problem Willem, tell me what your family would like to eat and I'll tell the waitress what to get you," Maddox felt a little sorry for him, it had to be hard to be in a new place and not know what all the names of the food really were.

"Were you behind this?" Willem sneered.

"No, but how many people do you know actually eat a live octopus?" Maddox twitched his mouth trying not to start laughing again.

"No one, which is precisely my point, this was a joke," Willem hated feeling like he was the butt of every ones jokes.

"Listen, it's on the menu because a lot of people come in here to play little fun jokes on their friends..., they call it "Oc'ed. If you've been Oc'ed then it's like you've become one of us. Everyone goes through it at one point or another. You just did it to yourself that's all. It's actually an honor around here," Maddox smiled.

"Honor or not I didn't appreciate that. Your menu's must be labeled with what is in them," Willem insisted.

"Right Sir we'll get right on that," Maddox joked a little irritated, "in the mean time would you like to eat?"

Willem didn't continue the argument, "Piper wants a hamburger and french-fries, Hailey wants some spaghetti, Preston wants Pizza, and I would like, Umm, do you have a steak?"

"Yes."

"Okay I'll have a steak," He stopped and thought for a moment then added, "well done please, I would rather not have the whole cow mooing here on the table."

It took Maddox everything he had to not laugh, "okay, I'll let her know," Maddox then made the order and then walked back to his table. Everyone at the table was still laughing as softly as they could, "Lets go," Maddox said covering his mouth so that he wouldn't start laughing. His back was toward the Karik family but he didn't need another problem. Everyone at the table got up and started walking out. Preston glared at Teag as they were walking away, but Teag just smiled and put his hand right up to his face then wiggled his fingers to say good-bye. Preston then shook his head and looked away. Zared then nodded at Teag as if to say come on lets go.

On the way back to their room The Daytons' and Estebans' Joined them walking down the hall. Amara Esteban started talking to Suraionee about what happened at the Karik Table.

"It was so funny when, Preston ordered the 'Sentient Oc' and his dad ordered the same. It turned out to be a live Octopus," Amara Giggled.

"And when it arrived the tentacles were flipping everywhere, did you see the looks on their faces?" Suraionee Added laughing so hard tears were rolling down her cheeks and every once in a while you could hear her snort.

"Then they caused such a scene and told everyone, "I didn't order that!" I loved watching them freak out," Amara Esteban hooted.

Everyone in the hall enjoyed a great laugh after hearing the girls replay the scene as they walked to their rooms to go to sleep.

Chapter 8

Somewhere on the Island Desdemona sat in a dark room as if waiting for someone. There was a knock at the door.

"Come," She demanded.

A large bulky figure entered the room, "I have news," he said in an Australian accent.

"Sit down and tell me," she instructed.

The man took a seat on the sofa across from her. A glass coffee table and wild flower arrangement in-between them, "the boy survived, he managed to escape the Dragon, two Spitniker dragons and the Dwarf LoRock."

"The boy's alive?" She started laughing, "wonderful, we'll go on with the original plans, but how did he escape? Wait, did you say LoRock?"

"Yes."

"How did he find his way into the dead mans pit and survive?"

"He said that they fought the Dwarf and managed to find the hidden mirror that took them to the Great Oak."

"Them?"

"Yes, he and another boy from the group, both were taken by the Dragon."

"And both survived?"

"Yes."

"What's the name of the second boy?"

"Preston Karik."

"Very good, arrange a meeting for the two of us. I want to find out what really happened. Does Teag have powers yet?"

"Not that we have been told about."

"Good then he will not be more powerful," after a few long seconds, "we're, done, do you need a written invitation to leave?" she sneered.

"No m'am, I was just leaving," he quickly jumped to his feet and walked for the door.

After he left she muttered to herself, "nothing worse than a great and powerful man who has no idea how much power he actually possesses...better for me though," she evilly laughed.

ZaBeth was preparing for the arrival of the new families into Makoto City. The Keno Tea she was making for each child was boiling and ready to go. In her room she stood in front of a mirror looking at herself. Her once leathered skin now soft and smooth in her reflection, her crouching old body stood straight and tall looking back at her. Her weathered old smile was now lush and warm. ZaBeth loved to stand in front of her mirror dreaming of the body she once had and desires to have again. The potion and charm she needed, requires several items not easily found or located in the City, "soon everything will be in place and the Pembroke's' will be turned back to their original form. Vidor will be broken and his power will be mine. Melanion hasn't come back for century's so why would he come back now?" She started to worry for a moment then calmed herself, "no he's dead he has to be. Vidor will be sorry he betrayed me," she swayed from side to side for a few minutes causing her dress to flow side to side, then she walked out the door.

In the morning everyone gathered in the Great Oak entryway ready to travel to Makoto City. Maddox lead them to a room just between the Restaurant and the Hotel. Inside, it was dark and felt small, though everyone fit inside comfortably. When the door shut Maddox pressed a button by the door. There were several buttons. One that said Eagle Heights School of instruction, and another said Crystal Cavern School of Mastery. There were buttons that said 'Home', 'Church', 'Castle', and many others. Teag couldn't quite make out which button was pressed but before he could even ask Maddox opened the door.

"We're here," Maddox motioned everyone out. They stepped out into the nice warm sun. The salty air was both refreshing and soothing. There were several homes on both sides of the road they appeared on. Each of them was luxurious and large. The landscaping on each yard was unique and creative with colorful flowers bordering each home. Animal figures made out of tall bushes were nicely clipped placed in every yard.

Maddox handed each of the men a wooden sign with their last names burned onto them. "Remember to put your plaque on the hooks on the porch when you choose your home," when no one moved Maddox snapped, "well, go on, make your choice. If there's a last name on the porch the home is taken."

With that all the families started walking, than in sudden competition one by one they started running to get the best home. The Karik's were pushing others out of the way to get to the home they thought was the best. The Trager kids slowly started walking. None of them knew what to do. They knew they couldn't live alone without parents. Maddox called to them to come back. "ZaBeth has a place for you to live. It's in town," Maddox said while walking with them, dreading that he had to leave them behind.

When they got there, the building was run down and neglected. It appeared to be abandoned and condemned, like no one had lived there in years. Maddox pushed the creaking broken fence open and walked them to the door. "ZaBeth said that they will take good care of you and you will get the best training here," Maddox tried to convince himself and the kids.

"I'm sure we'll be fine," Teag said as he looked at the run down building, "I'm sure it's much better inside," he tried to rationalize.

Maddox knocked on the door. As they stood there and waited for an answer, they could hear a slow creaking that slowly approach the front door.

When the tattered green door opened an old woman appeared. She was short and her teeth were rotten and a few were missing. Her breath smelled of rotten fish and her clothing appeared to have never been washed. Her hair was greasy and up in a loose bun but was falling all over the place. Everyone took a step back and covered their noses trying not to breath. When she spoke her voice was old and raspy.

"You must be the children, well come in, come in, thank you sir for bringing them, I have it from here," she said spraying Maddox in the face with her spit as she spoke. Then she slammed the door shut.

"This is your new home and you will do as your told or it will be off to the pit with you."

"The pit?" Teag asked, wiping a drop of spit off his cheek.

"Yes, it's in the basement. There's no light and no way out till I come get you. It's where you'll learn to behave should you misbehave," her look was cold and heartless. The three children looked back at the door longing for Maddox. "Well, he'll not be coming back, you live here now. I'll show you to your rooms," She sprayed before she led them around the broken down house. They walked up the rickety splintered stairs. "Watch your step," she warned as she skipped a step in the staircase that was missing. It looked like a long way down if you fell through that hole. When they reached the top, children scattered into the rooms down the long hallway. No one was to be seen after that. The three kids looked into each open doorway and they all appeared to be empty, even though they saw children run into the rooms. "Here is your room girl, and the boys will share this one across the way," lunch is at noon sharp, if you're late forget eating. Your training will start straight after lunch and end at dinnertime. Don't be late."

"Please, Ma'm, what do we call you?" Suraionee asked a little timid stepping back so she didn't get sprayed with her responce.

"Ma'm! No need for names, you get attached that way, and we won't be having any of that," she sneered and then walked away.

When the old woman disappeared down the stairs Suraionee walked into Teag and john's Room. She winced as she looked around at the filth, "oh, I don' t like this place, it's creepy."

"I feel like we're living in a haunted house. I can't sleep here, the spiders alone in a place like this…" John started.

"That's the least of our worries, I have a bad feeling about this place, we need to get out of here," Teag started proposing.

"No, don't even try, if you do, she'll hurt you."

The three of them spun around to find a little boy about ten-years-old. His face was dirty and he had spider bites all over his face and hands.

"Oh hi, who are you?" Teag asked surprised to see anyone else.

"We don't go by names here, just numbers," he said looking down. He didn't make much eye contact.

"What do you mean? You have to have a name." Suraionee said appalled at the thought.

"No, you see," he pointed to the carving in the bed posts, "those are your numbers. She doesn't use names because she thinks it creates a bond and softness in a person."

"What is your number then?"

"Seventy-Three."

"That's horrible!" Suraionee screeched. "I refuse to go by a number."

"I'm Eighty-Seven, and Teag is Eighty-Six," John said looking at the numbers.

Teag looked at the window and tried to open it. It was stuck shut.

"Please, don't, you don't want to make her mad. Besides she nailed them all shut, see?" Seventy-Three pointed to the nails in the window.

I can't stand this, If ZaBeth is the good Queen she claims to be, why is there a place like this? What could possibly be the point? I'm not staying here, not another second!" Teag demanded.

Seventy-three looked scared as he ran and hid.

Teag looked at John and Suraionee, "this ends here, lets go, we'll sleep in the streets if we have too, but…"

"Teag lets go already, stop talking about it and do something about it," John urged.

The three of them snuck down the stairs trying not to let the steps creek. Slowly they crept to the front door looking around to make sure they hadn't been seen. Teag slowly reached for the knob and turned it until it clicked. He quietly opened the door, but then it unexpectedly creeked loudly. The three of them froze looking around with their eyes hoping that no one heard anything. When no sound was heard He opened the rest of the door and stepped out onto the porch. Right in front of him stood the old lady and two large rotten looking men. They were all folding their arms.

"Going somewhere?" The woman asked.

Teag froze he wanted to hide what they were doing, but he knew he couldn't, and he refused to stay any longer. "Yes, were leaving." Teag said trying to walk by, but one of the large men put his hand out and stopped him.

"You're not going anywhere but the Pit boy. See this is what I was talking about when I said misbehaving. You can't just come and go as you please. You will follow the rules or you will be forced to stay in the Pit until you comply. And don't try to get away again. I know everything that happens in this house. The walls talk you know!" She smiled evilly as she commanded the men to take the kids down to the Pit.

Once downstairs they were thrown into a room that stunk like sewers. The old woman was true to her word, there was no light. They had to feel around the muck on the floors and walls to find somewhere to sit. Everything was damp wet and...gooey.

"Eeew, I think this is poop." Suraionee squawked as she grazed something slimly.

"Nasty! I can't handle this smell," Teag said getting sick.

"Either can I," John complained just before he began to vomit. As soon as he started upchucking so did Suraionee and Teag. Now the strong smell in the room was sewage and vomit.

They managed to find a bunk bed in the tiny room against the far wall. John and Teag shared the bottom bunk while Suraionee felt her way up to the top. They laid in the dark for what felt like hours.

"I don't get it."

"Don't get what Teag?"

"I don't understand, why we're being treated this way. I mean we were brought here to help them, and this is how we're repaid? Stuck with a smelly Hag and trapped in a tiny room with only two beds for the three of us, breathing in crap, I swear, my next visit to the doctor they'll do an x-ray and find poop stains in my lungs."

John and Suraionee laughed. "Only if you put your face in it Teag," John joked trying to make the time go faster.

Several hours passed and they were still stuck in the room. Unsure what time it really was they tried to just sleep so that the smell wouldn't bother them so much. They were stunned by a bright light that woke them up. They squinted to see out the door, but their eyes had a hard time adjusting, all they saw was a figure that came in and grabbed at them pulling them out. They were in the basement and they were slowly able to see that the old hag came to get them out.

"Get up stairs and wash up, it's breakfast."

"What happened to lunch and dinner?" John asked.

"Do you really want to sit here and ask questions that might put you back in the pit? Or would you rather go upstairs wash up and eat?"

The three of them looked at one another and then bolted up the stairs. The washroom didn't have showers, just a sink that trickled out water.

"How are we supposed to get clean? Suraionee asked frustrated that her hands weren't getting clean.

"That's the point. We're not. Think about it the old lady is dirty, the kids are all dirty...no one showers here." Teag said in realization of the situation they were really in.

In the dining room Teag counted sixty-seven kids. The room was quiet except for the light clanking of spoons in the bowls of mush they were required to eat. The three of them looked around and shook their heads not daring to break the silence in the room.

After breakfast the three of them ran upstairs to Teag and John's room and sat on Johns bed against the wall in silence. No one knew what to say or do. They had an hour before their classes started, but they had nothing to do. A half an hour passed and Suraionee decided to look out of her muddy window. It was hard to see anything but she could make out a figure coming to the house. "That looks like Maddox," Suraionee said as she waved her hand for her brothers to come over.

They heard several pounds on the door down stairs. The three of them looked at each other with excitement. "He came back for us," John said as he had a burst of abrupt excitement fill him. He jumped to his feet, ran out the door then started down the stairs with Suraionee and Teag close behind him. They stopped on the stairs when they saw the old woman reach for the door to open it.

"I want the kids back," he demanded.

"Oh I don't think so, ZaBeth made it clear that I was to care for them."

Maddox shirked at the smell of her but he quickly shook it off and then demanded again. "I'm not asking I'm telling you, they *are* coming with me, call them down."

"*No!*" She said then slammed the door in his face. She started walking away and was startled when she heard a loud lions roar and then the door was suddenly pounded in. With her mouth wide open in shock, all she could do was stand there.

Teag, John, and Suraionee raced for the door where he was standing. "I spoke to my wife Sarah, how would you kids like to come live with us?" When he took a second to look at them he asked, "why are you filthy?" He caught their stench and winced, "why do you smell like dung?"

"Well when we tried to escape yesterday she put us in the Pit where there was muck all over the place." John was quick to inform Maddox.

"Why didn't you just avoid it rather than rolling in it."

"How could we? There were no lights and it was all over the dag blummit walls." Suraionee reproached.

Maddox couldn't help but laugh a little at her choice of words, "dag blummit Suraionee?"

"It wasn't funny Maddox,"She growled at him.

"Oh I know, and I'm really angry about it, but the word girly, that's a good one."

We have plenty of room. Whado ya say? You want to come live with us?"

The three kids looked at each other and smiled. "Well ya know, we were kinda looking forward to livin in this dump, you're really ruining our plans," Teag teased.

Maddox smiled, "Well if you really want to stay here, I suppose there isn't anything I can do about it, but, who am I to think you might want to still be kids?" He said teasing Teag back.

Teag sighed, "well I guess we'll just have to give it a shot your way. You really twisted our arms, but we'll make the sacrifice for you we really liked the pit you know," saying it like he's really put out, only smiling.

Maddox wanted to give them a hug but changed his mind about it when he remembered what was all over them. "Thank you," Maddox said as he followed the children outside.

"No, you can't have them, you'll be sorry, I'll tell ZaBeth," the old woman stood in front of them with the two large men stopping them from leaving.

"Do whatever you want. They are coming with me," Maddox smiled at her and then pushed through them like they were nothing. It appeared the men were afraid to do anything to him.

"Oh Maddox, we are so happy to see you. That place is awful and those poor children that live there, there must be something we can do for them," Suraionee said feeling happy for her release but sad for the children they left behind.

When they got to the Pembroke Maddox pulled out the hose and sprayed them down until the muck was gone. Maddox showed them in while they were still dripping wet. Inside the smell of fresh apple pie warmed the air. The silence was broken to a buzzer in the kitchen. Milly used to burn candles that smelled just like it making the Trager kids all feel like they were home. Maddox called out to Sarah and said that he was home with company. Sarah ran out to greet them.

"Oh dear, all wet, let me get you some clothes to change into," she ran upstairs and brought down a set of clothing for all three of them.

She was a beautiful woman with beautiful long flowing brown hair. She had an olive complexion and vibrant dark blue eyes.

Once they changed and came back out she walked up to give them all hug, Teag was first and smiled when he found he was easily taller then her.

She hugged and kissed them all. Her demeanor was warm and open. "Welcome Children. Oh, I'm so happy you're here. I've heard so much about you. I hope you like Fruity Paste...I mean Apple Pie," she said pushing them to the kitchen to sit down at the table.

"After you eat Maddox will show you to your rooms. Teag and Johnny will share a room and Suraionee will have her own. I'm sorry that Isabelle isn't here yet. She is in school and won't be back till a bit later. Make yourselves at home and be sure to ask for anything you may need," Sarah went on. She was so talkative and loving Teag was happy to be there with them.

"Oh dear," Sarah suddenly blurted out, "I forgot to give Mr. Drummond his instructions for the day."

"Who's Mr. Drummond?" Suraionee asked.

"Oh he's the clerk behind the desk for the hotel. He's the one that is in charge when Maddox and I aren't there," Sarah said reaching for the papers on the desk and then heading for the door, "sorry, I'll be back later."

"Bye," They all repeated just before she shut the door.

"Your in charge of the Great Oak?" Teag asked excited.

"Yeah, actually we own it, and everything in it," Maddox said matter-of-factly.

"You own the amusement park, the restaurant and the hotel? Cool." John said in excitement.

"When did you built it?"

"About sixty years ago. ZaBeth and I argued about it for a while, but when I offered her fifty percent of the profits she allowed me to go ahead with it."

"Right," Teag said a little upset with ZaBeth and slightly shaking his head in disgust.

After they were settled in, Maddox took them and the other new families to register at the Eagle Heights School of Instruction. When everyone was registered they all loaded into the Giraffe Carriages that were waiting for them in front of the school and were then taken over to the Castle where ZaBeth lived. Teag started noticing as they traveled along the streets of homes, there were a few faces he recognized at random houses minding their yards, yet couldn't quite remember where he had seen them before. 'Maybe it was at the Great Oak, where I saw them,' he thought to himself forgetting about it. A moment later he saw someone who put it all together for him.

"The Captain!" Teag pointed, "that's the captain from the ship," John and Suraionee positioned themselves to see where Teag was pointing. He was a tall, strong bulky man. His gray hair was short on the sides, but longer on the top, and nicely groomed. He was dressed like a lumberjack, plaid shirt, khaki jeans, and large bulky brown boots. He was out sweeping his porch. There was no mistake, "what is he doing here?" Teag opened the door to the carriage and started to climb down before Maddox realized what had happened. Maddox immediately stopped the carriage and tried to call Teag back but it was too late, Teag was down and running up to the man on the porch. When the Captain noticed him coming he tried to pretend he was really busy.

"Captain! How did you, what is this? You live on this Island?"

"Hello there, you must have me confused with someone else," he replied acting nervous.

"No, you were the captain of the ship, and I've seen some of the other crew on this street too," Teag insisted. The captain looked over at Maddox who had just climbed down from the carriage and was walking up to Teag. Maddox nodded that it was okay to talk and so he didn't deny it any further.

"Okay, so I'm the Captain," he said. He picked up a gardening tool and started pulling weeds out of his flower garden. They appeared to be his prized possession as the garden was beautifully put together, pink stargazer lilies, blue irises, and lavender chrysanthemums were presented in just the right way to make it appear that they all came off the same plant like a bouquet, full and beautiful, wrapping itself around his home.

Maddox glanced over at the captain and then back to Teag. "Well the crew from the ship are always the same members from this Island community so that we can have as few deaths as possible."

"What? So then what's up with the old beaten up ship?" Teag asked.

Maddox again looked at the Captain, "my boy, each time we use the same ship, and each time that ship sinks."

"Why don't you just use a new ship, it might actually help the passengers enjoy their stay a little better."

"We don't have that kind of man power or magic to do that."

Teag nodded his head in disbelief, "Right, so pulling out a ship that has been underwater for say five years at a time, airing it out and repairing it and then sinking it all over again, is how much harder than just building a new one each time?"

"Well of course when you put it like that it does sound better," The Captain chuckled. Teag thought back to his time on the ship and remembered the musty smell in the rooms, the way the ship appeared tattered and worn, the painting above all the beds of the stormy sea...He remembered his feelings of torment while he panicked inside as his awful dream of the storm and drowning came true, the horrible loss he felt when he lost his parents. Tears filled his eyes. "Your so concerned with having as few deaths as possible, yet my parents, my parents died, no one else's, just mine. Why is that? Do you really think that playing with others emotions is that fun? Is life just a joke to all of you?" Teag looked at the Captain and then back to Maddox. His heart was killing him. He felt like he wanted to die. Tears rolled down his cheeks. He closed his eyes and tried to calm himself because he was showing an emotion that a sixteen-year-old boy doesn't often like to share with others. When he opened his eyes the Star in his left eye was glowing again then there was a sudden burst of energy that shot out from him like an explosion. Surprised at the shock of force that left him Teag gasped.

"What was that you just did?" The captain shot at Teag. Surrounding Teag in a twenty-foot radius circle every living plant died. The Captain looked at his prized flower garden to find it wilted and dead. The big large gruff Captain dropped his jaw surprised at what he saw. He dropped to his knees before his wilted treasures and spoke to them as if they were his children. "Oh my babies, I'm so sorry," Then turning his attention to Teag, "what did you do?" he growled then picked up gently the crispy remains of the flower garden cradling in his hands carefully. Everyone that was watching from the caravan of carriages started laughing at the site of the big large brawny man who was so concerned about his frilly flower garden. It looked so out of place.

Angry that no one seemed to care that they were being played with like dolls, their choices were never really choices, Teag snapped, "so the trip that my mom got from her friend was really meant for us? How does that work?" Teag questioned his heart still pounding.

Maddox waited for a moment thinking, "well, all I know is that ZaBeth made sure that you would get on the ship, and that our Island is somewhere between Alaska and the Bismarck Sea I don't know how she did it.

Teag remembered the strange weather, and how unusually warm it was, "so that's why the weather was so much warmer than it should have been, we were actually going south west direction instead of North West."

"That's right."

"I can't believe that I didn't notice the sun coming up on the wrong side of the ship."

"No, you wouldn't have, the ship was enchanted so that it appeared that you were going north."

Teag was intrigued at the amount of work to get him to this Island. 'Why me? There's nothing great about me.' He thought. "Maddox, there has to be more to this story."

"What do you mean?"

"Well, it just isn't adding up, why would someone go to all this trouble to bring me here, just to get a potion from a wizards mind to turn you back into human?"

"Well because, I've been desperate to go back to my human form, and ZaBeth, being the kind queen she is, well, we've tried everything else."

"But Maddox, What's in it for her?"

"Teag, not everyone has motives for wanting to help a friend. Why did you help Preston?"

"He isn't my friend."

"I know, but you helped him just the same, why?"

"Because I couldn't live with myself if he had gotten killed and I chose not to do anything."

"You did it because you have a kind heart, because you aren't like him. You know that if the roles were reversed he would have left you behind."

"Easily. But, well actually, he had the chance when I tripped and fell, before the Dragon took me, I mean us. He did try to help me."

"Maybe he is just jealous and really wants to be your friend."

I don't know how you got that, he hates me, not sure why, but, what does he have to be jealous about anyway? He's the one with the muscles, and the girls."

"Yes, and I'm sure those girls are after one thing and it isn't his looks," Maddox smiled at Teag.

"Okay, but you must know that it was pure luck that we're still alive after all that."

"Hey mate," Maddox said to Teag, "you don't give yourself enough credit, it was your new abilities that helped you fight through those obstacles. And I don't mean your powers, it's your courage that made you talk to the Dragon, to look her in the eye. Your courage and intuition that helped you to know what the Spitniker Dorgoggin was about to do and persistence that got the door open to the Pony Hills, and saved both of you. It was your skills that fixed your own wounds and your courage again that saved yourself and Preston from the charging Spitniker. Had you not had these skills you would have died. And don't let me forget the conversation with the Dwarf; they never speak to humans, ever. But you, he spoke too, why?"

"Because of my powers."

"That may be part of it, but weren't you frightened?"

"Yes."

"Then what made you speak instead of fight back or run and hide?"

"I don't know, sheer stupidity?" Teag laughed. Maddox joined him laughing for a moment.

"No," he said seriously, "it was your heart, you weren't there to harm him or take anything from him, you spoke to him with your eyes."

"Yes, with my powers."

"No, Teag, with your heart."

"I don't get the difference. It all seems the same to me."

"It's the same as night and day. Do you think that the Dragon would have spared you if you had hatred in your heart? Do you think she would have cared at all to get rid of another human being? No, she said you were different, not because you could talk to her but because of your heart. It was broken when your mother and father had died that etched into your heart, the troubles you have faced before your journey here, and the choices you made of how to deal with them formed you who you are. You care about others and want to ease their burdens even if it means taking it all for yourself and suffering for them, if it's possible. Like all creatures they can sense a humans true heart," Maddox explained. Teag didn't speak. He didn't want to admit it might be true. That would be too much responsibility to live up too. He nodded his head, as to say he understood, and Maddox didn't say anything else.

The Castle was small compared to the ones Teag had seen in the fairytale books and in movies. The path leading to it was long and curvy and the Castle itself sat upon a hill. When they arrived, there were many servants there to greet them and others to take care of the Giraffes. The castle was cold and uninviting although you could tell that ZaBeth did everything in her control to try and make it appear otherwise. One of the servants escorted them all to a large Parlor room where they were invited to sit. ZaBeth had the Keno Tea ready and went in to give it to all the children. She stopped dead in her tracks when she saw Teag. Here eyes grew large and excited. "Oh, I am so glad that you are alright," She said. Then she seemed confused with the knowledge that the dragon never lets anyone get away, she was curious what powers he may already have.

Teag nodded and smiled listening to her every thought.

'Was he able to read minds before the Keno tea? How strong is he?' She laughed in her mind and then went on, 'No, he was just lucky, soon he will finish the task and Maddox and his sons will be cured and then who's to stop me.'

The servant then handed the parents regular lemon tea. The Trager kids knew what the tea was for but none of them were prepared for what it would do to them, and either was ZaBeth. ZaBeth knew that John and Suraionee didn't have any powers or abilities, so she allowed them to partake of the tea anyway. The tea looked purple and smelled like chamomile tea. After looking at it for a few minutes Teag took a sip and the tea tasted like a warm sweet watermelon juice. He wanted to ask for some ice to cool it down but decided against it.

After the pleasantries were over ZaBeth tipped her tea as though to say good-bye and then stood up and walked out the room. Slowly everyone finished the last sips of their tea and then trickled out in groups to go home.

In the living room at the Pembroke home Teag sat with Maddox while Suraionee took a bath upstairs and John played a card game called Triumph with Sarah, Ronan and Rylee. The living room was homely. It had pictures of their children on the walls and little nick knacks here and there. It looked like a home in the country, Modest and warm. The fireplace was roaring. And the sounds of laughter came from the other room. The front door opened and closed. Maddox and Teag looked over to the entryway of the family room, as the door was blocked from view by a large wall, expecting to see who had come in.

"Awe, that should be Isabelle," Maddox said still watching the doorway. An instant later a beautiful creature came walking around the corner. Her eyes were large and light brown and her beautiful shiny dark brown hair had naturally mixed highlights of dark red and light brown that almost shimmered in the light. She had a slender build and walked with grace she strolled in with a smile that instantly pulled at Teags' heartstrings.

"There she is, how was school?" he motioned her over and gave her a hug. She looked over at Teag and flashed another grin.

"It was great daddy," She said almost embarrassed, "who's your friend?"

"Oh, this is Teag Trager. Teag, this is my daughter Isabelle," he looked back at his daughter and said, "he and his brother and sister are going to be staying with us for a while."

"Oh?" She smiled again, "and where may I ask, are they going to sleep?"

"In Ronan and Rylee's old rooms. They moved their stuff out and moved into one of the new houses down the block."

"Sweet, I want to see their new place," she looked over to Teag, "welcome to the family," She shook is hand and then asked her father, "Where are the guys?"

"In the kitchen, they're playing Triumph with John," Maddox motioned to the kitchen.

"Nice to meet ya," she said throwing him a flirtatious smile then walked out the door.

"Yeah, you too," he said back at her but she was already out the door, "she seemed nice," he remarked as he floated back to his seat.

"Don't go gettin' any ideas, she's my daughter you know."

"Yes sir," Teag smiled and tried to clear the pink from his cheeks. When he had settled down and Maddox took a seat he asked, "Can I ask you a question Maddox?" Teag asked hesitant.

"Sure."

"Do you trust ZaBeth?"

"Yes," Maddox paused then asked, "why do you ask?"

"Well, I don't know, there was just something about her today that seemed strange. She was surprised to see me alive and she was thinking and wondering about the powers I might have now, before taking her Keno Tea."

"You need to be careful about listening to others thoughts because you may not get the whole story and because thoughts are personal. You need to learn how to control it, how to shut it off," Maddox instructed. Seeing the discouraged look on Teags face he added, "I'm just saying be careful, I'm sure she was just concerned like the rest of us. No one expected you to come back. It was a surprise to us all."

"Yes, but she can see the future right?" Teag asked.

"Well, yes, to a degree, there are a lot of things she can't see. And she can only see what could happen. Everyone has their free agency so if they make a different choice she can't see that until the choice is made. It's all very complicated."

"Why is it that my parents died and everyone else's family stayed intact?"

"Well, I don't know sometimes things just happen. That's a question I really can't answer."

"Yes but The Esteban's, Dayton's, and Miles families all had small children to hold on too and, I just find it strange that all of them had help to stay alive, yet my parents died," Teag's tone was angry.

"Try not to be bitter Teag. I know it's hard but what's done is done, I don't know why it happened, but it did, and I'm so sorry that I couldn't save them."

"And the other thing I have questions about is Johnny is thirteen and Suraionee is ten, how is it that she didn't see them when they have been in this world for that many years?"

"Well you're the only one with the abilities so maybe that is why, I don't know, there are a lot of things in this world that we don't understand, and we may never understand them. We should try our best to get over it and move on. I'm not saying you shouldn't feel angry, because it's a natural feeling because of what happened to you and your family. What I am saying is that you should try to understand it, and if you can't, then find it in your heart to let it go. You need to let it go, because those things can build inside of you and can change you in bad ways. Anger and fury tend to create monsters out of good people. Justice will come, maybe not at your pace, maybe you'll never see it actually happen, but it will, and when the time is right it will happen for you."

A blast of thoughts from all the rooms shot out to Teag in a sudden wave of chaos. One stuck out to him though, it was Suraionee from all the way upstairs. Her thoughts carried down like someone screaming in his ear.

"Ahhh, What's happening to me, I can see right through the door, and the floor," the anxiety Suraionee was feeling, kept getting stronger and stronger.

"Uh, Maddox," Teag said calmly, "Sura is about to scream, you better send Sarah up there fast," Teag warned him.

Just as Maddox had called out for Sarah, Suraionee Screamed, "Stop it! Stop it! Make it stop!" She yelled. Maddox looked at Teag with curiosity. Sarah ran upstairs to comfort Suraionee and help her out of the tub.

"How did you hear her all the way upstairs?" Maddox asked, "you were envisioned to only hear thoughts in the same room. This is quite unusual."

"I don't know, I just did. You don't think the Keno Tea had anything to do with it do you?" Teag asked, "in the carriage you were concerned that John and Suraionee didn't have any powers, but Suraionee is upstairs with the ability to see though things. How can that be?"

"What? She has powers? I need to tell ZaBeth right away," Maddox said jumping to his feet.

"No please, Wait, we don't know if it will stay. Lets not say anything until we know for sure, please," Teag pleaded.

"Are you still unsure about ZaBeth?"

"Yes, but if it's just a strange reaction to the tea and it goes away, why get her all mixed up into it all?" Teag reasoned.

"Alright, but only for a few days," Maddox wasn't sure if that was a good choice but decided to go with it out of respect for Teag.

When Suraionee was calmed down and her new ability under control she went downstairs to join in the card games. She took John's place while it was his turn to take a bath. Teag went up the stairs and walked past the bathroom door that was slightly opened. He heard John playing in the water. John heard Teag and called him in. Teag stood by the door not wanting to walk in. "What?" Teag asked not really wanting to be there at all.

"Look what I can do," John insisted.

"Wait! I'm not looking, I don't want to see you," Teag said with a disgusted tone.

"I have my pants on Teag, Eeew, did you think I would call you in here otherwise?" John said appalled but Teag felt the same way.

Since he wasn't in his birthday suit Teag decided it couldn't hurt so he peeked his head in. John watched for him and when he saw that he had the proper attention he placed his head in the water and stayed under longer then Teag was comfortable with. Worried, Teag reached in and grabbed John's shoulder and pulled him up.

"What?" John asked then finished, "it's so cool, I can breath under water."

"You can what?" Teag was stunned, "how long? Here I'll time you."

"Okay," John was excited that Teag was interested.

"Ready set, Go," Teag instructed as he watched the hands on the clock above the mirror. Ten minutes passed and Teag had, had enough he reached in and pulled him up, "I can't believe that."

"I could have gone longer Teag," John was upset that he was pulled out too soon.

"Yeah well I didn't want to be here all night," Teag chuckled.

"Yeah, I did it in the ocean too, but I thought that was just a co-ink-ee-dink, but I guess it's not because I can do it here too."

"Nice," Teag said, "but, don't tell anyone but Suraionee do you understand?"

"Why?"

"Just don't, it's important. Swear to me that you wont tell anyone. Swear," Teag said now bending John's arm back forcing him to agree.

"Okay, okay, let go," John looked at Teag confused. Teag had never hurt him that way before so it must be important to him.

"Now get out and take an actual shower, you still stink, and make sure to use soap," Teag ordered then walked out of the room.

Teag walked to his room and found several new clothes lying neatly on his bed. John also had several new clothes folded on his bed. Teag put his away and then pulled out all the gems and treasures and hid them inside a folded shirt on the bottom drawer of his dresser. Then he laid down. The bed felt soft to the touch and he knew he was going to sleep good that night. His room was comfortable; it was a dark blue with white trim around the ceiling and floor. It was large enough to give both boys the space that they needed and both beds were full sized giving them each room to toss and turn. Above him was a ceiling fan with lights so that when it became too hot both boys could have air moving. The Pembrokes' were so generous to get them all new clothing and rooms to sleep in he found himself wondering how much worse things would have been if Maddox would have left them at the old haunted house. Though he couldn't think of anything worse then being forced to stay in the Pit. Pleased that he really didn't have to think about that anymore he stood up and walked into the hall heading for the stairs. John was finally in the shower he noticed as he passed by the bathroom, John was singing horribly. Teag smiled, shook his head and continued to the stairs. When he reached the middle of the steps he heard voices in the living room. They were coarse and full of anger.

"What do you think you are doing housing these children?" ZaBeth yelled, "I had a perfectly good home set up for them. Agatha was going to teach them everything they needed to know."

"Have you seen that place or actually spoken to that woman in person? I couldn't leave them there she was rude and uncaring, these kids have been through so much already, why would you want to put them in a place like that? Especially if you need Teag to help you with your task. She had them in a Pit full of dung for the whole night. Did you know about that?" Maddox asked sternly.

"I know of the Pit. It's there to punish the bad children who don't do as they are told. It's been a wonderful discipline tool. The children behave so much better after serving out a short sentence in the Pit." She defended.

"That's atrocious!" Maddox roared. I can't believe I'm hearing this from you. Don't you think you should gain his trust and then ask him if he's willing, rather then treat him poorly and force him to do your will?"

"I don't have to explain myself to you, I've seen the future and I know what will become of him and his family," She looked around for a moment making sure that no one could hear her, "Do you really think that the cause is worth your insubordination? I can find someone that would love your job. I believe that Mister Karik was hinting upon this very thing, don't think your above being dropped if you don't do as I ask," ZaBeths' tone was dangerous.

"I am doing what we had talked about, you said nothing about treating these children with contempt, in fact you said nothing about their parents dying either. Are you hiding something?"

ZaBeth put her nose in the air her eyes grew large with anger at his question. "I saw nothing of the other two children, what makes you think I've known his parents would die in the storm?" She turned from him and faced the roaring fire trying to hide her face, but Teag herd every thought. Rage grew inside of him as she stood there feeding him her thoughts.

'You insolent man, if his parents were around do you really think they would let him go on a dangerous journey? No.'

Teags' eyes lit up as he heard her next thoughts as she evil-mindedly grinned.

'Besides, they aren't dead, I took his parents and locked them in the dungeon because I may need them to make the boy do my bidding should he choose to defy me, but I wont be telling you that.'

"You're right, I'm sorry, but you must please allow me to keep the children with me. I can train them or I can take them to whomever you like to train them, they just get to live with us here."

ZaBeth turned around and cunningly smiled at him, "Fine, they may stay with you, but first thing in the morning I want Teag to report to Nevina to train him, do what you want with the other two," she waved her hand and then disappeared.

"I'm glad she's gone," Teag exclaimed as he came around the corner surprising Maddox who thought he was alone.

"Oh, did you have to hear that? I'm sorry," Maddox sank into the recliner and couldn't look Teag in the eyes.

"I'm not, I was right, and the best part is my parents are alive," Teag eagerly told him.

"How did you get that out of the conversation?"

"It wasn't in the conversation, it was in her thoughts. She's playing you, she isn't a nice person there is something bigger going on, she mentioned that she didn't want my parents around because they would get in the way of her plan."

"So wouldn't that be more reason that she would kill them rather then keep them around?" Maddox suggested.

"No, because she said she wanted them alive in case I didn't do what she wanted and in that case she would use them to make me do her *bidding*," Teag tried to mimic her voice, "so lets go get them."

"No, slow down, you can't just march up there and get your parents, we have to play the game, here's what I suggest we do," Maddox leaned in, "let's call a family meeting," Teag nodded and ran to get Suraionee and John while Maddox called in Sarah, Rylee, Ronan, and Isabelle. When everyone was seated in the family room Maddox started, "it has come to my attention that ZaBeth is not who she claims to be. She made us believe that the Trager kids parents are dead while in fact they are living. It seems we have been fooled and we need to get them back."

"Well Maybe she had a reason to lie to us," Sarah said in disbelief of the news.

"No, She is after more than turning us back to human," Maddox informed her.

"Actually she is excited to get you turned back for some reason. Do you have special powers being lions?" Teag asked.

"Not really, other then brute force and seeing in the dark," Ronan answered.

"And being able to jump high and climb trees," Rylee added.

"Why would she want you turned back that badly?"

"What exactly did she think?" Maddox asked trying to figure out what was happening.

"Well at the castle she was asking herself questions like, *'was he able to read minds before the Keno Tea?'* and *'how strong is he?'* She laughed kind of malicious in her mind and said something about me just *being lucky,*" he paused and thought back again, "she said something about me finishing a task and that you all would be cured and then no one could be in the way to stop her plans or something like that."

Maddox bowed his head and shook it like he was saying no to someone. The room was silent for a moment and then Maddox asked, "what did she think when she was here?"

Teag thought back again trying to remember the exact words then spoke, "she called you an insolent man, and then questioned that if my parents were around do you really think they would let me go on a dangerous journey? Then she answered it for you, 'no,' then she said they aren't dead and that she took them and locked them in the dungeon because she might need them to make me do what she wants but that she wasn't going to ever tell you that."

"This is ridiculas," Rylee stated, "you don't' really believe that she is planning something and really acting this way do you? For years she has been our Queen and she has never acted that way before. I don't believe that Teag can really hear thoughts and I am really tired of hearing that you believe this nonsense," Rylee was clearly angry at the thought.

"Yeah? Try me," Teag snapped back wanting to prove that he wasn't lying.

Rylee sat there controlling his thoughts then let him have it, 'your too young to know what your talking about, you haven't been here long enough to know who any of us is or what we've been through, how dare you come here and make up lies.'

"But I'm not lying Rylee, I told you the truth, I'm not too young I'm sixteen and yeah I don't know what you've been through nor do I know you that well, but I don't need that to tell me that you're good people. I want to help you and I will do whatever it takes to help you become human again if that is what you want. But I have been around long enough to know when someone cares or doesn't. I heard her and the way her thoughts sounded and she doesn't care for you, there's something about your strength or something about you being Lion men that is keeping her from her plans and she wants to put a stop to it. Do you think for a second that if any of you change back to human that she will keep you around?" Teag was frustrated about everything that has happened in the past few days, wanting to see his parents again and knowing they are alive gave him strength, but he became worried that convincing the group of ZaBeth's true plans was going to be more difficult than he had anticipated.

"Fine, I believe that you can read minds, but taking them out of context, you don't know if that is the whole story. You only heard part of her thoughts; maybe there is a good explanation for everything," Rylee defended again.

"Okay, fine, have it your way, but do you think that calling your father an insubordinate and insolent man was a thoughtful thing for her to say, and that threatening his job and giving it to Willem Karik was a sweet thought coming from her? I may be young and I may be new to these parts, but where I come from, reading between the lines can be just as important as brushing your teeth. There are clearly two sides and you can't sit on both of them to keep the peace. Now is the time to choose a side.

"My mother told us a story before she died, I mean, disappeared. It was about a Queen and her sister. Their parents died but no one could figure the cause and when the eldest sister was about to be crowned queen the younger sister got up and told lies about her sister. Later the younger sister came back and apologized to the queen and played with the queen's heart then she poisoned her. The queen knew that her sister wanted something but refused to look at what it might be because she didn't want to take a side and didn't want to believe her own sister would want to hurt her. The queen died because of that choice. If it smells like a skunk, walks like a skunk and acts like a skunk, it's a skunk," Teag looked around the room at the shocked faces looking back at him, "what?" He asked.

"Your story..." Sarah started, "you say your mother told you that story?"

"Yeah we had an early birthday party on the ship and my mom gave Sura a necklace. She told us that story that went along with the gift it's just a story."

"Umm, no. Actually, was the name of the Queen, Alura?" Isabelle asked.

"Yeah," Suraionee answered.

"Was the sister's name Desdemona?"

"Yeah, but how do you know?" Teag had a confused look on his face.

"Because it really happened, here in Makoto City. ZaBeth is…"

"Queen Aluras cousin. Right. So then what happened to Desdemona?" Teag cut Isabelle off in mid sentence but was having a hard time believing the story could be true.

"No one knows, after she was sent out of the castle there were a few sightings of her on Koki Island but after that, nothing for a couple of centuries," Sarah answered.

"Okay you're killing me, how can it be the same ZaBeth? She has to be like, over a million and two years old now," Teag exaggerated.

"Right two hundred and fifty six this year," Ronan commented.

"How is she able to still be alive and not look that old?" John asked.

"Well, when she and Melanion put a spell on the Islands making them invisible. It also changed the way we all age when we are children we age normal, but once we get to be about Twenty years old we look that young until we turn about sixty and then we look about thirty at age one hundred and so on. The invisibility spell is supposed to last until Desdemona is caught and put away in a place where she can't take control."

"Okay listen, with this knowledge, and the way that ZaBeth is acting, do you think it may be possible that Desdemona did something to the real ZaBeth and took her place?" Teag asked.

"Well maybe, but the only person who could tell us how that would be possible is Vidor Lysander or Melanion, and Vidor's crazy and out of reach right now and Melanion hasn't been around since just after ZaBeth was named Queen." Sarah informed them.

"We need to go to Koki Island and start asking questions," Teag commanded.

"Since when did this become an investigation? Besides, if ZaBeth gets a whiff of what we are doing she will shut us down fast she'll send you back to live with…" Maddox started.

"Agatha?" Teag blurted out.

"Yes, Teag, Agatha, and you don't want to go back there, do you?"

"No, but I have one more thing to tell you, actually John has to tell you," Teag looked over at John who looked dumbfounded at the whole conversation, "John, tell them now, it's okay."

"Tell them what?" John had forgotten about his new ability. When Teag gave him a look he suddenly remembered what Teag was talking about, "right, Umm, well I can breath under water."

"What? Really when did this start?" Maddox asked.

"When the ship wreaked, I didn't need help because I could breath."

"So your saying that both you and Teag had your abilities before you drank the Keno Tea?" Maddox asked stunned.

"Yes," John agreed.

"Who are you related too? I mean your mother knew of the story, but how?" Maddox started questioning, "only the original Islanders had abilities with magic without the Keno Tea."

"Actually I don't know my great grandfathers name, my mothers grandfather, we always just called him Grandpa Great because he was our great grandfather. I heard my mom use another name once, but that was when I was like five, and I don't remember what it was," Teag admitted.

"Well, then, here is what we are going to do. We can't very well go out there fighting without training. Teag your going to see Nevina tomorrow and start your training, don't tell her anything personal and don't give away too much information. Just practice and then come home and we will work together on what you have learned and see if we can't strengthen your abilities. We will pretend that all is well and in two months we will go to ZaBeth and show her what you have learned not everything mind you, but enough. John and Suraionee will go to school and then afterwards we'll all split up and work on your new skills. In two months time I want us to be ready to do anything. If we work together we can do it. We have the edge because she doesn't know about John and Suraionee. Is everyone in on this plan?" Maddox asked looking around the room.

"Yes," Ronan started the chatter of Yeses that quickly followed by everyone in the room.

"Good. So, with that said, lets get dinner on and eat, then get some rest because tomorrow we have a big day," Maddox said ready to take on the task.

* * *

In the Morning Teag got up took a shower and then put on a pair of blue jeans and a navy blue dress shirt, made his bed and then made his way down stairs. The house had the smell of vanilla, cinnamon, and bacon. He went down stairs and found everyone already sitting there eating. Sarah had made French toast with bacon, sausage, eggs, hash browns, milk and orange juice. Ronan and Rylee had come over to join them for breakfast. Teag sat across the table from Isabelle; he was trying hard not to look at her because he didn't want his stomach flying away. It wasn't long before he had forgotten what he was doing and looked up at her. She was staring back at him with her beautiful smile and his heart took a swing. He decided he wasn't hungry anymore and just sat there playing with his food while everyone else stuffed their faces. Back home he always had apprehension when it came to girls. With this girl he just feels so shy and embarrassed. He started to believe that it might actually be his first crush. His heart was soaring, things just seemed to be taking a turn for the better, his parents whom he thought to be dead were alive and he is on this incredible Island with awesome new creatures and magic everywhere. And he gets to live with the Pembrokes' instead of that horrible broken down house with that hag they call a woman. All in all he was feeling' pretty good. Now if he could just get the courage to actually say more then two words to her...that's the trick. He looked down at his plate and realized that he had been fidgeting with his food; it was a big mush of everything put together.

"What's the matter Teag, aren't you hungry?" Sarah asked concerned that he wasn't eating.

"Yeah, well," he looked up into Isabelle's eyes and while he seemed to be staring deep into them he continued, "I...I...well I...I guess not," he glanced up at the rest of the table and everyone was gone except the three of them, "oh, sorry."

Sarah smiled; she knew what was really going on. "It's alright, you go on and get to class, I'll take care of this, you too Isabelle," they both stood up and walked out the front door together both feeling giddy. Teag was about to reach for her hand when they stepped outside, but was interrupted when they realized her Father was standing there waiting for them to come out.

"Alright, let's get going, you'll be needing this," Maddox handed him a rock.

"What's this for?" Teag asked thinking it was odd.

"It's a pager for me, remember you throw it on the ground and I'll come and get you where ever you are," Maddox reminded him.

"Oh yeah," Teag nodded that he understood.

"Now remember, do what Nevina says, but don't tell her everything, just what she needs to know because she reports right to ZaBeth." Maddox reminded him. as he walked Teag down the street.

"How far is it?" Teag asked.

"Only two blocks," Maddox answered still walking a fast pace.

It didn't take long to get to Nevina's place. The house was a nicely built two story painted light green with white trim. The lawn was bordered with thick colorful rosebushes that bordered thick like a fence. They walked along rosebush to the driveway and up to a door around the side of the house and knocked on it. When she answered, she wasn't at all what Teag had expected. She was extremely voluptuous, she was dressed almost like a gypsy and seemed like she was a bit angry with him, though he was right on time. The woman grabbed him by the shirt pulling him inside, Teag looked back at Maddox as the door closed behind him with Maddox on the other side. Breathing a little heavy she sat down in a large sofa chair then took a long drink from her cup that sat on a table next to the chair. When she sat it down she asked, "Teag, right?"

"Yes m'am," he answered politely.

"You may call me Ms. Nevina, ve vill become good friends," her voice was sharp and crisp. "Now, I vas told zat you escaped a dragon, is zis true?" Her eyes looked probing as she stared him directly in the eyes waiting for an answer. The longer she had to wait for an answer the longer her eyes appeared to be bulging from her head almost like a pulse. It occurred to him that she might have a power too. Suddenly worried what it might be, he answered.

"Yes, well I wiggled out of her grip and she dropped me in the orange grass, I hid from her while she searched but couldn't' find me, then I found my way back to the group."

"Oh, it must have been more exciting zen zat, you vere gone overnight," her eyes were searching for something but he couldn't read her at all.

"Well, yeah it was spooky to be grabbed by a Dragon, but she dropped me, so I laid low for a while and then searched for a way out of the tall grass. There isn't anything more to it then that," Teag said defensively.

"Okay, okay, so then tell me, have you ever heard anyone's thoughts before?"

"No, can't say that I have."

"Have you ever had a dream zat came true?" Her motions and attitude seemed to be like that of a counselor counseling a student.

"Yes, the shipwreck, I dreamed about that before it happened," Teag said matter of factly.

"Vell zen, it seems you are on ze right track, zough you should have had somezing happen to you by now," she stopped and stared into space as she thought about what she was saying. "Perhaps, a bit more Keno Tea, vill help it along," with her face still staring at the ceiling she slowly moved her eyes to look at him, "you vould like some Tea?" She asked standing to go get some for him.

"No, please, I'm good thanks," he begged.

"I'm sorry, it was not a question, you vill drink some Tea," Nevina demanded as she walked to the kitchen and poured a cup. When she returned she handed it to him and said, "drink."

Teag hesitated for a moment, and then did as he was told, "Mmm, Thank you," he lied.

She watched him as he kept trying to sip the rancid warm watermelon tasting tea. His nose scrunched up and made him gag a little.

"Quickly now, hurry it up, ve don't have all day," she insisted.

Quick to obey he swallowed the last bit of it, and then took a deep breath negatively shaking his head, "yum," he said sarcastically.

"Now zen, ve must begin. I vant you to concentrate on zis room. Vat do you hear."

Teag listened intently trying to figure out what he was listening for, he had already tried to listen to her, but she must know that even if he tried he couldn't hear her thoughts, 'why couldn't he hear her thoughts?'

"I can't hear your thoughts, m'am, I mean, Ms. Nevina," Teag said trying to get out of her what she wanted.

"I know dear, perhaps if I make it a little easier?" She asked, then without waiting for an answer, she threw a shiny little black rock on the ground. In an instant Preston Karik appeared dressed all preppy. The shock of seeing Preston in the same room made the Keno Tea in his otherwise empty stomach turn uncomfortably. "Very good, now zat Preston is here ve can move on," Preston seemed just as upset that he had to work with Teag.

"Ms. Nevina, I didn't volunteer for this, to help him," Preston argued in a snobby tone.

"You vill do vat I tell you boy. You vill be revarded as ve discussed, yesterday," She turned her attention back to Teag, "now, concentrate on ze room, vat do you hear?"

Teag closed his eyes to make believe he had never done this before and he was doing what she asked. Preston was angry at the situation. 'I hate this, why did I volunteer, the reward, oh yeah the reward, a SkyBee, yeah, okay, I'll give this a shot....Oh that awesome machinery, the beauty of it and to think that man can fly without a airplane, I can't wait to have the breeze in my hair, and the chicks, they'll be all over me."

"Teag?" Ms. Nevina called, "vat do you hear?"

"Oh yes em', Preston is thinking about a SkyBee and how he'll look to the girls when he gets one."

Prestons' eyes grew large as his surprise caught him off guard, "you didn't tell me he could read minds. I don't like this,...no, I'm going home," he started walking to the door when Ms. Nevina held out her hand and gripped at the air, and he stopped. Not because she told him too but because she forced him too.

"You vill leave ven I tell you. If zere is somezing you don't vant him to hear zen control your zoughts, but you must zink somezing because he needs za training. Do you understand?"

"Yes, Ms. Nevina," Preston looked terrified, but Teag was happy to see that she had a power and what it was, but the question kept coming to him, why can't he hear her thoughts. Something was stopping him and it made him nervous that he didn't know what.

"Teag, I vant you to concentrate again, zis time I vant you to zink of zat vase, see if you can move it," Teag tried but wasn't able too. So he closed his eyes and tried again this time he waited longer before giving up but still nothing. He looked at Ms. Nevina and shook his head. "Keep trying," Preston seemed relieved that Teag was doing something other than listening to him he managed to settle down in an armchair that sat at a table across the room. Teag could still hear his thoughts, but he tried to tune them out, as he really didn't care what he was thinking.

After several hours of practice listening to Prestons thoughts and trying to move objects around the room Ms. Nevina called it a day.

"Go home now, but practice. Your homevork is, to listen to ze people in your home zen vrite it down and tomorrow you vill report to me vat they are zinking. Is zat clear?" Her demeanor seemed more to get the skinny on the Pembrokes' rather than teach him something, but Teag was sure that he could come up with something without giving her any important information. Preston stayed behind while Teag left to go home.

By the time Teag got home it was two o'clock in the afternoon. He found everyone in the family room talking about their first day at school. John and Suraionee thought that the classes seemed fun. It was a lot like their school at home only history was about the history of the Islands and not the United States. They had a lot to learn but were excited to attack the chore.

"Alright, it's time to work on the skills we know about. Johnny, go with Rylee to the pool downstairs, Suraionee go with Ronan to the Kitchen, and Teag you stay here with me. Isabelle, you go do your homework and then see if there is anything you can do to help Ronan," Maddox instructed.

"I'll be folding the laundry in my room if anyone needs me," Sarah nodded then walked out of the room.

John had already changed into his swim suite he followed Rylee to the basement. It was a large daylight basement with a high ceiling and a huge window with slat blinds that were slightly open. The view was of the ocean and other nearby Islands. Rylee turned on the lights then walked over and closed the slats. The room was huge. There was a slide and both low and high diving boards. There were several plants surrounding the room almost giving the feeling that they were in the middle of a jungle. You couldn't see the actual walls because of the thickness of the plants. The only wall that was visible was the full window wall and the hallway that they came down from.

"Jump in," Rylee instructed, "let's see what you can do," he smiled, Rylee was decked out in a wet suit complete with diving gear large enough for his entire lion body and face. He jumped in after John with a giant splash. When they went underwater, they suddenly found themselves in the Ocean. There were no walls to the pool, nothing to contain them. John was excited. Several different kinds of colorful vibrant fish cut through the water like a knife.

As John and Rylee enjoyed their swim Suraionee and Ronan were in the kitchen trying to control her vision.

"Just try to see what's inside the cookie jar, don't go so far through it that you miss the important items inside," Ronan coached.

"Okay," Suraionee concentrated on the jar with all of her might, "but I keep going through the floor, how do I stop it at a certain point?"

"Well, that's where practice comes in. I don't have your power, only you do, I can only teach you and talk you though it, only you can take the steps to the other side. You can do this! once you master it I'll take you for ice cream. So practice hard, when you're reading or doing your chores. No one will know what you're doing unless you tell them," Ronan empowered her.

"Cool, okay," Suraionee was so excited she immediately went back to work.

While Suraionee was working hard with Ronan, Teag was telling Maddox what happened at Ms. Nevina's place and about her instructions.

"Yes, I knew that she would want to know what we're doing, but mostly she would want to know if we are loyal to ZaBeth and if we suspect anything wrong. So be careful with what you say. Now let's get started, focus and tell me what you hear," Teag closed his eyes and focused so hard he could hear all the thoughts and voices of everyone in the house and then suddenly every piece of furniture in the house lifted off the ground. "*Stop!*" Maddox roared surprised. "What's going on?" His deep Australian voice seemed confused.

Teag opened his eyes as everything came falling down. His left eye still glowing, "what the…" Teag gasped, "who did that?"

Ronan and Suraionee ran in from the kitchen concerned with the raising items and crashing of the furniture. Right behind them Sarah and Isabelle ran down the stairs and into the family room, "Did you see that?" Isabelle said excitedly, "what happened?"

"Who did that?" Sarah asked looking at Suraionee and then at Teag.

"I don't know," Maddox said, then it came to him, "but I have an idea, everyone take a seat."

Everyone in the room found a seat and sat down, "not you Teag. Come over here."

Teag did as he was told.

"Now, try that again."

Teag closed his eyes and focused. Once again all the thoughts in the room flooded his mind, though the conversations weren't there because no one was talking. Suddenly he felt himself lift off the ground and he heard everyone gasp. He opened his eyes and again everything came crashing down.

"Oww," Ronan whispered when the sofa came down jerking him.

"Ouch," Suraionee said as the jolt of her sofa chair hit the floor.

"Ooo," Sarah whispered as the sofa she shared with Ronan crashed to the floor.

"Hey," Isabelle said as she lost her balance and fell to the floor from sitting on the arm of the sofa chair she shared with Suraionee. "Ooh cool, your eye is glowing, that's neat trick," she said as she noticed the star in his eye.

"How am I doing that?" He asked Maddox.

"Your powers are stronger then we thought they could be. If it was going to gain strength like that it shouldn't have happened that fast. Changes like that come with time and practice."

"Well would drinking Keno tea do that to me?" Teag asked.

"Maybe, but not in the small amount that ZaBeth gave you," Maddox was intrigued.

"But what if I drank more of it today," Teag asked.

"How? Who gave it to you?" Maddox asked.

"Well Ms. Nevina did when she thought I didn't have any powers. She forced me to drink the whole thing fast."

Maddox laughed, "Well then that would do it. But how did she get her hands on it? Only ZaBeth knows how to make it and she never gives second doses because of the effect it can have on people."

"What effect?" Teag seemed a little worried.

"Well, you can get hives, and vomiting, it has been known to make a lot of people deathly ill for weeks. How do you feel?"

"Fine, I was a little sick at first, but I'm fine now. Here's the other thing, I could hear thoughts and conversations," when everyone just shook their heads like it was no big deal he added, "conversations that everyone was having in this house and down the street."

"Interesting," Maddox folded his arms and then switched positions and placed his fingertips on his chin playing with the fur and then the other hand rested on his hip pensively. "Try this, focus again but this time focus on the sofa and see if you can bring it to your feet."

Teag was excited. First he looked at the sofa across the room and then he closed his eyes and thought about the sofa. In his mind he told the sofa to 'come here,' immediately it moved but in jerky sporadic movements. Isabelle and Suraionee giggled as they watched Ronan and Sarah's heads bob all over the place. By the time the couch made it over to Teag's feet Sarah was sick to her stomach.

"Next time let me off the ride first," she said as she dizzily found her way to the bathroom off the kitchen.

"Bravo," Maddox applauded, "bravo! Work on that while you are at home and you'll be a master in no time thanks to Nevina and ZaBeth. So let me see, put all of your abilities together so far, you can understand the thoughts of animals, or creatures if you will, you can hear thoughts and conversations anywhere within, we'll say a block radius, though we should test that too, and you can move objects with your mind. Mighty nice mate, mighty nice," Maddox said with enthusiasm.

Suraionee and Rylee went back to the kitchen to continue working and Isabelle went back upstairs to finish her homework.

"Maddox?" Teag asked remembering Prestons' thoughts earlier in the day, "what's a SkyBee?"

It's a, well, I don't know how to describe it. You stand on it and surf the wind. Let me see I think I have a picture here somewhere," Maddox flipped through some books that were on a nearby shelf, "aha, here it is. This is a SkyBee, fun little devils. We should take the family when this is all over and go surfing," The picture in the book showed a lady with long flowing black hair standing on what looked close to a standing Jet Ski. It had a rounded but pointed nose that had handlebars that stemmed up to standing height. Along each of the sides of the platform extended small pointed triangular wings. Out the back of the platform was a large turbojet engine that appeared to be making it speed through the air.

"Where did you hear about a SkyBee?"

"Oh I heard Preston thinking about it this morning. I didn't know what it was or what it did, I was just curious."

The next day Teag went back to Ms. Nevinas' place.

"Sit down," She pointed to the sofa against the wall. Slowly nodding her head she asked, "So vere is you homevork, I trust you did it."

"Yes," Teag pulled out a piece of paper from his pocket and handed it to her but she wouldn't touch it.

"No, I vant you to read it out loud," she said as she stuck her nose in the air and waved her hand for him to go ahead.

"Maddox thought a lot about what he will do when he changes back to normal. Sarah thought about the business at the Great Oak and about what needed to be cleaned or made for meals. Ronan and Rylee weren't there much but when they were, they both thought about when their next building job would come along or the cute ladies they seemed to like," Teag stopped.

"And what about Isabelle?" She pulled her nose out of the air for a moment to observe his eyes.

"Oh sorry, she thought about homework and practicing the piano and what friends said about other friends at school."

"Let me see zat," she demanded as she held her hand out for the paper in his hand. She gazed over it quickly as though she didn't believe there was writing on it, when she was done she smiled and handed it back, "you may zrow zat away. You did very well."

The lessons continued when Preston showed up and they practiced, but became harder when Preston practiced his new power of closing off his mind while still having thoughts, and making different sounds happen from the other side of the room, causing Teag to lose his concentration several times.

Within a two-month time of special training on top of their regular schoolwork John's abilities grew as well. He found he had a photographic memory and second favorite to breathing underwater, he could turn invisible. During the month he learned how to control them and worked hard to develop them. Suraionee though didn't gain any new power but wanted to learn how to defend herself so she was enrolled into the art of Koikochi, a type of karate on the Island.

She faithfully went to her classes and quickly caught onto the techniques making even the old members fight for their place in the chain. Teag's telepathic, psychic and telekinesis abilities strengthened quickly, within the month he could move any object with ease and hear any conversation or thought from anyone within a five mile radius.

Chapter 9

After three months of special training, John and Suraionee were sent to school while Teag and Maddox climbed into a giraffe carriage and left to meet ZaBeth for a review, just as they had planned. It was August and the heat made the days almost unbearable. Teag sat there enjoying a large amount of cool wind that came from a tiny bird that did nothing but stay close to him. While stationary, spun super fast to create a wind. Teag felt bad for Maddox, who sat there filling a bottle of water, from a large bucket that sat by his side and never seemed to lose its level. He took the water and threw it over the top of his head and then turned his head side to side while the fast air from his own bird, blew over him.

"At least I'm shaded by the canopy," he remarked noticing Teags' growing concern, "don't worry, I'll be alright," he smiled back at him.

"What do you call these birds?" Teag asked loving all the new creatures he saw everyday.

"Windyflitters," Maddox said just before dumping another round of water over his head.

Teag nodded and then stayed quiet for most of the way there, contemplating what might happen.

When they approached the Castle Teag started to get nervous, "so what's the plan?" He asked Maddox.

"We act like everything is normal. When she gives you the assignment you act surprised because you aren't supposed to know about it. Then just before we leave we will pick up Johnny and Suraionee and head out. Imagine her surprise when she finds out about their abilities," Maddox laughed, "You three will make a great team."

The Carriage stopped and the two of them climbed down the ladder. They walked up to the door and were greeted by the door servant.

"ZaBeth is waiting for you in the Parlor room," The servant said motioning them in that direction.

When they walked in ZaBeth was irritated, "well, I thought you would be here five minutes ago Maddox."

"Sorry, The traffic was terrible," he said smiling.

"I'm sure it was," though irritated, ZaBeth pretended to laugh knowing full well that there isn't any traffic at all in this area and not really finding it funny. "Well now, Let's see Teag, Let's see what you can do...Goodred," she called to her servant waiting by the door, "bring in the troubled Monkey."

Maddox tried to make eye contact with Teag, but Teag was too interested in seeing the Monkey on the other side of the room. However ZaBeth seemed to catch a glimpse of Maddox's attempts and ordered him out of the room.

The servant Goodred brought in a spider monkey in a cage and then left the room. The monkey was whimpering. Maddox tried to remind Teag with his thoughts 'No! Don't, you didn't work on that in your classes,' but Teag was too interested in hearing what the cute little monkey had to say.

"What's wrong little fella?" Teag asked talking to the Monkey in his cage.

'My hand hurts,' The monkey thought handing Teag his hand.

"Where does it hurt?"

'I have a splinter right here,' he replied pointing to the spot on his finger.

"Well let me help you," Teag reached in the cage and pulled him out. Then seeing a pair of tweezers that were placed conveniently on the table he started pulling out the splinter. There you go, good as new," Teag said as he put the monkey down.

'Thank you,' the monkey said before he went back to his cage and shut the door.

Teag looked at ZaBeth whose mouth was on the floor. "I knew you would be telepathic but I only thought it would work on humans, I didn't believe it when I heard you could speak to animals too, so I decided to test it," she said in awe.

"Who told you?" Teag asked with anger and curiosity as his heart tried to jump out of his throat. He was now concerned he had given away too much information.

"I started with the animal because you made it past the dragon, and no one lives once captured by her. I didn't know of your ability," she lied, "but I thought I would try it anyway and when you failed that one I was then going to bring in the human who can't speak," there was a short pause and then she went on, "this means so much more. You have no idea." ZaBeth got up from her seat and started pacing thinking of all the new plans she has for Teag. "You will of course be famous you know," she added trying to get him excited. Then she remembered the business she had for him first. "Oh yes, back on task, I have a job for you and Maddox. Will you accept it?" She looked around for Maddox, "where is Maddox?" Then answering her own question she shook her head in disgust, "bring him back in," she demanded, put out that he wasn't in the room.

When Maddox returned he made eye contact with Teag, but Teag shrugged his shoulders, as if to say *sorry I didn't hear you*.

"Are you listening?" ZaBeth was clearly irritated that she had been talking and no one was listening to her, "will you accept it?"

"Yes," Teag said without hesitation.

ZaBeth nodded, "you will need to travel to the Black Wizard Forest. Inside is a fortress that will be hard to break into. Find Vidor Lysander and when Maddox approaches him listen for the ingredients to the antidote that will turn him and his sons back to human. Next, find the tunnel in the basement that will lead you to the Diamond Rock. Take this vial and capture some of the Suns Rays. Also some where inside the Diamond Rock is a special diamond in the shape of a sun. You will know it because it glows an orangey yellow color. Third you will need to travel to the Polar Hawk Mountains. Find the Fresh Water cave and inside there is a icicle in the shape of a moon. You will know it when you see it because it glows blue. Also, in this large container you will need a Crumble Rock to save for later crushing," she handed him the jar, "from there you must travel to the Golden Turtle Lagoon. Somewhere at the bottom of the lagoon are four Shimmering Silver Stars. They may not all be in the same place. There are many dangers ahead. Do you think you can make this journey?"

"Yes," Teag agreed.

"Then I will see you when you get back," ZaBeth said with confidence waving him out of her sight. "Maddox, stay for a moment," she commanded. Maddox watched as Teag walked out of the room the door shut behind himself. "Maddox, after you get the recipe for your antidote you are to come back here so we can put it all together."

"But I thought I could go with Teag and finish the rest of the quest. He's too young and new to the area to be out there on his own. He doesn't know all the dangers."

"He can rely on the creatures around him. He can clearly speak to them so they will help him. I want you back here do you understand?"

Maddox hesitated but then agreed.

John and Suraionee were waiting outside for Teag and Maddox to show up. They climbed up the ladder and quickly sat down anxious to hear where they were going. Their smiles quickly turned to frowns when they heard the words, "Black Wizard Forest."

"That place is spooky, are you sure we have to go?" Suraionee asked.

"With all of our abilities together I don't see how we can lose. We can do this," Teag said with confidence, with no idea what was ahead.

"We will spend the day at the Great Oak and then attack the task at hand in the morning," Maddox told them as they made their way to the portal down to the Island below.

That night was a hard one for Teag, the thoughts of what would happen, and what creatures they might have to face kept creeping into his mind. Trying to shut them out so he can sleep he listened to some soft classical music while he lay in bed. He suddenly found himself back in the tall orange grass, riding in a giraffe carriage with John, Suraionee and Maddox guiding the giraffe as if the dragon never took him. The other survivors were also there riding in their giraffe carriages.

Suraionee reached her hand out of the carriage and touched a blade of grass. It felt like normal grass. She reached out again and tried to break off a piece but failed, "why can't I break it?" She asked forgetting the earlier conversation.

"Hello? If a Dragon can't burn it down with fire do you really think you can break it with your hands?" John teased.

Suraionee felt sheepish and sat back in her seat.

They came to the edge of the Orange Dragon Field then turned right. Now they were traveling southeast. On the right side of them was the tall grass and the left, millions of thick large spooky trees the ones they had seen when they first saw the island. They were on a run-down dirt road between the two. It was very shaded and had a dark and spooky feeling to it.

"What's that?" John asked getting everyone's attention.

"That there, is Black Wizard Forest. You won't be wanting to go there by yourself. Its got all kinds of creepy crawly things that you'd just wish you never knew about," Maddox warned them.

"Isn't that where you said Vidor lives?" Teag asked.

"The very same," Maddox watched all the droopy trees go by as they traveled along the edge of it.

Teag got a funny feeling that someone or something was watching them even though no one could be seen. The feeling turned into creepy when he caught a glimpse of something hiding back in the trees as soon as he looked in that direction. It turned his stomach to think that he would have to go there to read Vidor Lysanders' thoughts. He suddenly had no desire to ever go there. 'I want to go back', He thought unable to say it out loud. "Why didn't we just go right through the Orange Dragon Field? It would have saved a lot of time." Teag asked knowing that the Dragon wouldn't have hurt them.

"Well, we have never been friends with the Dragon, and she has killed many of our people. We don't want to provoke her so we go around. The first hour we spent in the grass because she would have seen us when flying to North Beach," Maddox informed him.

"Well from now on we can travel through it can't we?" Teag asked.

"If what you say is true about the dragon being good then I would have to say, maybe. But, tell me this, where does she live in there?" Maddox asked.

"I can't remember exactly where, but she's got a lair that's inside the ground."

"Well, that may or may not cause a problem, because we wouldn't want the Giraffes to stumble upon it and fall in, now would we," Maddox reached under Teag and John's chairs and pulled out a medium sized pole. He put it in the hole that was in the center of the carriage. Then behind Suraionee's seat he pulled out a round wooden tabletop that was folded. He unfolded it and placed it on the pole until it clicked into place. Then he placed a map on the table and looked at it.

"This is where we are," he said pointing to a spot between the Black Wizard Forest (E) and the Orange Dragon Field (Mid East). Then he went on, "this is where we were," he pointed to Pony Hills (Mid-North) between North Beach (NE), Polar Hawk Mountains (N) and Orange Dragon Field. He continued, "and this is where we're going,"he pointed to the Great Oak (SW) between Golden Turtle Lagoon (Low SW), Pinapple Falls (W), Orange Dragon Field and South Beach (S).

"Where's Makoto City?" Teag inquired excitedly.

"Yeah, I don't see it on the map," John added trying to pin point it with his eyes.

"It's most secret, to outsiders, which you aren't now," he said smiling, "okay I'll tell you, but don't tell the others, I'd like to see the looks on their faces when I tell them to go inside a tree to eat and relax."

The three of them looked at each other then nodded in agreement.

"Okay, inside the Great Oak is a special room that will transport us."

"Where does it transport us to?" John asked with his eyes full of excitement.

"Look up in the sky. What do you see?"

"A bird?" Asked Suraionee, "what does that have to do with anything?"

Trying to hold back the laughter, Maddox pointed and said, "no dear, think bigger."

"That huge cloud over the ocean?" John asked.

"Yes," Maddox said wanting to keep their suspense. He was enjoying the looks on their faces.

"You're telling us that we are going to live on a puffy cloud?" John said disbelieving.

"Yes, but it's like a regular city with a great view of the Ocean," Maddox corrected him. All three kids looked puzzled.

"On the bottom it looks like a cloud, but on top, it's a city, not a cloud, or at least it doesn't look like a cloud," Maddox started to confuse himself.

"Cool!" John exclaimed.

Now more excited then ever they were looking to see if they could see the Great Oak yet.

"There's more," he said and they sat down to listen. "The Great Oak has a restaurant, a hotel, and a large amusement playroom with."

"Playroom? That's for babies," John said upset that it wasn't like a six flags.

"Oh you think do you? Just wait and see," Maddox informed them with glee.

"You said something about a room that will transport us, what does it do, move like an elevator?" Teag asked changing the subject.

"No, it's much better, I can't explain it, besides I want to see your faces when you see it for the first time.

Looking at the Cloud in the distance, Suraionee asked, "doesn't the cloud ruin the ground below because it never lets through sunlight?"

"No, because it just stays over the ocean by Pineapple Falls."

"Pineapple Falls?" Teag asked with interest looking at the map to see where it was.

"Oh look we've made it to South Beach. Only six more miles left to go," Maddox said showing them the large beach.

"That doesn't look so dangerous," John said seeing nothing different from North Beach.

"Ah, that's because you don't ever see the trouble until it's just upon you, and by that time it's too late. You've got to be the best of the best to make it through one of the attacks of those creatures."

John and Suraionee stared out in the hopes that any second there might be an attack of some kind they could see. Teag studied the map memorizing everything. It was as if it was his only chance to see it all. The map was old but well taken care of, the drawings looked as if they were done in a black calligraphy pen. It almost had the appearance of a pirate map, the kind he saw in the movies. It wasn't anything like the maps back at school.

The time passed quickly. There were so many things to look at and wasn't a moment to sit and twiddle their thumbs. The Great Oak was just over the next bridge. The tree looked like an ordinary oak tree from a distance but the closer they got the bigger the tree became.

"That looks like it swallowed my house," John said, "That's not easy you know, it's two stories high and wide too.

"You haven't seen anythin' yet." Maddox smiled then helped the kids out of the carriage.

Everyone was unloading and looking around for Makoto City that Maddox promised to be amazing.

"What are we doing here? I don't see any city," Sneered Willem Karik

"Be patient Sir, I'm sure you will be more then happy in a moment," Rylee assured him.

Maddox tapped on a knot on the tree and a door that looked like the tree opened up to let them in.

Surprised and excited everyone, ooed and awed. Teag John and Suraionee smiled with anticipation, and were the last to step inside. The others followed close behind, with Ooo's filling the room as they were all taken back with the beauty inside. But oo's and awes were not what Teag had in mind. When he stepped inside he found himself in the Black Wizard Forest standing with John, Suraionee, and Maddox. With his adrenaline pumping he had the sensation that something was hunting them, something evil. He turned himself around in slow circles searching for what ever it was that was watching them, but nothing could be seen.

Every once in a while he could hear twigs snapping and thought he heard someone say, "keep coming, right into my trap, you'll pay for trying to bamboozle me, you fools."

Then like a flash all kinds of Dorgoggin's clomped out from behind the trees surrounding them back to back the four of them stood facing their opponents not knowing how to fight them. Somehow they got away and were now running, the Spitnikers' were spiting bones and the Makotice was spitting venom, just missing him. The sound of clomping had stopped and the voices were gone. Teag felt relieved and stopped to catch his breath. He turned around to face his companions, but no one was there. Shocked and worried for them he frantically searched the trees for any sound, but nothing came. He ran back the direction he had come and came to a clearing where it appeared three bodies were lumped on the ground. Teag slowly sauntered twards them, fear taking over, 'it can't be,' he thought as he realized it was his family. Teag fell to the ground in tears; his heart felt like it was about to burst. There lying on the ground was his sister, brother, and his new friend Maddox, horribly mutilated. They were hardly recognizable. Teags heart couldn't take the pain he felt. 'It's all my fault, I shouldn't have brought them here, I should have protected them,' he thought. Not knowing what to do he threw himself over their dead bodies refusing to go any further. When suddenly a sharp pain hit him, he turned and looked in the direction it had come. His vision was blurry, but he could barely make out ZaBeth standing next to a Spitniker Dorgoggin. Slowly he faded out of consciousness.

Teag sat straight up, sweat glistened his body. He was breathing heavily as though he had been holding his breath. He quickly jumped out of bed and ran to Suraionee's room to check on her. She was lying there peacefully sleeping, and then he ran over to John's room. He also appeared to be fine. Shaking off the horrible feeling that lingered, he went back to his room. The clock next to his bead said it was five am, so he went to take a shower. His heart was still pounding he couldn't shake the unbearable feeling the dream had left him. After his shower he tried to read a book to clear his mind, but the pictures of the dream kept flashing in his mind. He stood up and decided he had to wake up John and Suraionee and talk to them about what had happened in his dream. He wasn't sure if he wanted them to go with him now. He couldn't bare it if they died out there.

After waking them, the three of them gathered in the living room of their hotel room. Suraionee and John had their robes on and were still yawning.

"Why did we have to wake up so early?" Suraionee asked yawning yet again.

"Because we have to discuss, this trip," Teag said.

"Why, we're still going, so what's the problem?" John asked rubbing his eyes.

"That is the problem, I had another dream and this time all three of you died."

"You saw yourself die?" Suraionee straightened up.

"No, I saw you die, you and John, and Maddox, killed by the Dorgoggin's."

"Which one?"

"All of them, besides does it really matter? My dream about the shipwreck came true."

"Yeah but you didn't see anyone die in that dream except yourself and that part didn't come true, you're still alive," John made sure to point out.

"True..." Teag agreed.

"So, that doesn't mean that we will die, it just means that we may have a harder time getting through to Vidors lab," Suraionee said matter-of-factly.

"I don't want you to go!" Teag insisted.

"That wasn't the deal Teag. We all know the dangers, we knew what they were when we decided to go the first time. You need us and we're going," Suraionee said in a motherly tone.

"No your not, I'm calling it off."

"You can't do that!" John argued.

"Call Maddox in here, well talk to him about it," Suraionee insisted.

"Fine," Teag grabbed the rock from his pocket and threw it to the ground. Maddox suddenly appeared, already dressed and reading a book. He was wearing khaki pants and short sleeve shirt with pockets. He almost looked like he was ready to go on a safari hunt, all he was missing was the hard khaki hat.

"Oh, hello, I was going to come and get you in another thirty minutes," he started, but noticing the disgruntled looks on their faces he went right for the problem, "what seems to be the trouble?"

"Maddox, Teag had another dream and says now that we can't go, just because he saw us all killed."

"What is this all about?" Maddox asked looking at Teag.

After explaining his dream to Maddox, Maddox sat for a few moments contemplating the situation. "Tell me about your first dream about the ship," Maddox asked calmly. When Teag described it to him Maddox spoke again. "It appears that your dreams warn you of the danger ahead, but the outcome is not completely written," he said. All three of the kids looked perplexed, "what I mean is, it's a warning that there is trouble, yet each one of us has a choice when that problem comes about, which can either be for good or bad, but history isn't written yet. There is a chance that you can still get through it alive. You did, in your dream about the shipwreck," Maddox said calmly.

"See I told you!" Suraionee snarled.

"We don't need to be fighting like this just before we go. Teag, are you willing to let them choose for themselves?"

"I don't want them to die, it would be all my fault, and then I wouldn't be able to face my mom and dad ever again. I would have a guilty conscience for the rest of my life."

"Would it be you killing them?"

"No, but it might as well be."

"No, that isn't how it works. If you were the one killing them then it would be your fault."

"No, but it would be my fault because I'm letting them go."

"I have news for you, they have freewill, that means that even if you tell them they can't go, they will. They'll just hide somewhere until we're there and then they'll come out and you'll have to just deal with it," Maddox explained.

"Yeah," Suraionee smarted at Teag.

"All I'm saying is that you need to let them choose, and take the consequences of their choices, wither they are good or bad. I don't feel that things will turn out the way you dreamed them. We need to get going though so what is it going to be?"

Teag thought for a few moments, "fine they can come, but if it even starts looking like it's a trap, I'm sending them home. Deal?"

"Deal," Suraionee and John said simultaneously.

The air was cool and crisp when they walked outside bright and early. The sun was just coming up. Suraionee rubbed her eyes as they walked out into the sunshine. Just outside the Great Oak, their Giraffe Carriage awaited to take them to the border of the Black Wizard Forest.

"Maddox, why don't I just call for Nyla and have her take us there?"

"That wouldn't be a good idea, she's too big to walk into the thick trees."

"Well she could just burn them down for us," Teag smiled.

"No, that would just give away your position and you wouldn't have anywhere to hide. It's best to call her when your out of the Black

Wizard Forest," Maddox instructed and then changed the subject. "Now, are you sure you have everything? Canteen, tent, all of your supplies and your food?" Maddox asked one more time.

"Yes, Maddox, it's all in our back packs, besides you act like your not coming with us," Teag teased.

"Well, I am while we go to deal with Vidor Lysander but after that you have to do the rest on your own. I have to report back to ZaBeth," Maddox sadly informed them, "I'm sorry that I can't go with you any further, but you have my pager and you can still call on me anytime you get into too much trouble."

The thought of doing it on their own wasn't sitting well with the Trager kids. But they still had him now so they all decided to think ahead to the task in front of them and then worry about the rest when the time comes to separate. They all climbed up the ladder and sat down in the carriage. They started to move towards the Black Wizard Forest. The ride was smooth and way too short. Before they knew it they were there and it was time to move on. As they were all standing there putting on their backpacks and getting ready to go in, Teag felt eyes on him again. He searched the wilted droopy trees but couldn't find anything.

"Keep your eyes open. It's been a year since I've been here and lets just say the creatures aren't friendly. John, it would be best if you went invisible we don't need any creatures attacking you from behind. This place is hard to find. Suraionee, can you see the door to his Castle?" Maddox asked.

Suraionee searched as far as she could see, "no, not yet, it must be further in."

"Okay, Keep your eyes open," Maddox instructed.

Walking in to the Forest was like walking into a blanket. The trees seemed to close in behind them as if to keep them there. Suraionee scanned the area searching for the door when she suddenly slammed into a tree and fell down.

Everyone ran to her aid, "are you okay," Maddox asked concerned she had hurt something.

"Yeah," she said laughing, "I guess I forgot to watch where I was going too."

"Be more careful next time," Teag said irritated that they had to stop and feeling the eyes getting closer.

'I know you're there, I'm gonna get you, you can't hide, this is my home, you can't hide from me,' A voice in Teag's head softly spoke as if it knew he was coming.

"I think Vidor Knows we're here," Teag warned to the others, "we better get in there fast."

A tree branch broke behind them making them turn around to see who was there. Nothing was seen and the Path seemed clear to run. "Go, go, go now," Maddox whispered. While Maddox was running by their side he fell into a deep hole in the ground.

Teag and Suraionee Stopped to help him.

"No! Keep going, I'll be fine," he yelled back to them. John was still running and moving fast, but because he was invisible no one else knew where he was.

Clop clop, clop clop, the sound of hooves quickly moving from tree to tree began to get closer and somehow Teag knew they didn't have much time to find the door. Though being inside didn't have the promise of safety either. Thoughts of his new dream crept back into his mind. He looked at Suraionee and envisioned her mutalated face staring back at him. He gasped feeling sure the dream was coming true at that very moment. Trying to shake the feeling he concentrated on making sure they weren't being surrounded.

"Teag can you hear who ever it is around us?"

"No, whatever it is isn't thinking anything."

Another branch snapped behind a large round tree to their right. Teag turned around and lifted the tree with his telekinesis, then tossed it aside. Behind it was a creature that looked like a horse, but it had scales all over its body. Its neck was a little longer and it had the head of a huge snake proportionate to its own body. It had two large horns on the top of its head that curved and pointed forward and a long tail with a rattle on the end. It stood there, it's beedy black eyes just glaring at them for a moment. It stood up on its back hooves, spread its ginormous bat wings and hissed while rattling its tail.

"Who are you?" Teag asked in hopes that he could make friends with it.

'My name is Thayne, but I'm not here to make you my friend,' he said back hissing. Knowing what Teag would try to do.

"We don't want to hurt you or invade your space, we just have a few things…"

'I know why you're here, you want my masters magic and inventions.'

"No, we just want to ask him a few questions and we'll be on our way," Teag was worried that Thayne wasn't going to let them through. He and Suraionee started slowly backing up. "What are you?" he asked hoping that the question would distract the strange horse like snake creature.

'I'm a Makotice Dorgoggin," Thayne informed him then noticed them moving away, 'hey! where do you think your going?' He hissed and then started to chase them.

Suraionee and Teag split up to try to confuse him. Teag looked behind him hoping to find Thayne chaseing him but found that he was no where in site. Teags' stomach was suddenly in his throat at the realization his little sister is the one being chased. He flashed back to his dream again and feared that she might get hurt. So he ran searching for their thoughts to lead himself to her.

Suraionee felt his breath on her neck. She quickly dropped to the ground then jumped back up and ran the other way when Thayne jumped over her. He turned around staying fast on her trail. She knew she couldn't out run him and that she would have to try to fight him if she wanted a chance to live. She turned around and faced him as he came at her she turned to the side and kicked her leg out. Missing him, she ran to hide behind a tree. Breathing heavily and scared to death, she peeked around to see where he was but he wasn't there. She backed up against the tree. Her heart was pounding so hard she was shaking with fear.

Thayne came up behind her on the opposite side of where she was looking, leaned in and bit her arm pushing venom into her body. Suraionee screamed so loud, with pain, it echoed through the Forest.

Meanwhile-

John heard suraionee scream and took off towards her. He saw her hide behind a tree. He watched in terror as the snake-horse like creature was about to attack his unknowing sister but before he could do anything to stop it, it bit her. When Thayne released her to get a better grip John became visible then stabbed him in the back hip with a sharp rock, making Thayne hiss and turn his attention to him.

"Uh, oh," John said as he hadn't thought that far in advance and didn't know what to do. He didn't want to go invisible again because the creatures attention would go back to Suraionee, so he started to run. Thayne followed close behind.

Teag heard Suraionee's screams, the fears of his dream coming true erupted through his body, and then he heard John's thoughts. He ran as fast as he could frantic to find him, but instead caught a glimpse of Thayne. Teag used his power to pick up the Makotice Dorgoggin and threw him against a tree. Thayne flopped to the ground then got up shaking himself off and started towards John again. John felt he was far enough away from Suraionee that it would be alright to go invisible so he did. With surprise Thayne searched every direction but couldn't see him but instead found Teag and started towards him.

"You won't win Thayne," Teag prejudged, "John, go see to Suraionee," he commanded suddenly empowered.

Thayne didn't speak but instead spit a great amount of venom at Teag. Teag stopped it in mid air then threw it a side onto the ground. When it came into contact with the ground the living plants that were there shrivelled up and died. The ground sunk in a little, creating a small dip in the earth.

'I see your powers are strong, but you can't defeat me, I've been here for centuries and know every tree and stone on this island.'

"How is that going to protect you? You've never met me before," Teag said confidently as he and Thayne paced in a large circle directly across from each other, never taking their eyes off one another.

'ha ha ha ha, you're nothing but a human, you're the weaker species, magic or not.'

"I'm tired of this conversation," Teag said as he picked Thayne up, his eye glowing a bright blue, and threw him so powerfully that he flew out of the forest and into the ocean miles away, "take that you piece of slime," Teag mocked, as he swiped his hands together like he was wiping off the dirt. He was proud of himself for the accomplishment.

"Are you okay?" John asked Suraionee who was crying.

She was bleeding profusely and needed to get the venom out and a bandage on. John reached into his backpack and pulled out his first aid kit to attended to her wounds. Teag caught up to them hearing their thoughts he knew they were there but he couldn't see them.

"Suraionee? Johnny? Where are you?"

"We're right here what's wrong with you, your looking right at us," Suraionee said irritated because she was hurt and coughing.

"Your invisible."

"I know," John started, "Maddox told me to stay that way remember?"

"Yes, but Suraionee is invisible too?" He said making a statement and asking a question at the same time.

"Cool! If I touch you, you disappear too? Awesome," John said excited to find a new trick. Then remembering the venom, "we have to get her some help now. I don't know how fast his venom takes effect.

"I'm so sorry Sura, I didn't think…"

"I'm fine, Teag, it's just a flesh wound, it'll heal. He just caught me off guard it wont happen again," she said back, trying to be tough.

"I found the entrance not to far from here," John said matter-of-factly while finishing up her bandage. Maybe we can find and antidote in there.

"Can you walk?" Teag asked holding his hand out to help her up.

"He bit my arm not my leg Teag," She said still mad that she let her guard down at all and taking it out on her brothers. She reached up with her good arm and accepted his help up.

They heard another snap behind them. Suraionee looked over but there was nothing there.

"What's going on?" Maddox asked surprising them from behind, "what's the matter with Suraionee's arm?" He reached down holding her arm up as if he could see it better.

"It's a long story but a Makotice Dorgoggin, named Thayne bit her," Teag informed him.

"What? The Makotice Dorgoggin is in here? That's strange, he bit you Suraionee?" Maddox asked with concern.

"Yes," Suraionee said becoming weak and a little loopy.

"Oh no, I didn't plan for this, his kind has never come into this forest before, at least not for the last century…quickly where is that entrance? We don't have much time."

While they walked, and with out hesitation, John told Maddox about the new trick he found.

"This might work to our advantage," Maddox said thinking up a plan to get them inside without being seen.

John lead them to a large rock and told them to watch the door. He threw a rock at it and it rebounded with a jolt of light like there was electricity all over the door. A few moments later the door opened and an old man with long silver hair and a long beard that touched the ground walked out. He was in a long black robe that had a hood, loosely hung around his neck.

"I haven't seen him in a long time, but that is Vidor Lysander," Maddox whispered.

Vidor walked out looking around. A large bird walked out behind him. It was about six feet tall and had feathers on its head that looked like quill pens. It's body seemed small compared to it's long feathers that tightly held to it's sides and a long tail of feathers followed behind it. It had unusually long legs and was mostly white with a little red in color. Vidor pointed and the bird walked out looking around as if it knew what it's orders were.

"That's Vidors Secretary bird, he uses it as his eyes while he stays safely out of reach. Somehow the bird sees things and relays it back to Vidor. I'm not sure how it works but I remember that was what happened last time. The bird told him we were here and then…"

"Shhh, here it comes," Teag whispered with warning.

John had one hand on Suraionee and his other on Teag's back. Maddox put his hand on Johns' shoulder. The secritary bird flew to the rock they were hiding behind. They all slowly got up and walked to the door that Vidor left open. The stork searched the area but couldn't see anything. Quietly the four of them sneaked past the bird and into the open door. They walked down the hall and after a few left and right turns, came to a large opening in the wall. They all jumped when they heard a door slam behind them down the hall.

"The Secretary Bird must be coming back," Maddox warned them, then looked around into the large room in front of them. It was large and had millions of different inventions inside. Stairs lead down into the deep room. At the far end of the room stood a wall of shelves full of bottles of potions and ingredients to make them. Vidor was sitting at a desk next to a large machine, reading a book. The Secretary Bird walked past them and flew down the stairs than stood close to Vidor. It looked as if it was telling him something. Teag heard the bird, but he was confused he thought the bird told Vidor that, *Maddox is here,* but how did he know?

Teag whispered to Maddox, "he knows you're here."

"Good then, I'll just go down and we'll see if I can get him to think about the ingredients for the potion," Maddox stood up and walked down the stairs to talk to Vidor. Almost as soon as he stood up Vidor looked up at him and smiled falsely.

"So good to see you again Maddox," Vidor lied, "I'm glad you came for another visit, I have just the potion for you."

"I'm not here to die Vidor, I just want the potion to turn my sons and me back to normal."

"I'm afraid that is impossible, the ingredients you need you will be unable to get…, and I am not going to give it to you," Vidor slammed the book closed then tossed it on the table in front of him keeping a smile on his face.

'One small crushing rock, two dragon livers, seven drops of Blue Moon Icicle, one ray of sun, and three crystals from the Crystal Cave, and a blade of grass from Dead Mans Pit,' Vidor thought with a smile, 'you'll never get the ingredients because most of the ingredients are the same for the Universitas Dominium Monile.'

Teag once again remembered the story his mother told them on the ship.

'I can't have ZaBeth get a hold of that pendant. The only other items she needs to finish it is the Diamond Shaped Sun and the Four Silver Twinkling Stars. If she gets her hands on those last ingredients the world will be under her control, or maybe it's Maddox that wants the control, I better terminate him quickly,' Vidor's smile faded. His anger began to grow. "You will not see the light of day.""Noooo!" Yelled Teag, "stop Vidor, don't do it," Teag stood up and walked down the stairs.

"Teag, what are you doing?" Maddox questioned upset that he didn't stick with the plan

"Oh, do you know one another?" Vidor asked with a smile pretending to be happy, then quickly changed it to a look of fury, "good, you can die together."

"Wait, I now understand what happened to you. ZaBeth was after your power."

"Teag, you don't know what your doing be quiet," Maddox tried too quiet him.

"No Maddox, he thinks you're the one that wants his power not ZaBeth," Teag tried to explain.

"What do you know of ZaBeth?" Vidor said curiously.

"Teag, stop it now don't you see, he's trying to turn you against her?" Maddox played along when he saw Vidors' curiosity.

"He didn't know I was listening, I got my information from a fresh source. Maddox don't you see? Why did she give me orders to go to Diamond Rock to get the Ray of Sun?"

Vidor's interest grew.

"Why did she tell me to get the Blue Moon Icicle, the Diamond Shaped Sun, the Four Silver Twinkling Stars, the Crushing Rock? The only things she didn't tell me to get was the Blade of Grass from the Dead Mans Pit the Dragons Liver, and three Crystals from Crystal Cave. I'm guessing that, that those ingredient have nothing to do with the Universitas Dominium Monile."

Vidor's eyes were large, "How did you know of those ingredients and of the, the Monile?" There was a short pause, "I didn't say it out loud. I didn't, how could you know of such things?" He was confused and frustrated.

"Vidor, I know there is some good in you, I know that you were forced out by ZaBeth. She was trying to get your powers, she planned the whole thing and now she is trying to use me to get her the ultimate power. I won't let her do it. Join us and we will help you and get rid of her."

"Teag Trager! You don't know all of this for a fact. Look at what Vidor made me. Do you think that he did that because he was good?" Maddox pretended to be angry.

"Maddox, You're a good man, I know that you can see this. Vidor was scared, he didn't know who was trying to get his powers, just that it was someone close to him. I believe that we can trust him and that ZaBeth is the one that is trying to fool us all. Please trust me."

John rushed down the steps, "can we hurry this up? Suraionee is in a lot of pain and needs medical attention now."

"Oh I forgot," Teag, rushed over to Vidor, "please, she's been bitten by Thayne, she needs the antidote or she'll die."

"Thayne? Who's Thayne?" Without taking a second to listen for an answer he went on, "Anyway, I don't care, another stupid human dead, all of you are worthless. You think that you can just waltz in here pretend that you know everything about me, get what you want and disappear? I think not," Vidor turned his back on Teag, facing the stonewall several feet away.

"Please, for once in your life, trust someone. We wont take your magic, or your inventions. We'll make sure that she never gets the Monile."

Vidor was struggling with himself, he hated humans and wanted them dead, yet knowing that somewhere out there was the original Monile, and someday she might end up getting her hands on it. He wanted to put a stop to it at once, "What is your name boy?"

"Teag."

Vidor was shocked at Teags trust, "your name is Teag, huh? I don't know you and you don't know me from anyone and you would put your trust in me? You would, believe that I wouldn't harm you? Why?"

"Because, If we don't then who will? My parents told us that '*if we don't stand up for what we believe in, our opportunities, freedoms, even our choices, our very lives might get taken away from us. We may not get another chance.*' And like you said Vidor, if she gets her hands on that pendant she will rule it all."

"I said that out loud?"

"Well maybe not, but I heard it anyway," Teag said with a smile.

"I do find it strange that she told me all the ingredients before we left here, if she knew the entire time why did she send us to come here to Vidor?" Teag commented something told him that she didn't really want Maddox to come back.

"Okay," Maddox agreed, "so Vidor, What do we need to do?"

"No I wont help you. If you get those ingredients then you will all betray me...no, I won't help."

"I will," came a voice from behind them.

When they all turned around, Vidor recognized him right away, "Melanion!" he hoarsely yelped.

Teag, John, and Suraionee looked at him closer and realized it was, "Grandpa?" they all repeated together.

"Yes, I know, you buried me, or at least you thought you buried me. I've come to help you," Melanion informed them.

"So that is how you had powers before the Keno Tea, Melanion is your Great Grandfather," Maddox chuckled, "it's all starting to make sense now. That is also how you entered the lost room, your blood," Maddox was putting some of the puzzle pieces together.

"What do you mean blood?" Suraionee and John asked together.

"The only way that you could have gotten into the lost room inside Dead Mans Pit was if you had the same blood as the royal family," Maddox replied.

"LoRock told me about that, he said I had Desdemona's blood if I could enter, but how is that possible?" Teag asked wanting more information.

"Because I am her uncle," Melanion informed him.

"I can't believe it, all this time we've been related to the devil herself?"

"Yes, and no, I prefer to think of it as related to Queen Alura and...," Melanion trailed off as if he was still hiding something, "Anyhow, there are other things we need to discuss right now," he became serious and changed his tone, "there is an evil force that you can't fight alone, even with your powers. You need the Monile to defeat it."

"Melanion, in the wrong hands it will do horrible things..." Maddox noted.

"But without it all will be lost. The Monile in the right hands can be an amazing tool for good. Maddox you have a choice, you can turn back to a human if you wish, but the strength and powers you have now will be gone. Vidor has a potion already prepared that will allow you to choose when you want to be the lion man or when you want to be human. If you wish I will give it to you. That way, should you need your strength again, you can call upon it."

"I've been questioning it for the past few days, why ZaBeth wants them gone so bad, what's in it for her, so, yes, that sounds wonderful."

"No Melanion, you can't just show up after centuries and give away my things!" Demanded Vidor

"Might I remind you that I am not out of practice of magic? All it will take is a flick of my finger to..." Melanion looked at his grandchildren and then back at Vidor, "well, anyway, you know what I can do," He warned seriously.

"Oh, Melanion the Great has returned, so now all must bow to him, Aye? I don't bow to anyone anymore, I created my own kingdom where I rule. These infidels will rue the day that they trespassed in my kingdom."Vidor pointed to Maddox and the children.

"Vidor, you've gone mad, I think you've spent a little too much time in this forest alone. I've had enough, give them the potion for little Sura, *now!*" Melanion yelled with such force that the walls seemed to tremble.

Vidor shook, it was evident that he was scared, but he stood his ground believing that he was not crazy and that he could overtake Melanion. He looked him in the eyes. "Vosha…" he started speaking. Melanion shook his head and before Vidor could finish what he was saying Melanion waved his hand in a large circle and Vidor disappeared.

"Where did he go?" John asked in surprise.

"Oh, he's still here, he's just in between worlds where he can't cast spells or hurt anyone."

"But if you could do that before, when the whole problem started with Desdemona why didn't you? Any why didn't you use it on her?"

"Because it isn't right to take away one's free will and choice."

"So then why did you do it this time?" Teag asked confused.

"Because he was about to kill us all, and we have a task to do," Melanion explained.

"Help me," Suraionee whispered. She had managed to drag herself down the steps to where everyone was standing and after speaking, collapsed.

Hearing her faint cry for help Melanion turned around. He had forgotten about her in all the commotion and was angry with himself for it. Bring me the Makotee Serum, it's the bottle on the fourth shelf from the bottom, five rows over from the right. It's a red potion in a bottle the shape of an apple. Hurry quickly, there isn't much time left, I hope it isn't too late," he got down on his knees and lifted her head up. Her lifeless body dangled about. Putting his hand over the bite the holes in her arm, her skin healed up but she remained unconscious. Teag found the apple red bottle of potion and handed it to Melanion. Without hesitation he opened it and poured the potion into her mouth. Suraionee had stopped breathing.

"No! No! You're not finished here yet, it isn't your time, fight it!" Melanion cried emotionally.

Teag for the first time in months, had someone else there to take the burden, yet his heart felt all the burden in the world. Again it was his fault. He knelt down by his sister and placed his hands on her cheeks. He tried to feel a pulse on her neck, but there was nothing. His sweet sister was dead.

Tears rolled down his face and dropped onto the hard stone ground. "Suraionee, we talked about this remember," he said sweetly wiping her hair out of her face, "you said you wouldn't die, you said...you would, you would..., make the choice, it was a choice remember?" He pleaded in agony. John stood over his shoulder crying. Then pleaded more, "please!" Teags eyes grew red and puffy with tears. His hands suddenly began to glow red against her face, frightened he was hurting her he pulled them away.

"No! Put them back," Melanion instructed amazed at what he was seeing.

Immediately obeying, Teag put his hands back on her face and the red glow came back. "What's happening?" Teag asked worried.

"I don't know but it looks like it's helping, look," Melanion pointed to her chest rising and falling.

"She's breathing!" John cried with joy.

Everyone watched her with anticipation. The red glow stopped and Teag pulled his hands away. Suraionee's eyes slowly opened as she smiled at everyone.

"What's going on? What happened," she asked airily.

"You don't want to know," Teag said wiping the new tears of joy off his face and then hugged her. John knelt down and hugged both Teag and Suraionee. Melanion held his hand out for Suraionee's. She took it and he helped her stand up, giving her a big hug once she was on her feet.

Melanion walked over and took another potion from one of the shelves. It was a small glass vial with a purple potion inside. Melanion handed it to Maddox along with two others. "Take this and give one to your son's, with this, you'll be able to choose who you want to be, when you need to be it."

"It's not going to change me back to a Lion at the full moon is it?" Maddox asked teasing.

"No," Melanion smiled, "but you have more powers then you know, find the powers and you'll know why ZaBeth wanted you changed back."

"What? No hint of what they might be?"

"No, I haven't the foggiest," Melanion smiled back. Then looking at the kids, "now ZaBeth is after the Universitas Dominium Monile is she? What happened to the necklace your mother gave you?" Melanion asked Suraionee.

Suraionee looked down in shame, "I lost it in the ocean."

"I have one, I found it in the Lost Room," Teag informed them.

"You found the lost room?" Maddox questioned in awe, "Why didn't you tell me?"

"I don't know?" Teag honestly answered, "Anyway, I found one in there, it is exactly the same as the one Mom gave Sura," Teag remembered.

"I wondered where that came from. Sarah came across it and destroyed it. In the hands of Desdemona it would have been, horrible, just horrible."

"What? So she just went through my things?" Teag asked a little irritated.

"No actually, I don't know how she came across it, she just did, she asked me if I went and retrieved it from the lost room and I assured her I hadn't been there for over a Century," Maddox defended.

"Great now what?" Teag said frustrated about the whole thing.

Melanion breathed in deep and then sat in thought for a moment, "I'm afraid then that you must make the journey to get the ingredients to make the Monile."

"Why? Can't we just defeat her without it, I mean if all of us gang up on her with all of our powers together...," Teag asked.

"No, you see, ZaBeth has more power than she is letting on. That is why I left so many years ago, I just knew something wasn't right but I had no proof, especially since she was being so kind and generous to everyone in the kingdom. Somehow I knew that if I didn't leave, she, or someone would use me, maybe even turn me into something against my will."

"How is that possible?" Maddox asked, "you're a powerful wizard."

"There are potions and spells that will transfer magical powers to another, they can even use them to change your personalities and sometimes even desires. Such use is against the law, but to someone in a high position like Queen ZaBeth, or even to someone like Desdemona, using them to hurt and get what they want can be second nature."

After a few minutes of quiet John spoke up, "we'll let's go get them," John said as he started walking out the door, Teag and

Suraionee nodded and then started to walk out after him. When John turned around and noticed that Melanion wasn't moving John asked with great concern, "Grandpa Great, aren't you coming with us?"

"No, I'm afraid I can't. I have a few other things I need to attend to. Please take care of each other and don't forget to use your resources," he walked up to them and gave each of them a hug. After he hugged Suraionee he looked at her arm. "Oh, much better, good bye kids and Maddox, be careful," he smiled at them all and then wistfully disappeared up the stairs and out of sight.

Once outside, Teag pulled out the map he found in Dead Man's Pit, and searched for Diamond Rock. He pointed at the map, "We're about here in the Black Wizard Forest," then moving his finger up the map a little further North, he said, "Diamond Rock is North East from here, it looks like about two miles," he pulled out his compass and looked at it and then pointed in the right direction, "so we need to go that way," he directed. The four of them started walking deeper into the Black Wizard Forest forgetting that Maddox had to get back to the castle. The trees were still gloomy. They walked through the thick drooping shadowy trees. The longer they were there the more gloomy they started to feel, like despair was setting in.

"I'm thirsty," Suraionee complained.

"So pull your canteen out of your backpack and get yourself a drink," John remarked back to her. She stopped and unzipped her large green backpack and pulled out the canteen full of water. When she tried to open it, she found it was hard to twist.

Teag noticed that she was struggling and said, "here let me help you," he held out his hand waiting for her to hand it to him, but she managed to get it and twisted it off. She tilted it to her lips, unexpectedly she lost her grip and dropped it on the ground spilling it all before she could pick it back up.

"Gosh darn it," she said in anger leaning over to pick it up, and then dusted off the dirt that accumulated on the mouth piece. "I spilled it all over," she said in frustration.

"Well find a watering hole and you can refill it," Teag said as he motioned her to keep walking.

To their left was a strange alligator like Dragon. Its body was long and legs short to the ground like an alligator. The scales all over its body were black with splashes of dark green so it could blend into the background. Its nose was long and teeth were sharp. It had long spiky horns all over its head starting just a little further back from the eyes. The spikes continued in a straight line all the way down it's spine getting smaller the closer it go to the end of the tail. They all stopped and watched as it blew fire at a large rabbit and then to make sure it was dead it scooped it into it's teeth, then a with a slice sound, the teeth grew, shooting through the large rabbit and out the other side then shrinking back to normal again so it could eat it. They all moved a little faster while the creature was eating.

A little later they saw a spitting Turtle. It was large and its colorings helped it to blend into the nearby rocks and shrubbery, it behaved differently. The turtle had sharp teeth and spit a thick tar like venom at its prey to blind them. It also had great speed, not normal to a regular turtle. The group saw more strange creatures the deeper they went through the forest.

The droopy dead trees were getting thinner and the light was starting to shine through. Maddox Stopped, "wait," he said, "I forgot, I need to go back to ZaBeth or she might become suspicious."

"But you can't, she'll kill you. You can't go," John started pleading.

"Listen, I can take care of myself, I'll tell her your on your mission and act like nothing is wrong, it'll be alright, you'll see," Maddox then took off running on all fours. They watched him until he disappeared into the thick trees.

They continued walking. Suraionee started whining again, "I'm tired can we just rest here for a few minutes?" She found a large rock to sit on and didn't care if they said 'yes' or 'no'. The sounds of a babbling brook were all around them, "where's that sound coming from?" She asked standing up and looking around. She peaked behind her rock and found a creek hidden behind the rock and hidden by bushes and trees. She leaned over to fill her canteen, but the closer she got to it the darker the water appeared. She stuck her hand in it and pulled it out. The water was black and slimy like oil. "Aargh, Eew!" She yelled as she tried to wipe her hand off on the ugly trees and bushes around her.

"What's wrong?" Teag asked a little worried about the tone in her voice as he ran up to her. She held out her hand and showed him the oil, "oh is that all? It's just oil."

"In the creek? That's gross!"

"Where's it coming from?" John asked trying to see which way the water was flowing.

"Vidor's Laboratory I would imagine. That would explain why the trees and so droopy here," Teag commented, "common, we still have a long way to go. He took one more swig of his canteen of water and then closed the lid tightly, wrapping the strap over his shoulder and neck so it would stay on. Then he started trekking through the trees again. Time seemed to go on forever. They didn't think they were ever going to make it to the end of the forest. He could smell reptiles and oil, 'a bad combination' he thought. Wanting to get out of there quickly he picked up the pace. John and Suraionee tried to keep up.

"Slow down, Teag, your going too fast."

"Sura, you're the one who wanted to come along, we need to get this done and I really don't want to be here longer than we have too, so can you just try to stop complaining just a little?"

"Sure, you know I only just got the poison out of my body, but, yeah, sure whatever makes life easier for you," She said manipulatively.

"That's it, Sura, when we get out of this forest I'm calling Nyla and she is going to take you home."

"No, I want to stay."

"Then stop acting like that, I'm not going to sit here and listen to you whine the whole trip."

"I'm sorry, I just wanted you to slow down just a little."

Teag took a deep breath, "fine, but keep up please," they took a few more steps and saw a little more light peaking through the trees. "I think that's the end just ahead," Teag said running towards it. The closer he got, the more light the trees let through, and the fresher the air smelt. "Hurry," he called to them, "I see the edge of the forest."

John and Suraionee caught up and were smiling, "we made it," she said, then looking at her brother Teag, smiled and said, "Good thing you stopped complaining, I was about to send you home," she laughed teasing. Teag grinned and shook his head, in a high-pitched voice he mimicked her "can't we just stop for a minute? I'm so tired," he laughed.

"That doesn't sound anything like me."

"Good, because if it did, I'd really start to worry," Teag laughed some more.

There at the edge of the Black Wizard Forest was a small round field. At the edge of the field was a straight drop down half way around. The only way out was back through the Forest. In the middle of the Field was a giant white shimmering Diamond.

"Holy Shmakers! That's Huge. Its got to be about fifty feet tall," John commented.

"Yeah and about, uh eighty feet wide," Teag said enjoying it's glittering beauty.

"Diamond Rock! Mom would have loved this," Suraionee remarked, "lets get closer."

Upon examining it a little closer, Teag could see one of the Sun's rays penetrating the top of the Diamond. "She said somewhere inside is the Sun Shaped Diamond. There has got to be an entrance here somewhere," he said feeling along the lower side of the large diamond. Suraionee joined him in searching for something that would open a secret door. All the way around the Diamond and still, nothing was to be found. John saw a stick on the ground and tried to pick it up. When he lifted it, a door in the ground next to the Diamond opened up. It had a twisty staircase that lead down. The hallways were a thick red brick.

"Lets go," Teag said leading the way. When he got to the bottom and stepped on the ground floor, a fire lit the way on torches that were attached to the walls on both sides of them. As they inched their way down the narrow hall, each torch they passed lit up until there was nowhere left to go. Teag reached up and pulled the last burning torch out so that he could look around for a hidden room. When he pulled it out, the wall at the end slowly slid opened. Heavy scratching sounds filled the narrow hallway as the door grinded open. When it stopped moving they walked in carefully taking each step. Teag touched his fiery torch on the unlit torch that was placed just inside the medium sized room on the wall. As he did, the whole room unexpectedly lit up. The room was empty. The walls were a thick round gray stone. Around the middle of the wall all the way around the room about every fourth stone was a protruding stone. It appeared to be someone's design. There were five stones on the right and left sides of the wall from the door. On the same wall as the door and the wall opposite, were only three protruding stones on each wall.

"Why is the room empty? Something had to be here," Suraionee asked inquisitively.

"I don't know. I've never been here before," Teag said sarcastically. On the wall to their right just after they entered the room, John leaned on the second protruding stone from the left.

The stone he was leaning on slowly moved inside the wall, "Uh, oh..." John said as he noticed it move.

"What did you do?" Teag yelled, "hurry we gotta get outta here," he exclaimed as he grabbed their arms and started to drag them out. "Who knows what kind of booby trap you just set off," before they left the room the ground started rumbling as the back wall moved aside and slowly disappeared into the other walls, revealing another hallway with a bright light that shone at the other end. They stopped to look at the bright light that seemed to call to them. Almost in a trance the Trager's slowly walked towards the light. At the edge of the doorway they saw that the sun rays were shining down through the top of the diamond and passed though then out through the bottom of it and into a large pool of what looked like a glowing orangey/ yellow kind of liquid.

"Its gotta be hot," Suraionee said.

Teag pulled out the large potion bottle, ZaBeth had given him, and then leaned in to scoop up a bottle full, being careful not to touch it. "It doesn't feel hot putting my hand next to it."

There was a sound behind them. When they turned to look they found a tiny little woman who stood about three feet tall. Her skin was like human skin but her hair glowed and appeared to be on fire. "Oh, hello there," she said, startled to see anyone, "we usually don't get humans down here."

"We? There are more of you down here?" John asked.

"Oh yes, but we like to call it up here," She stated.

"Your nice then?" Suraionee asked.

"Of course, we would never hurt a fly,unless they attack us and then it would be like, Attack!" She yelled catching the Trager's off guard, "and then of course we would go after it and make sure..." she stopped her dramatic monologue and glanced back at them realizing she was babbling, "sorry, I do that sometimes," she smiled.

"What are you?" John asked.

"Oh, please excuse my bad manners, I'm Suri, of the Sun People."

"Cool!" John exclaimed.

"I'm Teag, this is Suraionee, and that there crazy one is John," Teag pointed over to him, "I have a question."

"Sure," she said interested in what he had to ask.

"Can you tell us where to find the sun shaped diamond?" Teag asked hoping she would cooperate.

"Well there are millions of them at the bottom of the Sun Bath. That is where they're safe from anyone but us," she said.

Teag started towards it like he was about to climb in.

"Oh, *no, please*, don't go in it, it'll burn you," She pleaded.

"But I need that diamond to save my parents and it isn't hot, I'll be okay."

"Oh, Please, that may be a good reason to take it, but let me do it for you," she stepped into the liquid sun and waded in it for a moment. "You'll burn if you touch it." Then she dived under. The liquid was so thick it rippled when she dived in but didn't splash. When she came back up she had the sun diamond in her hand. She stepped out and dried it off with a towel that was hanging on the wall. Singeing it and leaving a burnt smell in the room. When she left the towel and walked over to give it to Teag, everyone looked at the towel she left hanging on the wall. It was singed all over. She looked over to what they were looking and then looked back at Teag and then tried to hand it to him again, but he was too afraid to touch it now.

"Go on now, here it is, you want it don't you?" She asked.

"Yes, but I don't want my hand burned off," he said, not sure he wanted to touch the stone or her.

"It isn't hot anymore. Go on and take it," Suri tried to hand it to him a third time. Teag apprehensively reached out to touch it, being careful not to touch her because 'she must be hot,' he thought. Suri touched his arm and made Teag jump and scream like a girl for a second, "see I'm not hot either," she said laughing. We are Sun People, but we aren't hot to touch. My hair isn't hot either, here put your hand in it," Teag then put the glowing diamond in a special pouch and placed it carefully in his back pack. Then he put his hand in her fire like hair and was excited when it wasn't hot. John and Suraionee then wanted a try.

"Oh forgive my manners, would you like to come in eat and meet some of my friends? They would just love to meet you."

"Well?" Teag started apprehensively knowing they needed to move on.

"Please Teag? We'll just be a few minutes," John begged.

Teag looked over a Suraionee who was clasping her hands together like she was pleading, and she was jumping up and down, nodding her head, with a big smile on her face.

"Okay, but only for a few minutes."

"Great follow me," Suri smiled and waddled out the way they came in. She made her way back into the medium sized room with the protruding stones and pushed one of the stones in the middle of the wall. And one of the small walls began to open up, heavily grinding stone against stone. Teag felt all turned around, "how can you tell which one is which? I mean you could have just as well pushed that stone on the other side and opened up a worm hole that would take you to the Milky Way in space."

"Oh no, that could never happen, the stone that does that is over there," she pointed to a short wall across the room.

Teag laughed, "I was joking, but you really do have a stone button for that, that's very interesting, I'll have to remember that for later," he smiled as he gave a weirded out look to John and Suraionee.

"Oh? Why is that? Do you have friends there?" Suri asked thinking he was serious.

"Uh, no," Teag wanted to bust out laughing because she wasn't getting that he was joking and kept it going, "I've never been there, I just thought that I might need to send a few people there?" 'To get rid of them,' he thought. Teag couldn't believe what he was saying, talking like there are people that live on the Milky Way. He was trying not to offend Suri, because he could see she was serious about every word she was saying.

"Oh that would be nice," she said, "it's a beautiful place, you should go there some time."

"I will," Teag nodded, really thinking it would never happen.

When the door opened all the way they stared into space, before them were several big and little stars brightly lighting the way, but the largest light came from the massive sun that sat a little far off from the right side of the doorway. They could feel the heat coming from it. directly in front of them was a purple pathway that appeared to be like some kind of brick. The pathway was about four feet wide and wound its way around toward the sun.

"Come with me," she said as she started down the path.

Suraionee panicked, "Um, I can't go, I'll fall, and it's too hot, we'll all burn up."

Suri turned around and looked at her, "don't be silly sweetie, there is plenty of room for you to walk along the path and we've had other people here before, and they didn't burn up," She smiled then walked up to Suraionee and took her hand, "see I'll show you," she started walking down the path with frightened Suraionee by her side. Teag looked at John and then walked over to the edge of the pathway and looked over the side. All he could see was space but every part of him was saying it was a dangerous trip. He looked back at the group and noticed they were disappearing in the light of the hot sun so he rushed to catch up with them. The pathway looked like a layered brick type of material but it was smooth and slick. He caught up to them but slowing down was a bit harder. He slipped and glided down the pathway at a high speed and was headed right for the edge. Beginning to panic as he got closer to the edge of the pathway, on his stomach he slid backwards trying to grab at the slick floor for something to hold on too. Then just as he was about to slide off, 'BAM' he smacked right into an invisible wall and crumbled up, relieved as he came to a halt. Right in front of him through the invisible wall was the sun. It was so big and bright he couldn't look directly at it.

"See Suraionee, that's why you wouldn't fall off the side."

Suraionee laughed at Teag, and then asked, "why didn't you just tell us about that?"

"Where would the fun be if I told you it was completely safe, that would have ruined the effect."

Suraionee and John laughed and giggled, "yeah, it would have been a shame if we wouldn't have gotten the chance to see Teag smack into the wall. That really would have ruined the effect for me," John laughed uncontrollably. Teag took it well, and laughed at himself.

"Is that protecting us from the heat of the sun too?" John asked.

"Yes sir," Suri smiled, "this way," she lead them around the corner of the sun and there was a door it was black and looked like some kind of metal. Flames from the sun were all around them, but all they felt was uncomfortably warm, they weren't burning up, though they couldn't stand there too much longer. The air smelt like gas and was a little over powering. Suri opened the door and walked in, followed by the kids.

Shimmering lights sparkled all around them. They stood in the middle of the street looking at a large diamond city, with skyscrapers and cars that glittered sending chills down their spines. Purple's, blues, yellows, and orange's painted in the sky giving the look of sunset. The temperature was just right for them and the air inside smelled like fruit. All the Sun People were moving about like business as usual. It reminded Teag of being back in Washington. It looked like a city of little people, only all of them had flaming hair.

"Is it almost night time here?" John asked noticing the colors of the sky.

"Oh no, we don't have a sun so to us the day is always like a sunset, and the night is just black. Sometimes when it's dark, we can see the stars through the walls of the sun, but that doesn't happen all the time," she smiled, "come, come, this way," she led them across the street to a small diner. The sign above the door said, Bistro's, Diner, when they walked in they smelled apple pie, and chicken with mashed potatoes and gravy. Their mouths watered as then were led to a booth not too far from the door. A tiny man approached wearing an apron and a name tag that said Bistro.

"What can I get for you?" He asked smiling. Suraionee couldn't take her eyes off his flaming hair. Everyone in the diner had flaming hair. It was so neat to all of them that they just sat there and stared.

"You're new around here. Let me guess, today is the first time you met a Sun Person," He said knowing the look. The three of them nodded their heads.

"Bistro, this is Teag, John and Suraionee, Kids, this is Bistro."

"Hello," Bistro said as the kids stared in awe, "let me give you a little hint for surviving around here, no one likes to be stared at," he said, playing with them, yet being serious at the same time.

The kids nodded, "sorry, sir, you, just look, well..." Teag started.

"You're the bomb!" John laughed thinking they were the neatest people ever.

Teag laughed, "yeah you're the coolest people we've ever met."

Their comments made the little man smile, "oh well in that case, dinner's on me."

"Sweet!" John said licking his lips.

"So, what will it be," Bistro asked.

"Um, I think we'll all have your fried chicken, mashed potatoes and gravy, with a slice of apple pie," Teag smiled as his mouth was watering.

"And what to drink?"

"Do you have sprite?" Suraionee asked.

"Sure," Bistro smiled at the kids.

"Greatest day ever!" John kept smiling.

"Anything for you Suri?"

"Oh no thanks, I ate an hour ago, I'm just here with the kids."

Bistro nodded to her then walked away to place the order.

Suri smiled at the kids. All three of them were mesmerized with the beautiful shiny city. It was like being in a diamond palace. It was so colorful, buildings and cars were clear like diamonds, but the sparkles splashed random spurts of colors, in every direction.

The traffic looked like New York City the way the people rushed around walking along the streets and hailing taxicabs.

Before they knew it, the delicious food was placed before them. They looked at the wonderful food that sat in front of them and then started stuffing their faces almost like they were racing to the finish. Suri was pleased with their, sound effects as they ate. Bistro was wiping down the counters and listening with a huge smile on his face.

When they were done eating Teag and John started playing with Suri's hair again.

"Sorry, I wanted you to meet some of my other friends, but they must have had other things to do they're usually here, you met Bistro though," she smiled.

"We have to go to the Polar Hawk Mountains and into the Golden Turtle Lagoon, so we better get going," Suraionee reminded her brothers.

"Oooh? Your traveling are you? Come, Come, I'll walk you back," she stood up and started out the door.

"Bye Bistro, it was delicious, thanks!! Teag said waving at the little man.

"Bye, thanks," Suraionee smiled as she walked out the door behind Teag.

"Bye, thanks," John said as he walked out behind Suraionee.

When they got back to the empty room they hugged Suri and thanked her for everything then they started back down the hallway that led to the twisty staircase.

Suri suddenly remembered something, "wait a minute, I have something I want you to take," the three of them looked at each other wondering what it could be. Suri disappeared through the door but then came back again holding three squirt guns. "These will protect you," she said, "they're filled with Liquid Sun Rays so be careful with it. A little goes a long way. Spray it at your enemies and they will leave you alone. But be careful not to spray one another or you'll either end up with a third degree burn or you'll become a crispy critter," she warned. Then after drying off the outside of the squirt guns she handed them over.

"Thanks Suri, you're the best," Suraionee said thinking they just got the coolest weapon in the world.

"Your welcome, be careful out there, I do hope you come and see me again soon," she said smiling and getting louder the more she said so the kids could hear her as they walked away down the hall. They waved back at her.

Once outside they wondered how they were going to get to the Polar Hawk Mountains and the Golden Turtle Lagoon. There were miles that needed to be covered and they were already getting a little tired. Teag opened his backpack and sat on the ground rifling through it. He pulled out the map. When he opened it up, he tried to calculate the miles in his head. Knowing it was too many to travel in even five days walking he thought about calling for help. He folded his arms and started meditating.

"What's he doing?" Suraionee asked John.

"I don't know, I've never seen him do that before."

Teag started floating in the air keeping his legs crossed and arms folded, then he gently set himself back on the ground and opened his eyes, "It's done."

"What's done Teag," John wondered.

"I called Nyla for help."

"The Dragon? Sweet. But what can she do for us?" John asked.

"Well, she can fly us there for one, and it will take us less than a half an hour to get there,"Teag answered. Moments later Nyla appeared just over the trees of the Black Wizard Forest. The air swishing loudly beneath her wings

'Hello there Teag, it's good to see you again,' she said as she slowly landed.

"I was wondering if you could give us a ride to the Polar Hawk Mountains?"

'Sure, but let me call Blaze and Moya to come help…, cover your ears,' Nyla warned him.

"Cover your ears," Teag warned John and Suraionee because they couldn't hear what she was saying. The two of them looked at each other and were confused but followed directions.

A sudden Loud almost sonic boom came out of Nyla's mouth and within a few short minutes they were softly landing and talking to their mother. The two baby dragons were now the same size as Nyla.

"Okay guys, get on," Teag instructed while he climbed on Nyla and sat at the base of her neck. John climbed on Blaze, and Suraionee climbed on Moya, "Where is Alaura?" Teag asked.

'She went to keep watch, she'll join us later,' Nyla said as she started flapping her wings and took off. Blaze and Moya followed close behind her.

The wind flipped through Teags' hair and clothing as he soared through the sky. The wind lightly gliding across his body. It was an amazingly free feeling to be flying through the heavens. Over the Black Wizard Forest, they seemed to be free from the creatures below. A worried feeling began to grow in his gut. He felt secure and sure that as long as they were with the dragons they were safe yet something kept nagging at him. Teag got the feeling again only this time, that something was watching them, then following them. But suddenly Alaura flew along side of him and Nyla,

'Mother, a Makotice Dorgoggin has been watching you,' Alaura warned her mother through her thoughts.

Alarmed Nyla looked behind her seeing nothing there, 'Get into the grass and stay hidden, your not strong enough to fight the Dorgoggin.'

'But mother, you will be killed if you face him.'

'If I don't we'll all be killed,' Nyla said as she checked behind her again.

'Mother we want to help fight him with you, together we are stronger than one alone,' Moya said concerned for her mother.

"No! I couldn't live with myself if any of you including the children were harmed or killed. No! The answer is no!" She roared. Then forgetting about Teag on her back she instructed, 'Now all of you get down in the grass and hide,' Nyla was so at this point so concerned about getting her children and the Trager kids safe that she wasn't watching her surroundings.

Again Teag felt like something was following them. He turned around and saw Thayne, the Makotice Dorgoggin, chasing them and catching up quickly. "Hurry Nyla, it's a Dorgoggin, he's coming up fast," Teag warned.

'Now! Hurry, there's no time to argue about it, go Hide!' Nyla yelled as they zoomed through the air. Hot on her tail the Makotice spit venom at her, but her quick reflexes and zig zagging moves kept him just short of hitting her and Teag. In and out, up and down faster and faster they went, and Teag started to become sick to his stomach as he tried to hold on.

Blaze and Moya had disappeared into the grass below, Teag was relieved that they were out of the way and that at least they wouldn't get hurt.

Teag tried to grab a hold of the Dorgoggin and throw him, but this time he couldn't hear his thoughts and he couldn't take hold of him. He was powerless. 'how is he suddenly able to do that, what changed?' He thought. He took out the squirt gun and tried to spray it at the Makotice, but missed. A quick unexpected turn made him loose his grip and he dropped it. He watched his only defense fall into the Golden Turtle Lagoon.

"Darn it!" He yelled mad at himself.

'I have to drop you,' She cautioned Teag.

Teag looked down, they were miles high in the sky but was still more concerned for her safety, "How are you going to get away?"

'Don't you worry about me, I'm a tough old girl, besides I'll move much faster if I don't have to worry about losing you,' she said with concern in her voice, 'don't worry, you wont hit the ground,' she said as she dropped him. And quickly flew the other direction so as to keep the Dorgoggin from seeing him vulnerable. Nyla continued to dodge the Makotice's advances and took him as far away from the rest of them as she could.

* * *

Teag was free falling. His stomach was in his throat once again. Panic erupted through his whole body. A feeling he was starting to get used too happening these past few months. Not knowing how he he was going to stop before he hit the bottom, scared him. his arms and legs were flaling in the fast air, there was nothing to grab onto and his speed seemed to get faster and faster as the earth was getting closer. Closing his eyes he knew he had to stop himself somehow but nothing was coming to him. All he could think about, was the ground he was about to slam into, and how much it will hurt. 'I'm gonna die, I'm gonna die,' He thought as he started to give up hope.

'Think Teag, if you can float in the air when you meditated, maybe you can use it now to stop yourself,' A panicked voiced from above called out to him.

'Oh, okay,' With the ground growing closer he was seconds away from pounding into it, he closed his eyes and thought as hard as he could. His mind felt like it would melt. His heart felt like it was about to stop or even pop out of his chest. Sharp pains filled his entire body, and then suddenly they stopped. He opened his eyes and he found himself hovering over the ground just two feet from blaze and John hiding in the tall orange grass.

"WOW!" John exclaimed, "how are you doing that?"

"I don't know, Nyla told me I wouldn't hit the ground, and I guess I figured if I could hover when I meditate, why not stop myself from falling."Teag reasoned as he floated to the ground.

"Maybe you can fly too," John said excitedly.

"No, I doubt it," Teag said a little distracted as he tried to look out and see how Nyla was doing, "Moya," Teag called changing the subject, "can you see Nyla?"

Moya peeked her head over the tall orange grass and looked around.,'no I don't see her.'

"Can I come see?" he asked.

'Sure climb on,' she laid her head down on the ground and allowed Teag to climb on. She then lifted him just enough so he could peek out of the grass without being seen.

Searching the skies he became worried, when something just a few feet above his head whizzed past in an awful hurry, and as quickly as

200

the first flashed by another right on her tail. "He's too close!" Teag yelled. Alaura and Blaze lifted their heads so they could both see. Nyla was getting tired, and it was evident by the way she wasn't moving as fast as before.

'I'm going to help,' Blaze said.

'No! Mother said No Blaze, stay here,' Alaura demanded.

'I can't just let her die, I have to help, you stay here.'

Teag knew he should try to stop him, but he didn't want Nyla to die so he let Blaze go. He caught up quickly and was right on the Makotice's tail. Nyla made a quick turn around just missing the Dorgoggin by inches. She saw Blaze behind the Makotice knowing he was trying to help. A shot of adrenaline boost her tired body into overdrive. 'What are you doing? I told you to stay hidden, He'll kill you! Go back *now!*' She roared at blaze.

'No, you need help!' He said weaving in and out following the Makotice Dorgoggin and feeling very confident that he could put an end to it.

'Blaze if you don't go back and hide so help me I'll...'

'What? You'll what? If I don't you'll be dead, and if I stay, I can handle any punishment you throw at me, so what can you do?'

'Darn it Blaze, I don't want you hurt!' Nyla was becoming distracted because of his defiance. 'If you won't go back I have to end it now,' She shook her head in sadness. She quickly made a turn up, and Thayne followed, and then she did something no one expected, she quickly switched directions going back down, and collided right into Thayne.

"No!" Teag cried out. Nyla and the Dorgoggin fought as they plummeted to the ground Blaze was in shock didn't dare try to jump on the two fighting because he might hurt his mother. The Makotice was biting her neck and Nyla was ripping at his body with her sharp talon like claws biting back where ever she could. They hit the ground with a loud thud. Moya and Alaura ran through the tall grass with the Trager kids on their backs. They made it to the edge and peeked through the tall grass and found they had made it to the border of Golden Turtle Lagoon, Pony hills, and the Orange Dragon Field, where the three areas meet. The Makotice Dorgoggin had landed first on a huge rock breaking his back and killing him instantly. He had deep cuts and wounds all over his scaly lifeless body. Nyla was badly poisoned and had several puncture holes and large chunks missing from her neck and torso. She was barely Conscious.

Alaura appeared wanting to help. 'I'm sorry mother,' she said.

'We should have helped you,' Moya whined with tears in her eyes.

'No. You all did as I asked you too,' Nyla praised softly.

Blaze landed and with tears, walked up and nuzzled his mother, 'Why? Why did you do that?' he cried.

'Because,' she started as she struggled to breath, 'I couldn't, take, the chance, of him, turning, his attention, to you and,' she struggled to get the words out because of her emotion and pain, 'killing, you. I told, you to stay, hidden.'

Tears welded up in everyone's eyes.

'Get the, children, to the Polar, Hawk, Mountains, and, take care, of one another,' Nyla struggled for her last few breaths. Teag ran over and pulled out a scale throwing it on the ground in front of Blaze.

"Quickly just blow fire, hurry!" Teag told him. Blaze did as he asked and watched Teag as he used his shirt to pick up the scale and broke it open. He poured the metallic silver color gel onto the wounds on her neck. When it touched her deep gashes it dissolved quickly but there was no change.

'No, no, mother please,' Moya cried.

"Why isn't it working?" Teag asked upset, "here, blaze let me take a scale from your body, maybe the poison tainted her scales," he hurried over to Blaze and took a larger scale from his side. The scale removed with a *crunch* scraping sound. "Thanks, Here blow fire on it," Teag said as he threw it to the ground. Blaze blew fire and heated the scale just right. Teag picked it up using his shirt to protect his hands from burning and snapped the scale in half. Being careful not to spill any of the gel, he walked it over a few feet away, and poured it over her wounds hoping that this time it would work. Still nothing happened.

'I don't, think it's, going to work, on me,' Nyla struggled to say, 'thanks, for trying.'

"No! No, fight it!" Teag yelled as he hugged her neck. He remembered what he did for his sister and how he was able to heal her. He put his hands on her face and concentrated. His hands started to glow red. Hope filled all of them as they watched.

"Is that what you did to me?" Suraionee asked amazed at the cool light and hopeful that if it worked for her it would work for Nyla.

"Yeah," John answered for Teag.

Nyla closed her eyes and went limp, "*No!*" Teag yelled as he watched her. Everyone else gasped. "Come back, come back!" Teag tried so hard to bring her back but it was useless Nyla passed away. The three dragons wailed a loud cry into the air. It was a painful and sad roar. They bowed their heads in respect for their lost mother. Teag was still trying to bring her back. Blaze nuzzled his head under Teags arms causing Teag to let go of her.

"Teag, she's gone," Blaze solemnly said and then Nyla disappeared from sight.

"It worked before, why didn't it work this time?" Teag struggled to understand.

"Maybe it doesn't work on dragons," Moya started, "we know you tried, it was more than we did," she said sadly. After a few moments of silence Alaura, pushed on, 'she's gone, and we need to move on before any more Dorgoggins' come along.'

Teag climbed onto Alaura and said, "time to go."

Suraionee climbed on Moya and John climbed on Blaze, and with great force lifted off the ground and set off for the Polar Hawk Mountains. Everyone looked at the spot where Nyla disappeared in sadness as they flew out of sight. Over the tops of the Pony Hills they glided in the air, to the far left of him, Teag could see clearly where the Golden Turtle Lagoon was. Then they soon came to the foot of the Polar Hawk Mountains. The mountains were so tall that clouds covered the top half of them. Alaura dropped Teag off at a small pathway that went between two of the large Mountains. 'This is as far as we can go, It's too cold in there for us, we wouldn't survive,' she informed them.

"Thanks, we can take it from here, do you know how far Fresh Water Cave is from here?" Teag asked knowing she probably didn't know.

'I'm sorry I've never been in there before. I'm sorry,' Alaura wanted to help more but couldn't.

"That's alright, we'll call you when we're out if that's okay," Teag smiled sadly.

'Okay be careful I do know that there is an ancient Dorgoggin in there called the Hoarfrost. He's brutal and never takes prisoners, my mother told us about him,' Alaura warned them.

"Thanks, I'm sure we'll be fine," he thanked her and started walking through the passage. John and Suraionee followed close behind.

The passage way was thin. The mountains towered on either side of them leaving them no other way out but back the way they came. The pathway was solid rock. A few small plants grew on the ground between the cracked rock. There was a heavy cool breeze pushing it's way out the way they came. Suraionee was glad she brought a coat, she pulled it out of her backpack and put it on. After hiking a few miles up hill they found a larger opening that looked like it had been used for a camp site more than once. There was a large log on the ground and on the other side of it a medium sized fire pit with rocks placed neatly around it. About twenty feet away from the fire pit was a large flat debris free, sandy pit perfect for tents. They looked around for a moment while they kept walking through. Again they found themselves on the thin passageway. They walked through a large man-made tunnel that ended up being about thirty feet deep. Up and deeper into the mountain they walked until they came to a steep climb. There was no where to go but up. Without any ropes they started to climb the large boulders. Until they came to a summit that had three other paths they could take that lead them three different directions. Teag looked around to see if he could see a cave down any of the paths but there were too many trees and the base of the mountains, and was not visible from where he was standing. So he took out his map and tried to figure out where they were.

"It looks like we need to go straight," Teag said as he rolled up his map, put it in his bag and then started walking down the path. The path was steep and they had to be careful not to fall as they carefully slid down the hill walking sideways. There were trees and bushes everywhere. Teag pulled out the map again trying to see how much further it was.

"Teag you just looked at the map."Suraionee complained.

"I know but it just didn't look like it was this far in, I think we took the wrong path," Teag looked at the map. John and Suraionee joined him pointing and trying to figure out which path they took, but the map didn't show a place where three different paths met.

"What were you doing Teag? How could we get lost?" John sourly asked.

"I don't know, you saw the three way path, you know it was there, somehow, well, I can't explain it. I don't know why it isn't on the map anymore," Teag argued.

"Let's just follow the path we're on and see where it takes us," Suraionee said trying to ease the tension between her brothers. She looked away from the map and looked down where the path was, but it was gone.

"Where'd it go?" Suraionee said with panic in her voice.

Teag and John looked away from the map and looked at Suraionee, "where'd what go?" John asked still being sour.

"The path is gone, we were standing right on it. Where'd it go?" She repeated. Teag and John looked around. There was no path to be found. A canopy of trees surrounded them making it hard to see which way they should take. The three walked for hours through trees, up and down hills, and through thick brushwood, trying to find a path of some kind.

Frustrated, tired and hungry Teag decided, "listen we need to find somewhere to make camp because it's getting dark. We can't find anything in the dark."

"We passed a place just up that hill that is flat enough for a tent," John remembered.

"Great, lets get up there and set up camp before it get's too dark," Teag directed. They hiked back up the hill and found their spot, then began to unpack. It didn't take long to get the campsite set up. They sat on the ground and ate the peanut butter and jelly sandwiches and donuts that Sarah had made them and then talked about what they should do in the morning.

The Night air was chilly. It was pitch black except for the fire Teag had built. The three of them sat around the blazing fire talking about the events of the day until they grew tired. They turned in leaving the fire going for safety.

Teag was again troubled about the encounter with ZaBeth. When it suddenly It dawned on him that he never heard her thoughts. She did something to stop him from reading her thoughts. He looked over at John and Suarionee wanting to talk to someone about his discovery, but they were already snoring and he didn't want to wake them. He pulled out the map and looked at it again. Something else triggered a panic in him. The map was different again. Everything was turned around. Any direction he placed the map in didn't fix the problem. Puzzled he watched the map but nothing happened. He became sleepy and started to doze in and out. Every time he would wake up something else was different on the map. So he decided to pretend to be asleep while he peeked through his eyes. Suddenly it happened. The lines moved, changed even.

"I knew it! He yelled, loud enough it startled John and Suraionee waking them up.

"What's wrong," John asked.

"Oh sorry, we have a problem. This map is changing on us."

"What do you mean it's changing on us," he repeated suddenly awake.

"Exactly what I said. The lines are changing and moving around," Teag explained saying it out loud triggered another possibility in his mind, "what if the map and the trees and shrubs all moved around? That would explain why we were suddenly lost when we started on the path and hadn't moved.

"How is that possible?" Suraionee asked now fully awake. "I mean how could it all move without us hearing it or seeing it all move?"

"I don't know," Teag answered.

"Isn't that the map that Maddox gave you?" John asked.

"Yes, the one specially for the Polar Hawk Mountains."

"You don't you think he is in on the whole thing?" Suraionee asked John suspiciously.

"*No*! Don't even think it, Not him," Teag jawed at them.

"Well how do you explain it then? Someone had to jinx it, who would do that knowing that he was going to give it to us?" John said trying to justify himself.

"I don't know, anyone could have done it. Why didn't I hear any of ZaBeth's thoughts when she questioned me? I'm so stupid I didn't even see it coming. Maddox is in trouble," Teag grabbed his backpack and rifled through it searching for the pager rock. He threw it to the ground. But only silence followed.

"Let me try," John asked grabbing the smooth cream rock from the ground. He then threw it down, and still nothing happened.

It isn't going to work, remember," Teag reminded them, "he said it would only work if he still had his with him."

"This can't be happening," Suraionee whimpered.

"She knows," Teag frowned believing the worst, "she's known all this time. Someone's been telling her our secrets."

"Maybe not, do you think someone could have read your mind?" John asked trying to think positive now.

"No, or they wouldn't have needed me...I see it now, they were testing something. It started with Ms. Nevina. She was the first one I couldn't read. But how could she have known about my powers being able to communicate with animals and stuff. I don't get it at all," Teag struggled to find the answer but nothing came. He was so tired now almost drained and it was starting to get light out, "Let me sleep for fifteen minutes and then we'll get going. We have to find the ingredients and get out of here."

"But what are we going to do? How can we help Maddox, she's too powerful." Suraionee asked concerned.

"Shhh, I'm sleeping," Teag hushed her.

The dungeon was dark and drafty. It smelled of rotten Hay. Teag heard crying coming from somewhere close by. He walked toward the sound, "who's there?" He saw a shadow of a figure in the corner behind bars,"who's there," the crying stopped.

"Teag!" yelled the woman. She ran to the bars. "Your alive! That wicked woman told us you were dead. I'm so sorry about Johnny and Sura, we tried to save them."

"Mom, no, we're all alive. It's okay," he lovingly brushed her messed up hair off of her dirty face, "where's dad?"

"I don't know, they separated us months ago, I haven't heard from him since," she was crying now.

"Mom, It's alright I'm here, I'll get you out of here. Where're the keys?" Teag asked looking around.

"I don't know, I don't think she had one. She would wave her hand in front of the lock and it would open."

Teag looked at the lock but the light was so dim it was hard to see. There was a creaking of a door down the hall.

"Shhh, mom I'll be back for you, don't worry, it'll all be okay,"Teag whispered.

"No don't leave me," She whispered back reaching out her hands for him.

Teag hid in the darkness staying out of sight. The figure was large and familiar but was too dark to see his face. He kept his voice down Teag listened for his thoughts but couldn't hear them. It was frustrating that his powers seemed worthless lately. The large man let his mother out of the cage and guided her down the hallway. As they passed a light Teag could see his mother clearly. She was dirty and way too thin. They had clearly treated her poorly. Never in his life had his mother been untidy nor would she ever have allowed it. She was always so groomed and beautiful to look at. This made Teag angrier than ever. His rage consumed him. The lights from the fire torches flickered. The figure guiding his mother out stopped and looked back as if he knew he was here. Then walked on. Teag looked around in all the other cells trying to find his father but still had no luck. Then suddenly a voice whispered, "face the sun at dawn, Follow the mountain wall to the right. It will guide you to what you seek, follow it to the left and be lost forever."

"Who's there?" He asked.

"Hurry Teag, hurry."

"But I'm not in the mountain…" Teag suddenly remembered that the last thing he thought about before the dungeon was being in the mountain.

Teag jolted awake, jumping to his feet, "Hurry, we haven't a minute to lose."

Surprised, "you were only asleep for three minutes," Suraionee questioned, "I thought you wanted to sleep for fifteen minutes," she was chasing him around the campsite helping him as he raced around putting things away. John pulled out his canteen and dumped the water left in it over the fire that was still lightly burning. The night sky was getting brighter.

"Hurry, help me pack, we'll miss it if we aren't ready to go," Teag rushed.

"Ready for what? John asked thinking he was crazy, "we're lost remember?"

"Yeah but I was told how to get out of here. I saw mom, she needs us."

"Wait, how did you see mom, you were with us the entire time."

Frustrated and not wanting to talk it out at the moment, Teag snapped, "just hurry, we'll talk about it later.

* * *

They finished packing just seconds before dawn. Teag faced the direction of the sun and then walked straight toward the mountain the sun peeked over. When he got to it a while later he followed it to the right. They came to the large mouth of a cave. "This has got to be it," one by one they walked in. Teag pulled out his flashlight and pointed it, looking in every corner. The light sounds of water trickling came from somewhere deeper in the cave.

"What are we looking for here again?" John asked.

"Crumble Rock and a glowing blue ice cycle in the shape of a moon," Teag reminded nicely.

"What do you think the crumble rock looks like?" Suraionee asked.

"I don't know a rock that crumbles easily?" Teag guessed, "if you see any boulders feel free to pick them up and chuck them against the walls to see if they crumble." There was a crack behind them and a large boulder was lunged at them. It missed and hit the cave wall shattering into smaller pieces. When they looked at where the boulder came from, a large Ogre stood snarling.

In a deep voice he yelled "Dis is me home, gee out!" he demanded picking up another large boulder. He stood about nine feet tall. Big round thick tree trunk legs and feet. Huge round stomach, thick arms with large hands a bald head and stubby round nose. His eyes were extra large and very angry. He had little ears and wore a pair of pants that looked like someone made for him lovingly but they were well worn.

"Please, we mean you no harm, we just need a couple items and we will get out of your way."

"No!" roared the Ogre, "*now!*" He threw the boulder just missing Teag by inches. It crumbled all over the ground.

John winced as another boulder missed his head when he ducked behind a large rock

"Look I think that's the crumble rock," Suraionee pointed out as she watched another rock crumble against the cave wall.

"Can you reach any of it?" Teag asked as he peeked around the large boulder he was hiding behind to look at the Ogre.

"I think I can, if you and Sura distract him," John answered for her. Suraionee ran from behind her boulder and watched the Ogre to see where he was throwing the next rock so she could avoid it. The Ogre looked at her and smiled.

"Pitty har," he started, "so bootiful," he started walking towards her. Suraionee screamed and ran to hide behind the boulder with Teag.

"I think he likes you," Teag smiled at her.

"What!" Suraionee steamed at Teag. The Ogre saw John trying to collect a crumble rock and he threw the next rock he had in his hand at him. John jumped to dodged it hiding behind another nearby boulder.

"I said keep him busy guys," John complained.

Teag reached into his bag and grabbed a donut Sarah and made from scratch. It was his favorite but he thought it might help them get out of this situation alive. He held it out to the ogre, "here, are you hungry? Eat it."

The Ogre gained a little interest. He sniffed the air and walked closer, "num nums?" He whispered. Teag threw it high in the air at the Ogre and the Ogre caught it and tossed it in his mouth, "*Morr?*" He cried.

"Okay, Okay, here you go, but will you take us to the blue moon?"

"Moon?" The ogre snarled, "no moon, she said keds moost die."

"Keds must die? Who's she?" Teag tried to understand what he was saying.

Suraionee took the donut out of Teags hand and grabbed her squirt gun then came out of hiding. She started to approach the Ogre with her gun pointed at him.

"Sura! What are you doing?"

"Trust me," she said.

"Pitty girl," the Ogre smiled, "Keds no die, me like pitty girl," Suraionee sprayed the liquid sun rays at a plant next to the large Ogre, singeing it instantly.

"He's saying Pretty girl, he called you beautiful," Teag deciphered his mumbled language. Suraionee held out the donut to him as she got closer and closer.

"Ogre, will you take us to the blue moon?" Suraionee asked batting her eyes and being very sweet. The ogre's heart melted.

He leaned over and picked her up and held her like a baby, "Wha yer mame?"

"Sura," she told him not thinking he could pronounce her whole name.

"Suea." He said as he cuddled her. She patted his nose sweetly and tossed the donut into his mouth, "num, nums," he smiled gleefully. He took the gun from her hand and threw it out of the cave.

"Oh no!" Suraionee gasped.

"Great, Sura, now John is the only one with a squirt gun," Teag yelled.

John searched his back pack that felt a little light, "oh, no!"

"What?" Teag asked worried.

"It's gone."

"What's gone?"

"Everything. I think the gun was leaking, because there's a singed hole in the bottom of my bag and there isn't anything in it, everything's fallen out."

"Great, so no one has a squirt gun," Teag shook his head mad.

"Ogre, can you take us to the blue moon?" Suraionee asked again. The Ogre nodded his head in agreement. The ogre started walking them deeper into the cave. The sound of rushing water became louder the deeper they went. The smell of the cave was stifling damp mildewy mist.

"We must be getting closer," Suraionee observed still in the Ogre's arms.

"Dis ay," The ogre waved to Teag and John to keep following.

When he came to a cliff, he stopped They were at the opening of a huge cavern that had to be hundreds of feet high. He could see the bottom of the cavern but it was too far and steep to climb down. There looked to be an indoor lake at the bottom and Teag wondered where the Ogre might be leading them. At the edge of the cliff to the right was something that looked like a twisty slide like the kind you would find at a water park. It was made of slipery mud and rock and had lots of rushing water flowing through it. Water was falling from the side of the cave and swishing and swirling down to the bottom.

"So where is it?" Teag asked.

"Don dere," he pointed down the slide.

"What? I didn't know we had to get wet," Suraionee complained.

"Shhh," Teag whispered. He turned around and heard a voice in his head.

'Strangers are in my mountain.'

"Go noo, dagogin coom, huwee!" The ogre grabbed Teag and John and tossed them down the slimy mud slide then he tossed in Suraionee. He looked behind him to see the Hoarfrost Dorgoggin closing in on him. The Orge jumped onto the slide and quickly caught up with the kids.

"Who was that?" Teag asked.

"Dagogin, bad!" the ogre warned, "me and dagogin eminees," he yelled so they could hear him over the rustling water.

"What?' John asked confused, "eminees? What's that?"

"Enemies," Teag corrected him, "Their enemies, and he's talking about the Hoarfrost Dorgoggin," Teag repeated remembering the type of Dorgoggin Maddox and Alaura had said lived in these parts.

"What's that?" John asked because he wasn't paying attention.

"You know the Dorgoggin Alaura and Maddox told us about, the one that lives here in these mountains."

"Oh Yeah," John started remembering.

Round and round they went down the churning slide, twisting and sliding water splashing into their open screaming mouths. Then *splash*, into a small pool of water. The Hoarfrost Dorgoggin was flying down towards them. With no where to go they all watched her get closer and were frightened. The water in the pool spilled out and they were all dragged into a larger rock tube, twisting and sliding. It appeared that the Dorgoggin couldn't follow them this time. Suddenly they plunged into another pool, this one much larger and the water was much cooler. Not sure what was going to happen next they felt themselves being dragged out of the water.

"Run," the ogre instructed.

"Where?" Teag asked. The ogre pointed to a small blue light that came from the other end of the large dark cave they were in. They started running. As soon as they cleared the door the Ogre tried to get a boulder in the way of the door to block them in. He showed great strength moving the large boulder.

"Wait! What about you Ogre," Suraionee asked concerned for her new friend who was closing himself on the outside.

"He tried to lock us in here," John demanded angrily.

"No, I think he tried to protect us from the Hoarfrost," Teag said as he peaked between the rocks.

The Ogre didn't answer her and stopped moving the boulder suddenly leaving about two inches that they could see through. The Tragers' could hear the Ogre talking to the Dorgoggin and could see the Ogre's back.

"Leev da keds awone," he said forcefully.

'You are defying Desdemona Ogre, She said kill the kids and take the ingredients,' The Hoarfrost Dorgoggin hissed, ice steam slowly spurting out of his mouth as he talked.

"Don't care, good keds, not gonna kill dem," The Ogre roared.

'She told me this might happen,' the Hoarfrost growled. And then without a fight the Ogre stood there knowing what was coming. A cold white like gas filled the cracks that weren't covered.

"Stand Back!" Teag yelled as he saw the white steam lightly swirl into the room, "looks like our Dorgoggin breaths Ice," he commented as he looked at the poor Ogre that stood there frozen in place. Teag was starting to feel nothing when it came to death. His heart felt cold. He knew he should feel something, but so many people and creatures that he cared about have died, or at least he went through the grieving, and the emotion of it was so draining that he just didn't feel like he had it in him anymore. John felt the same way.

"No!" Suraionee said sadly as she looked at her new frozen friend, "he was nice. I really liked him," she cried.

"Too many people are dying on this trip," Teag said sadly as he went over and tried to comfort his sister, but feeling no emotion himself, "quick lets just get what we came for and get out of here."

"Did anyone get any of the crumble rock the ogre threw at us?" John asked worried.

"Great, What are we going to do now?" Teag was upset that they forgot it. Suraionee looked mad too. Watching their faces John smiled, "It's okay because I got some while you weren't looking."

"Good Job, John. Now lets find our Blue Moon Icicle and get out of here before that Dorgoggin finds it's way in," Teag praised.

"I can't believe you too, the Ogre just died for us and your laughing about a stupid crumble rock!" Suraionee yelled.

"A lot of people have died for us, Sura, I don't mean to be cold, but it's gonna keep happening until we get rid of ZaBeth and Desdemona. The only way through this is to just finish the task, please," Teag said coldly. Even John thought he was a bit too cold, though he thought he was right.

"Fine, finish your stupid scavenger hunt, but don't plan on talking to me anymore," she waited for a moment then added, "you're a jerk!" Teag shook his head and then let it go.

The room was brightly glowing blue. There were only a few blue moon Ice cycles. The room was small and bones were scattered all over the ground. In one corner a person had died and their bones were the only ones in the room that were still in tact.

"Ewww, lets not end up like that, please," Suraionee shivered.

"I thought you weren't talking to me," Teag snapped.

"I wasn't, I was talking to John," she lied glaring at him. She had already forgotten that she was mad and wasn't going to talk to him anymore.

There was a large pool of water that would fill up quickly and then empty every thirty seconds, into a medium sized tube, much like the ones they slid down earlier.

"There that looks like our door," Teag pointed. He walked over and took two Blue Moon Ice Cycles. It was strange because it wasn't cold at all, "hurry, the Dorgoggin's coming. I hear its thoughts," he suddenly rushed.

John was the first one in the water. He held on to Suraionee to help guide her.

There was a loud crash and the shimmering blue Hoarfrost came crashing through the thick ice wall, into the cave. Shattering ice pieces mixed with rock flung everywhere. The Dorgoggin lunged at them with his fangs snapping inches away.

The water flushed just in time to escape the cold rush of icy breath. Angry they escaped again the Dorgoggin let out a sonic cry that could be heard underwater.

Teag, John and Suraionee were now in deep freezing water being rushed quickly through the suffocating walls. Just when Teag and Suraionee felt they couldn't hold their breath any longer they were shot out of the cave and into a large pool of deep water outside. It was sometime in the afternoon, and the sun was shining brightly. The wind wasn't blowing very much but the air smelled sweet like fruit. Teag and Suraionee came up gasping for air before the three of them swam for the side. John helped Suraionee climb out. Teag looked around. The Polar Hawk Mountains were too their left now. They were miles away, on top of a cliff. All around the large pool of fresh water were Pineapple trees. Pineapples were floating in the water and going over the large waterfall across from them. "This must be Pineapple Falls."

"What," Suraionee asked, "how do you know what the name of this place is?"

"Remember when we were travelling by carriage and Maddox showed us the map?" Teag reminded them not waiting for a reply, "well, he showed it too us, I remembered it because I wanted to see why they called it Pineapple falls. If I remember correctly," Teag said as he stood up and walked over to the cliff side looking out over the land.

"No, Teag, that never happened, you were taken by the dragon remember?"

Thinking back he remembered, "Oh yeah, it was my nightmare that happened in, anyways I was right, and the Golden Turtle Lagoon is, just down there," he looked at his watch, then back at his brother. "This is your job, it's just after lunch time if you hurry we can be done and home before dinner. You're the only one that can do it. Find those four Silver Shimmering Stars. We will be walking around, down to the bottom."

"Okay, see ya," John said as he jumped over the waterfall and dived into the lagoon below.

Teag started walking around the long way down the ever so slight hill while Suraionee stared out over the cliff side. "It's so beautiful. Look there's North Beach way out there, and the Black Wizard Forest, and over there's the Pony Hills and there the Orange Dragon Field."

Teag walked back and looked out again. "There's the Great Oak. That's where I want to sleep tonight. So, hurry lets get down there and meet Johnny."

Suraionee skipped most of the way enjoying the deliciously juicy fruit from all the fruit trees along the way.

Chapter 10

The air was cool as it pressed his wet clothing against his body. John stood there over the cliff and smiled. Knowing he couldn't drown made him feel invincible. He leaned forward and jumped; free falling tickled his stomach. He enjoyed the cool air that whizzed past him as he fell from the sky. He splashed as he dived in. The water enveloped him like a warm blanket to his icy windblown skin. As soon as he hit the water he turned invisible just in case there were predators he didn't know about. The water was murky and made it a little hard to see. Inch by inch he went, knowing they had to be somewhere. John shuffled his hands through the sand and seaweed, and tussled a few small fish, they seemed to be trying to determine boundaries. The job began to feel overwhelming because of the size of the lagoon. As he disturbed the sand on the ground of the lagoon he came across Teags gun that fell from the sky. He went up to the surface and tried to squirt it at the grass but nothing came out. 'it's all dried up,' he thought then looked at it closer. It looked like lava rock was inside, 'the water must have hardened the Liquid Sun Ray into a rock,' he thought as he tossed the gun onto the grass above and then dived back in to keep searching.

After three hours of searching he pondered where they might be. Remembering how Teag found the lost room by skimming his hand along the wall he decided to try it. He touched the steep muddy walls of the lagoon and slowly skimmed along finding nothing at first. Shortly after starting he went right through the lagoon wall and into a small water filled cavern. Inside he found millions of tiny golden turtles floating about that appeared to be pure gold. There were several large oval rocks that lit up the room. The lagoon walls had, random, built in mud shelves that held treasures from sunken ships. Forks and plates were on one shelf down low, while a ceramic water skiing figure and boat sat by its self on another shelf up high. In another area he found beautiful seashells and coral. It was all like a collection of some kind by someone he didn't see anywhere. He went through a large hole that lead to another larger cavern. He didn't spend much time searching the room because as soon as he entered it a glimmer caught his attention back further into the cavern. He swam over to it and found that it was the first shimmering silver star. The next two he found hidden in the sand, another room. In that same room he noticed a large hole in the top of the cavern that appeared to be open. He swam to it and pushed his way through to the top, poking his head out of the water. There in front of him was another large cave that was filled with air. Billions of Diamante Púrpura crystals were everywhere shimmering in the lining the walls of the cave. 'Now I know where they get them from," John thought to himself. The fourth star proved much harder to find. He looked everywhere in the lagoon, but it was no where to be found.

As he started back toward the exit he spotted a giant golden turtle; it was massive and was looking right at him. He moved from side to side and the turtle watched him closely even though he was invisible. It's eyes grew narrow, and it snorted air out. It started charging, chomping its giant snapper at him. He was swimming for his life, but because of his training he was able to swim a little faster than a normal person keeping him just ahead of the large chompers cracking down behind him. Mostly because he could breath and didn't have to come up for air. With the turtle hot on his heels he found himself trapped between two cliffs and turned to stare at the angry turtle. When it made another attempt to bite him in half he saw it. 'The shimmery silver star,' he thought, 'how am I supposed to get it from there?' he pondered. He moved just in time to miss the jaws of the monster. When it clamped down its jaws got stuck on the rocks. John felt this was his chance. He poked his arm into the jaws of death and reached for the star. 'Just a little more,' he thought as he worried about the large mouth breaking free. The turtle was starting to wiggle out. 'Hurry Johnny or your chopped sea weed,' he told himself. His hand clasped over the fourth star and he pulled it out just seconds before the turtle crushed down. He swam to shore as quickly as possible. Weaving side to side he tried to dodge the turtle that came barrelling down on him. John looked behind him slowing himself down, and then looked up and saw Teag standing there on the water bank looking down. He popped up and reached out to grab a hand. Teag clasped his hands and pulled him out; both of them falling to the ground just moments before the turtle jumped out of the water chomping after John.

"Wooah!" Suraionee yelled at her surprise. The large golden turtle raised out of the water with such force it jumped ten feet into the air before falling back into the lagoon.

Teag tried to talk to the beast but it refused to talk back.

"Why weren't you invisible?" Teag asked a little irritated? "You could have been killed."

"I was, but it saw me anyway."

"Really?"

"Yep, but we're alright now, I've got the stars," John said as he held them out and gave them to Teag.

"How could you see these down there, they're so small and the lagoon is so big," Teag asked as he looked at the tiny shimmering stars.

"I don't know I just did," John shrugged as they stood there next to the water. Suraionee was walking around with a stick in her hand wasting time and hitting the nearby bushes with a stick.

"Guys, come here!" Suraionee called out to them. She was standing by some thick bushes and looking into them like she had found something.

"What?" Teag asked as he and John both turned around to look at her. Without waiting for an answer they ran to catch up to her. When they looked inside they found, "four SkyBees," Teag said remembering the picture Maddox had showed him, hidden behind the thick shrubbery. Teag reached in and tried to pull them out, but they were heavy. It took all three kids tugging and pushing to pull them all out. When three of the SkyBees were in the open, Teag stood on one and turned the key lock with his mind. The engine revved and glided on.

"Wait Teag, these aren't ours," Suraionee said still standing in the bushes next to the fourth SkyBee.

"Yeah, but we need to get to the Great Oak and find Maddox, and it's getting dark. We have to hurry, and it's too far away to walk," Teag said rationalizing his purpose.

"Teag, No, It's stealing," She cautioned him.

"Suraionee, maybe Maddox put them here for us so that we could get back faster," John concluded, excited to try the awesome machinery before him. Suraionee started walking forward pushing her way through the bushes and stopped when she saw a paper on the ground.

"Wait, there's something here," She said as she bent down to pick it up, and read it out loud…

Dear Teag, John and Sura,

These SkyBee's are for you. I thought it might make the last part of your journey a little more fun. Dad told me you asked about them. I'm sorry I couldn't be there to help you along the way, but I hope you'll find it much more exciting coming to the Great Oak in style.

Your Friend,
Ronan Pembroke

P.S. I'll bet your wondering what the fourth SkyBee is for. Dad said he was going to try to meet you out there, so I thought having an extra one there just in case would be a good idea. If he isn't there just leave without it and we'll get it later.

See you soon

"Wow, they were from Ronan," she exclaimed as she read the letter out loud. Attached to the letter were the keys.

"Greatest day ever!" John said climbing aboard his SkyBee.

"Yeah, Teag you don't have to hot wire them with your mind, here are the keys," she said as she dangled the clinking keys from her fingers.

"Sweet!" Teag smiled, "best part of the trip if you ask me."

Suraionee threw a key over to John and Teag as she climbed aboard her SkyBee.

Teag pushed a button marked up and the SkyBee floated up into the air. Slowly they all floated up, higher and higher. Trying to get the hang of how to manoeuver the machines they weaved in and out of the air. The higher they got the faster the wind, the faster the wind the easier the SkyBee's were to fly. John was having a hard time with his, and was hanging on for dear life, it appeared that the SkyBee was flying him rather than him flying the SkyBee.

"Lean back when you want to go up, and lean forward when you want to go down," Teag said as he got the hang of it, "then lean into your turns, that will make it easier," Teag yelled out. When big gusts of wind came Teag would ride them up and around. He bopped about like he was on water waves with soft sounds of thunder under his wings as he slapped about the air. They were in no hurry as they thought they that everyone was waiting for them at the Great Oak. "Ronan would want us to enjoy a few minutes of flying," Teag said a little earlier.

Flying so high in the air made it easy to see their way to the Great Oak so they slowly made their way there as they flew about enjoying their SkyBees. After dark they landed and walked up to the large tree trunk. Teag remembered his dream and how Maddox opened it up. So he taped on a knot on the tree trunk with a stick and it opened like a door letting them in. Though Maddox was no where to be found, there was a three bedroom suite waiting for them. When they got to their room all they wanted to do was sleep, but Teag heard someone calling them to the castle.

"Maybe when this is all over we can come back and spend the night here, but we have to move on," Teag said as he told them about what he heard. John and Suraionee understood and agreed. They walked to the transporter room on their level and pushed the button to the castle. But nothing happened. The buttons looked fried like someone had poured water over them rendering them useless.

"Come on," Teag said as he lead them quickly through the front doors heading back to the SkyBees'. "We've got to hurry, something's wrong," he said sensing the worst. John and Suraionee followed right next to Teag. Their dirty clothing and faces made people inside the Great Oak stare at them, but they kept going acting like nothing was different. Once outside they climbed back on their SkyBee's and took off for the Makoto City Castle. Shooting through the sky like rockets. The air smelled of rain. Thick dark clouds engulfed the Castle. Thunder and lightning filled the sky making it hard to get close without being struck down. They put the SkyBees on the ground right inside the locked gate and ran up to the castle doors staying low.

"These are locked too," Suraionee huffed, out of breath from running.

Teag tried to use his powers to open the door but something was stopping him. Quickly making a decision he said, "careful, stay close to the building and lets see if there's another way in," Teag instructed as he pointed John and Suraionee around the side of the tall stone structure. The wind was now blowing hard and the sky was well lit from the pounding lightning that hit random spots of the castle grounds. The beautiful flowers and nicely trimmed bushes were restlessly flipping in the wind taking the peddles from flowers, branches, and fresh leaves, and scattering them about the grounds. Dodging the lighting and terrible winds, it wasn't long before John spotted a hidden cellar door under some branches of thick leaves. The three of them quickly took branches and threw them aside. One of the branches was struck by lightning in mid air moments after John had let go. When Teag tried the doors they opened like someone was waiting for them to find it.

Once inside the gloomy cellar, the open doors slammed behind them. A large branch fell on top of it from the outside locking them in. The cellar lead to a long dark hallway that was empty and no one was sure which way to go, so they chose to go to the right. They followed it checking every door along the way only to find them locked until they came to a dead end. The ugly gray stone walls were cold and uninviting. The darkness made it hard to see. They held out their hands against the walls to feel their way back the way they came. Empty cobwebs attached to their hands and made them freak out every once in a while.

"Aaah," Suraionee said in fear, feeling the tickle of a spider crawling up her arm. She quickly brushed it off and shook at the creepy feeling it gave her.

The hallway twisted and turned until they came to a stairwell leading up. At the top they found themselves at the parlor room door. They slowly opened the door and just inside sat Maddox.

"*You!*" Teag yelled walking in and not looking at his surroundings, "I can't believe that you would lie to us and build us up. You made us think that you were helping, that you cared. We figured out your map and, as you can see we made it out of there alive, no thanks to you," Teag yelled while Maddox sat there and didn't say a word. "Well do you have something to say for yourself?"

'Run hide, save your family, she knows.' Maddox thought with all his strength.

Teag fell flush. He looked around the room and there stood ZaBeth. When Teag took a moment to notice, he saw that Maddox was badly beaten and appeared to be drugged.

"So you thought you could outsmart me? You thought that by being here a few months you would know more about my kingdom than I? I am surprised that you made it through each and every trap I set for you. How did you do it? You should have been killed by Thayne, you couldn't read his thoughts, so how did you do it?" She stood there and stared at him waiting for and answer to all of her questions.

"You sent the Makotice? How did you stop me from being able to read his mind?"

"Like I'm going to tell you that little secret, though I will say, you did well with Nevina and when you couldn't read her mind I knew it would work for me as well," She snickered.

"Who else did you send after us?"

"The Hoarfrost Dorgoggin, the Ogre, though he turned out to be a disappointment, and I warned Vidor of your coming but apparently I underestimated you, and was severely misinformed of how good your abilities truly were," she glanced over at Rylee. Then realizing that she went off on a tangent asked again. "How did you do it, how did you get away from them? Never mind, It no longer matters," she curled her lip and snarled her nose with hatred.

"Where's my mother and father?" Teag demanded not answering her question for the second time.

"So is this how you want to play it, answering a question with a question? This is my kingdom, mine! I was born the rightful queen and no one will take it away from me."

"So you really are Desdemona. I knew it. That's why you didn't want to be called Queen ZaBeth, you couldn't stand hearing her name being called as Queen so you played it out and made people think you were a good Queen, down to earth," Teag laughed. Then in a high pitched voice mimicking her, "call me ZaBeth, I never did like the whole formal name of Queen ZaBeth," he said smartly.

"What are you laughing about, I see nothing funny. You don't know, You weren't there, Alura took, *my*, kingdom," she snarled.

"No she didn't, it was hers, she was the oldest and the rightful heir. You lied and cheated to get what you wanted, you even killed didn't you," Teag interrogated her, but she stayed quiet, "you killed everyone that loved you, your mother and father, your sister and even your cousin ZaBeth."

"Yes I did. I had too. All of them stood in my way. Oh, you wouldn't understand. ZaBeth wouldn't have given up the crown that easily. I had too. It was for the best. For the good of our Island kingdom...listen to me," she piped up louder when she felt like no one was listening, and then remembered who she was,."Why am I trying to explain this to you?"

ZaBeth changed her appearance back to her own by overlapping her fingertips, her palms facing herself and started with the top of her head moving her hands slowly down her body, her blonde hair turned dark brown, her leathered skin on her face turned to soft olive, her cool blue sagging eyes turned light brown the wrinkles on her face smoothed, her dry pale pink lips turned to a voluptuous soft rose color. Her jaw line that was once almost non-existent turned firm. As her hands went further down her body, her clothing changed from dress pants and a nice white dress shirt to a flowing evening gown.

"Ahh that's better," she said looking in the mirror that was adjacent to her, hanging on the wall. The guards were surprised, and twitterpated at the sight of her. They would have never intentionally done something for Desdemona, but she captivated them with her beauty. They were quickly under her spell and compelled to do her every command. Her appearance was only a few years older then when she had first taken over so many years ago.

Rylee gasped, horrified as he watched her change right before his eyes. He just stood there staring at her in total shock. His heart hit the floor, he looked over to his father that was laying there in pain, feeling utterly embarrassed and stupid for his mistake in her true identity.

"I defended you, I believed you I did awful things for you!" He yelled angry and hurt.

"Oh, get over yourself, this isn't about you," she snapped at him disappointed that he was being so emotional. Rylee approached her like he was about to tear her to shreds. "Get back Rylee, or I'll kill you too," she warned. When he kept coming fury written all over his face, she then said quickly, "Rylee, I'll kill your mother, sister and your father!" Rylee stopped and looked back at his father. He closed his eyes and felt totally powerless. He didn't want anymore bloodshed. "That's what I thought," Desdemona turned her attention back to Teag. "Now, give me the items you acquired." She demanded holding out her hand.

"No, I don't think I will."

"Teagen Trager, Give me the items or I'll have to kill your mother for real," she waved her hand and Milly was dragged into the room limp and unconscious.

"My name is Teag," He started to reprimand her, but then seeing his limp mother concerned him, "what did you do to her," he demanded, running up to her. "Mom are you alright?" Teag was worried, he brushed the hair out of her face. she wasn't moving, his once beautiful mother was now crumpled up on the floor, her long hair tangled and dirty and her clothing scroungy.

"We'll call it insurance. Now hand over the items or I'll finish her right in front of you!" She demanded again.

"Teag, she's serious, please, just give it to her," Suraionee pleaded.

"Yeah Teag," John agonized.

"Look, she's going to kill us all anyway. We are the only ones that know the truth, she can't afford to keep us alive," Teag explained.

"Please?" Suraionee pleaded again.

Teag looked over at his sister. The thought of giving in made his stomach turn. They had come all this way and for what, to fail? Could he take the chance of Desdemona killing his mother if he didn't do what she wanted? Would she honor her agreement and keep them all alive if he did give her what she wanted? Suraionee's eyes were big and tears were flowing down her cheeks. He couldn't stand seeing her cry. The situation was impossible, and it made him even more irritated, 'I'll find another way to get us through it, to save everyone, I've got too,' he thought. "Fine, here," Teag handed everything over.

Desdemona sent over a servant to get the items and then commanded him, "get it to the jeweler and tell him I want it done in an hour."

"It's never going to work," Teag laughed, "your servant will probably run off with the items and make it for himself."

"He wouldn't dare!" She snarled but then she stood there for a moment worrying that Teag might be right. Frustrated that Teag's words got to her, she barked, "Guards, stay with them, I'll be back in a few minutes."

"Let them all go Desdemona, it's me you want," Maddox begged with what little breath he had. Teag glanced over to him, he looked miserable.

"No little nephew, it isn't. If I leave them be I'll be ruined, if I leave you, I'll lose my crown," she curled her lip and walked out of the room after the servant that took the items.

Teag looked over at Maddox, surprised at what Desdemona had called him and sad that he had ever accused him of betrayal, "Nephew?"

"Yes," he struggled to talk. The drugs in his body were wearing off as he started gaining strength he was able to talk, "Alura was my mother. She and General Flann were secretly married a year before my mother was killed. I was one month old when that happened. After Mothers' death Melanion took me and my father to Australia where I grew up learning about the islands and learned where my mother and father grew up, from my father. When I turned twenty I returned to the Islands to serve ZaBeth, whom I thought was a good Queen. My father stayed in Australia and died several years later. Melanion came back and forth in secret. Not even ZaBeth knew about it. However, one day she heard that someone matching Melanions' description lived in the states so she went in search for him. That was when he had to plan his own death, to protect all of you."

Teag nodded and then thought about the map again, "so if it wasn't you that gave me the jinxed map, who was it?" Teag asked him.

Maddox frowned and struggled to turn his head to look over at the door. Teag followed the direction and found Rylee standing there. Maddox looked back at Teag, "I had no idea he was feeding her our private conversations, and all of your abilities he knew about. I'm so sorry, but I'm glad to see that you made it out of the mountains safely."

"Thanks to you, If you hadn't called out to me and told me how to get out we would still be in there wandering around, or dead, that Hoarfrost is bad news. So how do you suggest we get out of here?"

"It wasn't me that called out to you," he whispered.

"Then who?" Teag was puzzled.

"I don't know," Maddox winced in pain.

Looking at Rylee, "but I don't understand, why did Rylee do it?" John asked sad that his friend would betray them like that.

Rylee was listening to the conversation and with a sad heart he walked over to defend himself. "I was raised to think she was a good Queen. There were no signs of her being cruel, heartless or even greedy towards any of the people of these Islands. She was a good Queen and, and I trusted her," he stuttered a little.

"But she said horrible things to your father," Teag argued.

"Yes, but she had never done anything like that before, I thought she was just upset because so many problems were occurring in her plan to help us return to our human form. I thought she was just stressed and overwhelmed. She said that it was for my family's own good that we get returned to normal as quickly as possible. She knew that dad would betray her so she needed me to inform her of what was going on," Rylee said with tears starting to flow, he scrunched up his face in sadness, he felt betrayed by ZaBeth and felt like he wanted to die because of his betrayal to is family, "I'm sorry dad, I didn't know who she really was. You've gotta believe me, I thought I was helping," It was clear that Rylee felt really bad. He didn't know what she was going to do to his family.

Maddox couldn't look at him because of the pain in his heart from his son's treachery. Rylee felt horrible.

"Stop talking," A guard yelled as he walked by. When he walked away Suraionee spoke up changing the subject.

"How are we going to get out of this one?" Suraionee asked quietly.

"We have only one chance that I can think of. Can you call Melanion? But not out loud," Maddox asked.

"Hey! Stop talking you two," Demanded the same guard pointing his long rifle at them and looking serious. Then after a moment of silence the guard walked away to talk to another nearby guard.

"Sure," Teag whispered, then closed his eyes and started to meditate.

"Try not to make it noticeable to everyone else, we don't want a welcoming committee waiting for him."

Teag nodded in agreement. He barely came off the ground this time and nothing else moved. His eyes were closed and a peaceful look was on his face. 'Grandpa, we need you, but there are guards everywhere, tell me what I should do,' after a few moments he opened his eyes and said, "It's done," his left eye was still glowing.

"Did you tell him what was going on so he can prepare himself?"

"Yes."

A voice came to Teag, 'wear the Monile.'

"What?" Teag said out loud bewildered, 'Wear the monile?' Teag remembered, he spoke back to the voice, 'It isn't made yet.'

'No son, wear the one your mother gave Suraionee for her birthday.'

'But I don't have it, it's in the sea remember?' Teag protested.

'No, it isn't, it can be used in stopping the second one from being made. It will also stop Desdemona's rule of terror,' the voice explained, 'look at the floor in front of you,' Teag searched the floor but nothing was there and then it magically appeared. He picked it up and tossed it carefully to Suraionee.

"Here Suraionee, use it to stop them from making the second Monile and then stop Desdemona," he whispered. Suraionee took the Monile and put it on.

"How?" Suraionee, asked.

"Use your vision and see where they are making it then just think about it, command it, and it will happen," Teag grew impatient.

"Suraionee closed her eyes. The walls began to open to her. She continued through the halls. She entered a small room where a little man was hard at work. The Monile was already done. 'There it is,' Suraionee thought to herself, 'now, come here,' she commanded Teag also helped and pulled the items toward them. There was a ruckus outside and the door opened. That made Suraionee lose her concentration causing the Monile floating in the air towards them begin to fall.

"Nooo!" Cried Desdemona at seeing the Monile falling. She lunged forward, throwing herself to the ground to catch it, and saved it just before it reached the ground.

Suraionee looked back down the hall and saw her father being dragged. He was unconscious.

Angry that they almost won, she screamed, "Seize him, kill him, I've had enough of this game!" She insisted in fury, pointing at Teag. Her rage engulfed her as she quickly started walking toward him.

When she noticed the Monile around Suraionee's neck she went to grab it. Suraionee yanked it off her neck and threw it to Teag.

Teag caught it and put it on. The power in the Monile instantly flowed through his veins causing his eye to glow brighter than ever before. He grinned as he looked at her. "Now it ends!"

"You have no power over me you stupid boy," she laughed, "I'm stronger then you'll ever be. Now give me the Monile and you won't get hurt."

"Like you would ever keep a promise, you a murderer and lier," Teag scoffed.

"Boy I'm warning you!"

The power of the Monile felt so good he thought he could fly. A moment later he began floating in the air. A bit shocked, and realizing the real relation to thinking something and it actually happening, made him feel invincible.

Teag and Desdemona faced one another and seconds later a white beam shot out of Teags Monile, while a black beam shot out of Desdemona's, both beams meeting in the middle. One force against the other. Teag concentraited with is eyes open, the star still shining brightly. He wanted her Monile crushed, but more then that, he wanted her powers. Not completely sure what they were, he felt he would use them better than she had. The blue instatly changed to white and shot out like a laser meeting the other two beams that fought in the air.

Both beams together created more power then Desdemona could fight. The white electric Beam took over her Black one causing her Monile to shatter into a million pieces.

Shocked and angry that Teag distroyed her Monile she comanded the guards to Kill him.

Guards from all over the building ran into the room after Teag. but he used his powers to throw them against the walls. Preston walked in the door smiling, "your orders my Queen?" He asked thrilled that he could do some more damage to Teag.

"I said kill him! Kill him! Kill him!" She hollered in a temper tantrum.

Preston made popping and clicking sounds all around the room to try to distract Teag, but because of their training, Teag had learned how to keep his concentration. He took a hold of preston with his mind and started to drag him against his, closer.

Preston struggled to get free, but was unable too. Preston stopped struggling and closed his mind and Teag was forced to drop him. But he was close enough to start fighting.

"Get his Monile Preston, and I'll give you control of the United States, wouldn't you like that?"

Preston ignored her and took a swing at Teag but he ducked just in time. Then he grabbed a hold of Preston with his mind and before Preston could force him to let go, Teag threw him against one of the nearby pillars, knocking the wind out of him. He took the Monile off and threw it back to Suraionee who missed it, letting it land in the couch cushions. She ran over to search for it.

"Someone kill that boy now," I'll...I'll give you a reward," She lied. Then after thinking for a moment she smiled, "the reward will be fifty million gold pieces, to the one that does it."

"Oh, I'm hurt, that's all?" Teag mocked her.

Several of the guards tried again to approach Teag including Preston, who was now recovered. A large group of men, encircled him slowly approaching with all kinds of weapons. A few shot at him from across the room trying to stay as far away as possible, but Teag just bounced the fast approaching bullets away like a rubber balls. The men ganged up on him all of them running to beat the other to killing him for the money. Preston made sounds of a shotgun come from the corner of the room making everyone duck. Teag deflected everyone. John went invisible and approached to try to stop some of the large men that were attacking his brother but was knocked aside, unintentionally. After several long minutes of fighting with all the men trying to kill him. Suraionee glanced over her shoulder, stopping her search for a moment, and saw Desdemona talking to a soldier. Then watched as he left the room in a hurry.

"I want to fight him on my own," Preston demanded to Desdemona, "please I can kill him, just give me another chance without these yahoos in my way."

"Very well, one last shot," she waved her hand and all the other men picked themselves off the floor and walked back to the walls to await their orders.

Preston looked at Teag, "no powers, one on one," he smiled evilly.

Convinced that he could take Preston on he agreed. Pacing around in a circle just five feet from one another they turned. Ready for the advance. Teag wasn't going to make the first move. He was tired and worn out from the day's adventures, but he forced himself to keep going or knew he would be killed. Preston sinched his way a little closer, until they were only two feet apart. The next thing he knew Preston had him in a head lock.

Teag grabbed onto his arms that were embraced around his neck and swung his body forward forcing Preston over his head and flipping him onto his back forcing him to let go. When Preston stood up Teag tackled him back to the ground and started hitting him in the face.

Preston kicked up his legs and wrapped them around Teag's chest then forced Teag backwards giving Preston the chance to get up.

A large man ran into the room and had short words with Desdemona then ran up and put both hands on each side of Prestons face.

Teag felt Preston break into his mind causing him to shift his powers. Teag jolted in mid air like he was being held up and beaten to death. Bruises began to appear and his body started looking mangled.

"Teag, concentrate your stronger than that!" John yelled.

Hearing this gave him the strength to fight back. The Monile still in his blood, made his eye continue to glow white, though he wasn't wearing it any longer. He looked at the man giving Preston his new powers and picked him up and threw him across the room. Not ready to give up to leave him alone yet, he hit him once in the head, so powerful it knocked him out cold. The last use of powers drained him. The Monile power in him disappeared.

While Teags back was turned Preston grabbed for a sword that was laying on the ground, and snuck up behind Teag.

'Look out Teag, behind you!' John silently but, urgently warned. Teag spun around and jumped just as Preston swung the sword low at his feet.

Preston was surprised and stood there stunned for a moment.

Then Teag decided that because Preston broke the rules by using a weapon, the deal was off. Teag used his powers to pick him up and throw him against the granite marble wall causing Preston to lose consciousness. Teag picked up all of his enemies off the ground and was getting ready to throw them when he heard a voice of alarm.

"Stop Teag, look!" Suraionee pointed to his Mother and Father who were being held by Desdemona and a guard. Teag put them all down.

"Yes, stop Teag," she mimicked, "or Mommy and Daddy will truly die."

"Who says they're not dead already. I haven't seen them move at all since we got here," Teag snapped.

"No! Teag what are you doing? Don't make her madder, she'll kill them."

"They're alive I assure you," Rylee stepped up. His demeanor looked as if he wanted to help. He seemed to look like he was trying to make up for what he had done.

"Like I would believe you Rylee, you betrayed us all, you acted like our friend and you took part in hurting those I loved. She almost killed us several times in the last few days, so why should I put my trust in you.

Rylee shrunk back. It was clear that he realized that he had done wrong, but his pride made it too hard to admit it out loud. He went back to the wall. Desdemona laughed, "you're all weak, letting your emotions rule you," she sneered.

"Leave him be!" Maddox roared gaining more strength.

"Give him the potion we made this morning, I want him human *now*," she hollered, then looking at Rylee, "give it to Rylee too and then kill them both."

Several guards seized Rylee and the other guards held Maddox down and forced him to drink the potion. The potion appeared to hurt Maddox as he shook and roared in pain. Rylee watched as his father struggled helplessly.

"Why can't he fight back, he's stronger than that," John asked bewildered.

"Because if he does he'll lose more than his life, he'll lose his wife and daughter. It didn't take much to convince him to obey when we showed him proof that Ronan was dead."

"What do you mean dead?"

"Dead, finished, no longer alive, put it however you like," Desdemona smirked.

"Ronan's dead? How? When?" Teag asked in shock.

"Well, Actually it was all thanks to Rylee, he has been so helpful," she smiled sweetly.

Teag looked over at Rylee who seemed to have tears flowing down his fuzzy face. Maddox was still in immense pain, he was jolting around like he was having a seizure, and then he suddenly stopped. He laid there lifeless as his body changed back to human. The guards went over to Rylee who was also being held by several guards. He was clearly having a change of heart. "No, never mind, I don't want to be human anymore. I'd rather stay like this," he pleaded as he struggled to get free.

"That wasn't the deal. Now my dear boy, I'm just holding up my end of the bargain, you wouldn't be trying to change our agreement would you?"

"No Ma'm, I was just thinking that we shouldn't waist the potion, you may need me this way, to help you," Rylee waited for an answer from her but when she said nothing he added, "Now that the Monile is destroyed," he tried to convince her.

"No dear boy, your services will no longer be needed," she sneered. Rylee looked over at his father, he was lying on the ground still lifeless.

"I'm sorry father, I was wrong, please forgive me," tears rolled down his furry face as he stood to take his punishment like a man. Desdemona gave him the potion to drink. He took it in his large paw and looked at his father. Then raised it to his lips. Maddox started to move and came too. He looked up at Rylee just as he started drinking the potion.

"Don't! stop! Rylee wait, I forgive you son. I know that you didn't do it to hurt us, you thought you were doing what was right," Maddox smiled at his son who smiled back feeling even more guilty than ever. He drank the last of it, then threw the vial to the floor smashing it. The pain set in almost immediately. Rylee roared with pain, his large lion body began to shake. Then the jerking and seizures set in. Suraionee and John's eyes were full of tears.

"Stop it! Stop it, Please don't, leave him alone," Suraionee cried as she struggled to get free of her captor to help Rylee.

"The Ironic part is that Ronan was merely given a potion to make him appear dead. It's amazing what you can get people to do when you have a little leverage," she cackled.

Maddox's eyes grew large as he realized that he had been tricked, "Ronan's alive?"

Suraionee found the missing Monile that ended up wedged deep in the sofa cushions

Desdemona laughed, "Like I could have killed you as lions. Why do you think I have been trying so hard to get you released, oh how did you word it? Oh yes, *"from your prison"*. Nothing could have killed you in your lion form...Like I would waist my time to turn you to human if I could just to kill you," she laughed again partly irritated. "Now that you are all human, I'll have no problem killing you and I'll be the one living happily ever after."

Teag closed his eyes. 'Sura, now, take her down now.'

Suraionee closed her eyes suddenly knowing what to do, and commanded Desdemona's powers to come to her. There was a rumble and the earth began to shake. Everyone scattered to take cover. Desdemona looked around the room.

"What is happening?" She asked. A tornado like wind started in the high ceiling. It came down over Desdemona and circled her pulling her powers out of her. "Nooo!" she cried and then disappeared. The tornado lifted and then came down over Suraionee spinning the other way giving her the powers. Then as quickly as the storm had started, it stopped. The ground stopped moving and there was silence in the room.

"Where did she go?"

"I don't know," Maddox said still looking around as though he was expecting her to appear from somewhere.

"Maddox is the true Heir to this kingdom," Teag turned to look at Maddox who was now standing hugging Rylee. Their clothing was much too large and drowned them, but they didn't seem to care as they checked out their human bodies almost like it was a dream.

Chapter 11

Milly and Jacob came too. They were happy to see their children all right. The reunion was so sweet as everyone seemed to be happy that the ordeal was over.

The door opened and Melanion walked in, "you did good kids," he said as he smiled at them. Teag, John and Suraionee ran over to give him a hug. Milly and Jacob's jaws hung to the floor.

"Grandpa?" Milly called not sure if she was seeing things or if he was for real. She looked at Jacob who seemed to be seeing the same thing, she ran over to hug him. "I thought you were dead. We buried you," she pulled herself away to looked at him again. "How? What's going on here? What happened?" She asked all at once wanting some answers.

Jacob was standing there pinching himself and looking at his hands as if he was sure he was in a dream.

Everyone took turns telling about the adventure, how Melanion was actually grandpa Great, and how they were connected to the KobiKobis Island. The mood in the whole castle lifted. Maddox, however, was still sad servants were searching for Sarah and Isabelle, but they had not yet been found. His concern for them grew with each passing second.

Melanion walked over to Maddox and shook his hand.

"Thank you for helping," Maddox said.

"There is something you should see," Melanion smiled and he pointed to the door and in walked Sarah, Isabelle and Ronan. "Sarah and Isabelle were found in a small raft a drift in the ocean without their Diamante Púrpura's and Ronan was knocked out and locked up in the dungeon."

Maddox and Rylee ran over to them, and they lovingly embraced. Maddox was so happy he didn't want to let go.

"Let us all go to the Great Oak, and get some rest," Melanion suggested. All agreed and left the castle.

The next morning at the Great Oak, Teag got up and went to speak to Maddox. He walked down the hall to the elevator and went to the first floor. He made his way to the foyer where he found Maddox standing at the counter talking to Mr Drummond. Teag was taken back when he saw Maddox in his human form. He was still a large strong looking man. His long dark hair hung just over his shoulders and was nicely groomed, the long mustache and beard he had yesterday were gone. He was in a black and white Tuxedo that fit him comfortably, "hi Maddox, I just wanted to say, thanks for everything."

"You're welcome, you would have done the same for me," he smiled.

"It's sad that you were forced to go back to human, and that you couldn't choose between them like Grandpa said you could," Teag frowned.

Maddox smiled, "Who says I can't?" Maddox then changed back into the Lion-man causing the new Tuxedo to almost burst all of the buttons, "Oops," he said as he changed back quickly checking to make sure he hadn't ripped his new suit.

"So when you drank the potion," Teag smiled, "you were faking the whole time?"

"No, the pain was real, but changing back into a human, was me. She had my family so I had to make her believe that the potion was working."

"But Rylee, is he human now?"

"Yes he is, he wasn't in a position to listen to me when I came back two days ago with the potion Melanion gave me. He'll be alright though."

"But how did they get to you to begin with?" When I left you at the Black Wizard Forest they were waiting for me at the castle. I didn't expect that she knew already, or how she knew for that matter. I told her I changed my mind and I wanted to stay human. ZaBeth was furious with me. She had drugged the tea I was drinking, and its effects set in fast so I couldn't fight back and then she threatened to make me by telling me her militia would beat me unless I agreed to co-operate. When that wasn't working she told me she killed Ronan, and she took Sarah and Isabelle and threatened to kill them too if I didn't do as she asked. She even showed me proof of the killing through an enchanted window, they had apparently staged it to get me to co-operate.

"What did they want you to do?"

"Change back to human and give up your plan; where you would be so once you had all of the ingredients she would kill you, your brother and sister. She didn't want to have any trouble with you while she put the rest of her plan together."

"Humph," Teag nodded with understanding. "But," Teag started politely, "if your Queen Alura's son, that makes you an original islander, and you said that only original islanders had powers without the Keno Tea…so what happened to your powers?"

"Well when I was young I told you that Melanion moved me and my father to Australia. We were in hiding mostly. Melanion was afraid that if I used my powers that Desdemona would find out about me and kill me. So he suppressed them with a spell and I never did ask for them back when I moved back to the Islands. I didn't know that she was Desdemona; after I became a lion I thought I could trust her and confided to her who I really was. She was a great actress because the news didn't even phase her. I would have never guessed that she was who she really was," Maddox explained.

Teag nodded with understanding, "so are you going to be King?"

"Yes, we'll have the ceremony in two days," Maddox looked up when he heard the laughing commotion of the rest of the Trager family entering the hall. Jacob and Milly were all cleaned up. Other than a few bruises, no one would have known the ordeal they suffered for the past several months.

Jacob walked up to Maddox and shook his hand. "Thank you so much for taking care of our children and for helping us all."

"Your more than welcome, I was happy to help, they're great kids. I'd also love it if you would all stay for the coronation, in two days."

"Sure we wouldn't miss it."

"And of course, you and your family are welcome to stay here as long as you like."

"Thank you, Milly and I were just saying this morning that we needed a vacation away from the vacation. Though this time we would prefer not to stay in a dungeon," Jacob said while laughing.

"I don't blame you. I think we could all use a little vacation from the past few months," Maddox smiled.

It was the day of the coronation; the sky was blue and the sun was shining. Birds were singing sweetly in the background and the flowers smelled fresh and heavenly. It was a beautiful and sunny morning. The castle gardens were lined with exquisite and colorful flowers and plants of all kinds. The people of Makoto City arrived and slowly filed into the castle cathedral to take their seats. Excitement grew as people were discussing the rumors of the events that took place a few days before and wondered who would take the seat. The Trager family arrived and took their place next to the Isabelle, Ronan and Rylee Pembroke. Ronan was also in his human form.

Teag made sure he got to sit next to Isabelle. She was dressed in a beautiful Red silk dress that was lightly form fitting and elegant. Ronan and Rylee were in black tuxedos and had top hat's with white gloves.

The room looked as though it was ready for a wedding. All the Island guests were dressed for the occasion. Sunlight poured in through the stained glass windows that bordered the walls. The room was full of talking and laughing people. Teag saw the Dayton and Mile's families seated amongst the crowds and happily chatting with others. He looked around and found the Karik family sitting in the back wearing black. They seemed to be upset with the whole thing. Melanion walked in and walked up to the podium in the front and the room became silent.

"Ladies and Gentlemen," he started, "we are here to witness the crowning of a new King and Queen. Many of you have known the Pembrokes' for many years, but what you didn't know was that Maddox is the son of Queen Alura," The room grew loud with chatter about the news. "Queen Alura and General Flann were married in secret a year before she died. And one month before Queen Alura passed away, Maddox was born. He was actually named after his father Scott Flann, but given a different name to protect him.

So with further Ado, I present your future King Maddox and Queen Sarah," he smiled as he held out his hand for them to enter. The congregation turned to watch the main entrance behind them as the doors opened. Maddox had his hand out and faced down. Sarah had her hand out face down over his hand as he guided her to the front. They carefully stepped up to their royal seats but did not sit down.

"Maddox please kneel before me," Maddox stepped forward and knelt down. "Do you promise and swear to protect and guide the people of the KobiKobis Islands, to do no harm and rule with just and a pure heart?"

Maddox nodded twice as he spoke, "Yes."

Melanion placed the crown on his head while he said, "Then I crown you King Maddox Pembroke, please arise," Melanion smiled and stepped aside. Maddox stood up and stepped back to his seat, then sat down on his throne.

"Sarah, please kneel before me," Sarah stepped forward and keeled down. "Do you promise and swear to protect and guide the people of the KobiKobis Islands, to do no harm and rule with just and a pure heart, and to support and guide your King?"

"Sarah nodded twice as she spoke, "Yes."

Melanion placed the crown on her head while he said, "Then I crown you Queen Sarah Pembroke, please arise my queen," he said as he bowed before her then stepped back. Sarah stood up and stepped back to her throne and sat down.

"I give you your King and Queen." Melanion said to the congregation. Everyone cheered as the King stood up and took the Queen's hand and guided her to the front. They bowed before the people. Suddenly all at once the crowd got up and bowed back. Staying down.

"Please arise," Maddox said as he motioned with his hand for them to come up. "We are pleased we can give back to this wonderful country, what so many of you have given to us. Thank you for coming."

Everyone clapped and cheered. Teag looked back at the Karik's and found Preston slouched in his chair clearly angry. The entire family sat motionless. Willem looked over and saw Teag looking at him. He motioned to his family to get up and leave.

As Maddox and Sarah made their way down into the congregation they stopped to talk and shake hands with everyone. People left their seats to go and greet them.

The next day the Tragers' were leaving by ship.

"Must you go so soon?" Queen Sarah asked, sad at the thought of losing them.

"Yes I'm afraid we must, we'll be back though, Melanion is here and we'll want to see him more."

"I'm so glad to hear that, then it isn't goodbye, it's a see you soon," Sarah smiled as she hugged Milly and Suraionee.

Teag was saying goodbye to Isabelle.

"I want you to have this to remember me by. She gave him a tiny mirror. Teag looked confused.

"So I can look at myself?" He asked confused.

"No," she laughed then looked to see if anyone was listening. When it was clear, she spoke quietly, "I found it in Desdemona's room, and it transports you where ever you want to go. Just look into it and then think of the place you want to be the most. It will take you there. So you can come and see me whenever you like."

"Oh, that's how she was doing it," Teag confirmed, "I'll see you after we get home. I don't think my mom will let me out of her site until we are all home and safe. I'll find you," Teag said as he stuffed it in his pocket.

"Isabelle, It's time to let them go," Sarah said as she motioned her over to them. Isabelle looked at Teag again then leaned in and kissed his cheek. Then she quickly ran over and stood by her mother.

Teag blushed. He and his family walked on board the big magical ship that would disappear after they got home. They waved as they set off into the deep blue ocean, headed to America.

Pronunciations:

Teag (Tea-g)
Suraionee (Sue-Ryan-ee)
ZaBeth (Za-Beth)
Dorgoggin (Door-gog-in)
Makotice (Mac-O-tea-s)
Hoarfrost (Hor-frost)
Spitniker (Spit-nick-er)
Makoto City (Mac-O-toe)
Keno Tea (Key-no)
KobiKobis Island (Coby-Co-bis)
SkyBee (Sky-Bee)
LoRock (Low-Rock)
Melanion (Mel-an-ian)
Vidor Lysander (Vee-door Lie-sand-er)
Thayne (Th-A-n)
Makotee serum (Mac-O-tea)
Alura (Al-oo-ra)
Nyla (n-I-la)
Moya (Moi-a)
Alaura (A-laura)
Willem (Will-em)
Karik (Care-ik)
Koikochi (KO-ee-Coch-ee)